"OH GOD, ... TO SAVE ME!

Yolanda would have made it to the roof if it hadn't been for the explosion. A collapsing wall slammed into her, and the baby dropped right out of her arms. Hysterical, she bent down through the smoke, wood and plaster to try to find him. When her hands came up bloody, she prayed it was her blood and not his . . .

By the time the firefighters reached Yolanda, the fire had gotten to her first. She was alive, but so badly burned, she hardly looked human.

She passed her days and nights at the hospital in endless misery. A surgeon told her—strictly off the record—about a new treatment currently under development, a treatment that was new, untested, and free of charge. He could not officially endorse it, but . . . her alternative was the pain, the expense, and the raw discomfort of her current situation.

In a low voice, he asked, "Would you be interested?"

She said yes. Who cared if anything went wrong?, Yolanda told herself. Nothing could possibly be worse than the agony I'm in right now.

Could it?

Fatal
BEAUTY

William Schoell

ST. MARTIN'S PAPERBACKS

FATAL BEAUTY

Copyright © 1990 by William Schoell.

All rights reserved. No part of this book may be used or reproduced in any manner whatsoever without written permission except in the case of brief quotations embodied in critical articles or reviews. For information address St. Martin's Press, 175 Fifth Avenue, New York, N.Y. 10010.

ISBN: 0-312-92138-1

Printed in the United States of America

St. Martin's Paperbacks edition/April 1990

10 9 8 7 6 5 4 3 2 1

Finally, this one's for Mom and Pop—who can never say I didn't warn them!

"... surely such beauty was a world of its own whose anarchy had a sort of godly license."

—Tennessee Williams,
The Roman Spring of Mrs. Stone

PART ONE
Laboratory

CHAPTER ONE

The laboratory was located in a former sanatorium in an isolated section of New England. Some would say that the inhabitants at the present time were no more sane than the inmates of old; they poked and probed and prodded at things better left undisturbed. "There are things man was not meant to know," they used to say in the old movies, but that was before science started saving lives and technology proved as much boon to mankind as burden.

Inside this Gothic structure, built in the late 1800s, with turrets and spires and large barred windows, there were converted chambers as modern as anything imaginable. Gleaming steel tables and fluorescent lights in the ceiling, polished pipes and tubing across the floor. Sinks that sparkled in the overhead light. Chrome fixtures. The very latest computer equipment. Vials and beakers and petri dishes. Machines that hummed and whispered and gurgled.

Four of the scientists housed in the building—they ate there, slept there, argued there—were now inside a particularly large chamber at the end of the first-floor hall. At one time this had been a sitting room for mental patients. A great deal of money had transformed it into an exotic and enormous laboratory, the third largest in the building, and shadows in the corners covered containers inside which small things slithered, hopped, and chuckled; it was as if they were imitating the raving lunatics who had spent their days there chittering and knitting and staring wide-eyed either at one another or at nothing.

Now these four scientists, two men, two women, were standing around the largest container in the room. This container was actually a large, rectangular glass enclosure, or tank, with a glass lid whose several sections could be swung upward on hinges so as to allow closer examination of what lay inside. The enclosure was about ten feet long and three feet wide. It was placed upon a long aluminum table that had been set up especially to receive it.

The first woman, Dr. Betty Lincoln, forty-seven, was a biochemist who had been stolen away (or so went the "official" story) from one of the largest pharmaceutical firms in the world. She was short, with heavy, unattractive features, thick limbs, and bifocals. An ugly woman. She wore her hair in tightly clustered ringlets. "The creature's skin is remarkable," she said with a thick Brooklyn accent. "It has a great deal of elasticity, yet it's tougher than anything I've seen before."

Frank Eddington was a bright-eyed blond doctor who looked two decades younger than his fifty years. His most arresting feature was his broad heavy eyebrows which met in the center of his forehead and made him resemble a benign, if agitated, werewolf. He tapped a pencil on top of the glass lid of the enclosure and spoke. "It could probably stretch to several times its original length."

"What amazes me is the facial structure," Dr. Susan Raymond said, barely suppressing a shudder. Of them all she was least comfortable with this animal, and the least likely to be taken for a scientist. She had fair smooth skin and blue eyes, full lips you'd expect on a model. Not beautiful—her face was too broad for that, her chin too large—but attractive. "I know we expected something like this, but . . . I don't know . . . when it's conscious it seems to be studying us."

Dr. Elliot Lester took this as his cue to introduce the subject with which he was most fascinated. "I really think we should do something soon about measuring its intelligence. I don't want to sound spooky, but I suspect this animal has mental abilities that may go far beyond what we'd expect—given its origin."

Dr. Lincoln spoke sharply, her puffy face scrunched up in irritation. "This animal is quite remarkable enough as it is, Doctor, without you adding your little bit of fantasy to it. Next you'll be saying it has psychic powers and can influence our dreams."

"How the hell do you know what it can or cannot influence, Betty?" Lester snickered. "There's never been anything like this beast before. We're dealing with a creature with totally unknown qualities." His pencillike neck quivered.

"Unknown, yes, but not from another solar system. We created this creature, accidentally I'll grant you, but we created it from the stuff of life all around us, from cells of known, living animals. We knew the hybrid would be freakish, to say the least, but there's no reason to presuppose the *supernatural!*"

"Betty," Susan interrupted gently, "I think all Elliot means is that we should measure the extent of the influence of the human cells. We have to do intelligence tests anyway, find out exactly what this creature is and what its various functions are. For instance, those seeping orifices on the top—are they used for excretion or is that fluid merely a lubricant or simple sweat variant?" She shook her head and smiled wryly. "This animal doesn't follow the lines of anything in the biology books, Betty."

Frank Eddington stepped back and reached for a notepad lying on a table behind him. "I did a few preliminary tests on those secretions last night," he told the others. "It's not a waste product at all; it's more of a by-product. In fact, this fluid seems to be an actual organ of the animal's body, a liquid organ that it constantly replenishes and expels. Don't ask me why."

"An organ?" Lester repeated.

"Yes, Elliot. Like the skin covering our bodies is an organ. And our skin cells die, fall off, and keep replenishing constantly. It's the same with this animal's fluid."

Betty muttered in frustration. "It's like nothing from any of the animals this hybrid creature is composed of."

"The fluid that oozes from the numerous orifices on top covers it almost completely, like a second sheath," Eddington continued. "But the animal produces far more of the substance than is necessary. Perhaps there's a glandular malfunction. Or something is stimulating it to produce more than it needs."

"What's the composition?" Betty asked.

Frank handed her a printout listing the components. She whistled with amazement. "Not dead cells at all," she said. "Not even dying cells, but living ones."

"Yes." Frank took out a large rounded glass dish from a drawer beneath the tabletop and turned to the glass tank containing the animal. He lifted the lid and scooped some of the oily fluid from beside the sleeping creature.

"When was it fed last?" Betty asked.

"This morning," Susan told her. "I'll feed it again when it's awakened."

"Still giving it insects and rodents?"

"Yes. Though I think it would like anything that was alive—and full of blood."

"Why do you think we keep it tranquilized?" Frank said.

No one spoke for several seconds.

"Speaking of eating," Elliot said, "I'm in the mood for coffee and a donut. How about a cafeteria break, everyone?"

He got no arguments. Though none of the four would admit it, they were glad to get away from the animal in the tank. It consumed far too much of their time as it was; it had only come into being as an accidental side effect of another experiment in genetic engineering, and it seemed to have no useful purpose. They each had other, more important projects. But in spite of their understandable revulsion, they were fascinated by the beast and felt compelled to study and observe it whenever they could. And perhaps Eddington was on to something; perhaps that fluid it secreted held some properties that could be useful to the people who paid them.

They left the room.

In the oval glass dish in which Eddington had collected the fluid, there was movement. The substance was quivering, solidifying. Taking on shape.

The creature in the tank began to stir.

CHAPTER TWO _____

Frank had just gotten his coffee and glazed donut and made his way over to the table where the others were waiting, when he remembered that he'd forgotten his notepad. There were things in it he wanted to bring up with the others while they were all together and relaxing. The various projects the four were supervising left them little time to compare notes.

He put down his coffee and donut and headed for the exit. "Be right back," he called behind him.

Upon entering the laboratory, he went to the table near the tank where he had left his spiral notepad. Putting it into the large side pocket of his lab coat, he heard a sound behind him, coming from the tank; it was a sort of gurgling.

He turned around quickly and looked into the tank, but saw no movement. The creature still seemed to be asleep; at least its eyes were closed. What an ugly beast, he thought, so large and long, grayish-red in color, the color of dried blood or certain kinds of clay. It had protuberances and appendages and orifices that seemed to be mockeries of similar organs one previously saw only in nature. And then there was the oral cavity that dominated the end of the beast which they assumed was the head, that horrible "face"! He could look the creature over and in some cases figure out which parent cells were responsible for which peculiarity, but he could not account for that face, that tubular mouth, the oil-secreting orifices that seemed as much wounds as natural openings in the creature's thick, mottled hide. The combination of disparate cells from different life-forms had created a strange, unnatural hybrid. This beast was really one of a kind and hopefully would remain so. For the first few weeks after its "birth" they'd been content to simply monitor its amazing growth and prevent it from dying, but now it was time to really examine every facet of it. He had no qualms about keeping it alive, safely contained, for study.

There! He heard that gurgling sound again. Now down at the back of the beast. It could have been some of that excess fluid plopping into the liquid that had already collected at the bottom of the tank. Yes, that was probably it. The beast usually opened its eyes before awakening for one thing. Susan was right—it did seem to study them. And even though Elliot had a habit of drawing hasty conclusions regarding brain power and psychic phenomena in all his experiments, there had been incidents that might suggest they were dealing with an animal perhaps as outré in the mental sense as in the physical: things in the lab had seemed to move by themselves when one's back was turned; odd thoughts had come into their heads and seemed to spring out of nowhere. He supposed a practical joker might account for some of it. Anyway, it was little more than a feeling, barely a suspicion at this point. Perhaps he, like Betty, was simply not prepared to confront the possibilities.

He turned away from the tank. Out of the corner of his eye he noticed something. He stepped over to the table where he had placed the large circular dish containing some of the animal's fluid.

He spoke aloud: "Oh my God."

His mind was reeling. It was simply unbelievable.

There could be no question that the fluid was one of the animal's organs, that the beast had control of the substance even when it was separated from its body, that it could read their minds, communicate with them, though whether that was proof of genuine intelligence or something more psychic and instinctual in nature he could not immediately ascertain.

He looked down at the dish again. *Incredible.* In its own unique way, the creature was reaching out to them, proclaiming with great urgency the need for a primal, basic requirement to be satisfied.

It was calling for its supper.

The creature was smart enough to play games, to be guileful. It had only been pretending to sleep, having long since shrugged off the effects of the tranquilizer. The gurgles had been a giveaway, had he been alert enough to decipher them. The creature had been slowly shifting its mass, flexing its muscles, preparing itself. Its appetite had grown far beyond what they had been feeding it.

As Frank turned back toward the tank, he had an irresistible urge to lift the glass lid and reach out to the creature, touch it, tell it with strokes of his hands that he was finally aware they were dealing with an animal that might possibly be as intelligent as humans. No longer would they treat it simply as a dumb, misshapen freak in a glass jar. Somehow he had to tell this man-engineered monstrosity that he *knew,* he knew it was more than what it appeared to be, he knew it was more than just a failed experiment, but rather was a sentient being with a mind and a soul all its own. He had to make sure this pathetic creature was aware of his concern and his compassion.

He lifted the lid. His ungloved hand reached out to stroke the beast's oil-sheathed outer skin.

The beast's face seemed to grow larger all at once, and Frank was perplexed until he realized it was just his disoriented perception. The beast wasn't getting bigger, it was simply coming closer to Frank's own face, hurtling up out of the glass enclosure and moving rapidly toward him. In a second the serrated teeth inside the mouth would be fastening on his neck. Frank jumped back quickly, in time to save himself but not fast enough to slam the lid back down before the creature could escape. It took a full thirty seconds for the beast to slither entirely out of the tank, a half-minute during which Frank could only stand to one side, transfixed, unable to move or even cry out. Then the animal was loose in the room with him.

The animal seemed to be everywhere at once. One part of it to the right, another to the left. The "face" seemed to peer out at Frank from behind every corner. He tried to run, but every pathway seemed barred by a section of the beast's body. He felt cornered, as if he were one of those bugs Susan fed the creature twice daily.

Then he fully understood the significance of what he had seen in the dish on the table.

Finally he tried to run.

Before he had gone three steps, he felt a sharp pain in his ankle and found himself being raised several feet above the floor.

He screamed.

The pain in his ankle was so agonizing he was sure if he looked downward he'd see his foot, severed, lying halfway across the room. But there was no time to look down. Suddenly he was whipped this way and that through the air like an hysterically flapping bird caught in an enormous net, only in his case it was not any effort on his part that caused the dizzying motion. The room flew past his eyes. He crashed into the wall of the lab across from the doorway, and then was swept over to the opposite wall to be pounded against that. He was then thrust up toward the ceiling, his body smacking against the rickety acoustic ceiling panels. The next second he was smashed down onto one of the lab tables, his body crunching vials and tubes to pieces, and from there onto the hard, unyielding floor.

His back was ablaze with pain. There were cuts and scratches all over his arms and legs, and two limbs felt broken. The pain in his ankle had risen to his thigh, as if something were engulfing, devouring, his leg. He was able to rest on the floor for a moment, and then the battering started again. He was like a fish at the mercy of a petulant fisherman who was determined to bash out the brains of the wriggling, uncooperative thing caught on his hook. Slammed into one wall after another, the ceiling, the floor, he was finally brought hurtling down onto the large glass tank from which his assailant had escaped. The glass ruptured, shattered. Pieces of it went flying in every direction. The force of the blow was so severe that even the aluminum table collapsed under the impact. The life whooshed out of Frank Eddington with his last breath, and his blood inundated the wreckage.

The thing on his leg worked itself up toward his groin.

CHAPTER THREE

People came running. The shattering noises, the screams. Something was happening in laboratory C. Lincoln, Raymond, and Lester arrived from the cafeteria moments later. They told the others in the room to stay back.

The creature was quiet now. Feeding.

Elliot Lester did not hesitate. Seeing the escaped creature feeding on his dead friend, he grabbed a fire axe and started hacking the animal repeatedly.

None of the others tried to stop him.

Betty was throwing up in one corner of the room. Susan, though abjectly terrified and repulsed, stood by Lester's side as he did his best to send the preoccupied creature from this plane of existence into the next.

Caught by surprise, the creature was not very effective in its attempts to defend itself.

Finally it was dead. There were parts of it scattered all over the room. Its "blood," a blue-green viscous fluid, had sprayed upon every table, tool, and instrument in the laboratory.

Using a scalpel and a small saw, Lester removed the animal fragment from what was left of Frank Eddington's leg. Men came with a stretcher and took the dead scientist away. The other three stood around the lab in shock and dismay, sobbing or looking numbly at the ruins of both the room and its monstrous subject, pieces of which were still strewn about the chamber.

Susan bent down at one large fragment, her eyes wide with astonishment. "Apparently it reproduces asexually," she said. "It was going to give birth." She pointed out the sausagelike protuberances jutting out partially from a nichelike aperture between two small appendages. "They're not dead yet," she said. "We could save them if we wanted to." She looked to Elliot for his opinion.

Betty spoke first. She was pale and shaken. "Why would we want any more of these? They already killed one of us. They'd serve no useful purpose. Surely, we can't be expected to keep working with these things." She looked at Dr. Lester. "You agree with me, Elliot, don't you?"

But Elliot was not paying attention. He was looking down at the same dish Dr. Eddington had seen before his death, the dish of the beast's fluid that had been miraculously untouched during the struggle. "We have to keep the babies alive," he said. He looked at Susan. "Her afternoon feeding was delayed because she was still sleeping soundly. But when she woke and we weren't there, she was hungry. She tried to let us know. She knew you were responsible for feeding her, Susan. And she cried out to you. When you didn't respond, she attacked Frank for sustenance."

Betty could not stand another of Dr. Lester's idiotic supernatural assumptions. "What are you talking about?" Her tears were still wet on her cheeks.

"This. I'm talking about this."

The two women went over to look at the circular dish. At first they thought Elliot had placed a mask over the dish, a mask made from a mold of someone's face. But then they realized—it was the oil, the fluid. It had come together, congealed, to form the shape of a human face.

It was all there: eyes, lips, forehead, nose, chin. A lovely face. The oil had taken on the color and property of human skin.

The face of Susan Raymond smiled up at them.

They knew they had to save the babies.

PART TWO
"Barrows Means Beauty"

CHAPTER FOUR

New York City—Several years later

It was four o'clock in the afternoon and Peggy Antonicci had still not put her face on.

It was a ritual she was unaccustomed to, but had begun to embrace—with fear and reservation—as she approached her thirtieth birthday. Now, three years later, she had still not perfected it. She still did not know if the things she did to her face were bona fide improvements or if she was merely fooling herself. She thought she could sense betterment in little things—there was certainly nothing wrong in covering up those tiny acne scars on her cheeks and the nagging blackheads around the bottom of her nose—but anything more elaborate just gave her the willies. It wasn't so much that she wanted to look younger as that she desired a more sophisticated, less "babyish" appearance.

She had once heard her voice on tape and been shocked at how dumb, inelegant, and appallingly low-class and infantile it sounded. She resembled a character in a sitcom, the silly girl from next door who never got a date, a homelier, Italian version of *Rhoda*. That voice! While she hoped a more mature appearance would offset the effect of her vocal peculiarities, she was secretly afraid it might only make it worse.

Was there anything more awful than one of those ever-so-pretty, carefully coiffed, beautifully made-up women who, upon opening their mouths, sound like chalk screeching on slate, or dipshits, or hell-spawned hybrids of the Bronx and Brooklyn? Her boyfriend once said her voice was cute, that *she* was cute and he liked her just the way she was. But then, David would say anything as long as she kept him fed and protected from the elements.

It seemed to take longer and longer to get ready, she thought. She had always been in awe of those girls back in high school who seemed to carry whole cases of cosmetics with them and would whip out a compact and lipstick and touch themselves up in seconds flat with the assurance and confidence that only came with the mastery of routine. It always seemed pretty silly to her. She also knew that the girls who looked best in makeup were the girls who looked best without it, a sad little catch-22 that had not yet sunk into the shopgirls who wore purple streaks on their cheekbones like the Bride of Franken-stein, or brightly painted lips that did not make their mouths more sensual but only accented their bad teeth.

And then there was this business of matching every-thing: matching eyes with lips, facial colors with the colors of your clothes and complexion. It was a bore. Half of her thought it was fun, trying to make yourself over so that you looked like a new woman. The other half didn't really want to bother. She winced at the possibility that she went through all of this just to keep a man, her David; but she knew that wasn't really the case. She wanted to look good for Peggy Antonicci. At least that's what she told herself. Well, she reminded herself, Gloria Steinem had been born pretty and didn't have to worry about these things.

She finally got away from the bathroom mirror, con-vinced she looked as presentable as was humanly possi-ble. She hadn't overdone it today. She wasn't going anywhere special and didn't really need to look glamor-ous. At thirty-three she was as dismayed by her looks as she had been at gawky, flat-chested twelve. Now her figure was more Rubenesque, her breasts quite large, but her face had not undergone much of a change since puberty. She tried to convince herself she was pretty. If she weren't, how could she have a boyfriend as sexy and attractive as David? She hated being a mass of insecurities, but in a society obsessed with youth and beauty, it wasn't easy being plain.

David was just getting out of bed. The bedroom was an unholy mess, as usual. There were books and papers lying all over the place, and little sunlight could come in past the almost barricaded windows and dingy yellow curtains. The paint on the walls was peeling, and there were numerous niches through which darted roaches and the occasional noisy, if unseen, rodent. The furniture in the room was ancient: a bed whose dilapidated springs groaned in protest even if you were to sit lightly on the edge of the mattress, a chest of drawers that probably dated back to the days of Boss Tweed, a night table devoid of a drawer and piled high with books and magazines, an old battered rocking chair in the corner upon which David left his rumpled clothing every night.

The living room was less of a disaster area, but hardly a room at the Helmsley. It had a small kitchenette attached, and a bathroom off the front door hallway. There were also three good-sized closets full of clothes she really should give away to the Salvation Army, but was too ashamed to show up with.

David groaned and stretched. "Got any orange juice?" he asked.

"I don't know."

"Can you go out and get me some? Please?"

"Get it yourself, David. You better get up or you're going to be late."

"I may not go tonight."

"What? David, we need the money. If you want to have money for new pictures you'd better go to work."

"Shit," he said. "Yeah, I guess I better. What about that check you were expecting?"

"It's in the mail. I wouldn't count on seeing that before Christmas."

"Shit."

"Yeah, shit."

"What are you going to do today?" he asked her.

"Don't know. I may go to a movie. Send out a few letters."

"You sure live the life of Riley. I have to work while you go to the movies."

She hated when he said things like that. She brought in far more income for the two of them than he ever did.

"David, I'm entitled to a little fun now and then. And you know damn well you're lucky if you worked a total of three weeks all year."

"Yeah, yeah, yeah." He pulled on his trousers and looked around for his shirt while Peggy picked up her purse and counted the little she had in her wallet. At least he hadn't taken any from her. "I wish I had some orange juice," he said.

"I said there may be some in the refrigerator. I'm not going to get it for you. You have two legs, David."

He got up and left the bedroom. "Bitchin' bitchin' bitchin'."

"Fuck you, David."

He shouted from the other room, while she counted coins in her change purse. "Did the mail come yet?"

"Not yet. I looked a little while ago. You go down this time."

"In a minute."

One hundred sixty-three dollars and fifty-three cents. She could get them through the next week or so, still have money for the movies and other things, but after that? If that magazine check didn't come, they'd be in trouble. Of course, they'd been in trouble before and somehow always found a way out of it. But it wasn't fun, it wasn't fun at all. How she wished he'd work at a steady job sometimes, even though she knew why he didn't and understood. Still, it wasn't easy counting pennies. In fact, the older you got, the harder it became.

She went into the other room and found David sitting down at the kitchen table, which was just a foot away from the couch. There had been some orange juice left. The empty container was at David's upraised elbow as he slugged the last of it. He put his glass down with a thud. "Ahhhh—just hit the spot."

"Good thing I didn't want any."

"The store's just down the block, sweetie. You're the one's got the money in this house."

"Yeah. Not much. Do you know where yesterday's paper is? I want to check the movie schedule."

"What are you going to see?"

"I'm not sure. I'm in the mood for a love story. Or maybe something to make me laugh."

He was pouring himself some cereal. "If you want a good laugh, just look in the mirror."

"Funny, David, funny."

"Seriously, I like the way you look today, babe. That's a nice outfit. Real pretty."

He gave compliments very sincerely and very often. "Thank you. It is a nice outfit, isn't it?" A gray skirt, blue blouse, blue kerchief around her neck. The blue contrasted nicely with her black hair and violet eyes. Every once in a while she did look good.

She warmed to him for the first time since arising, as they both knew she would, and went over to the table to wrap her arms around him from behind. She kissed him on the ear, the temple. "Davey, Davey, Davey. Do you hate that job at Hanrahan's so much?"

He leaned back against her bosom and took on a puppyish expression. "It's just that it's kind of boring. All they get in there is businessmen and secretaries. The night passes so slowly. Then I have to throw drunks out the door at eleven." He sighed and looked down at the floor. "I don't really like being a bartender."

"Poor baby," she said, kissing his hair. He didn't like being anything.

He was listed as a substitute bartender at half a dozen places, but he only got work occasionally, usually when a regular barman went on vacation. Hanrahan's was a pseudo-Irish bar down in the financial district of lower Manhattan. It catered to Wall Streeters and other yuppies. One regular bartender was hospitalized for the week and David had to replace him.

"If you don't go tonight," Peggy reminded him, "they'll get someone else to fill out the week."

"I know, I know."

"It won't be so bad. Want me to come down and sit with you for a while?"

He waved his hand in the air dismissively. "No, no." He always vetoed that idea for some reason, in spite of the fact that he always complained of being "bored" at these places, that the hours passed slowly and the customers wouldn't talk to him the way they would the regular bartender. "I know you want to see a movie and you probably have work to do tonight."

"It can always wait until tomorrow."

"No." He fiddled with the empty orange juice bottle. "Maybe you can come down tomorrow."

"Okay. Maybe tomorrow." She stood up and went over to the couch, hoping to find the elusive newspaper. David watched her as he ate his corn crispies. She knew he didn't want to work but she wasn't going to encourage him to stay home. Not if he wanted a spanking new set of eight by ten glossies to take on auditions. She couldn't afford to pay for everything and photos were not cheap.

She found the paper and sat down on the sofa to thumb through the movie section. "Is that all you're going to eat?" she asked as David finished his cereal. "Will they give you a meal at Hanrahan's?"

"A sandwich, maybe. Most of the good stuff is gone by the time I get there. They put out hors d'oeuvres and stuff like that for the after-work crowd, and the way they eat it you'd think they hadn't had a meal in a century. All the money they make, they still want freebies."

"That's the way of the world, honey," she said idly, focusing on the time schedule for a romantic double bill at the Biograph. "Going to do anything before you go to work, Davey?"

"If you lend me a couple of bucks, I'm going to buy the new issues of *Backstage* and *Showcase* and look through 'em."

"All right, but could you please *try* and clean up the bedroom a little bit? Most of that junk is yours, you know."

He always changed the subject when she mentioned cleaning. "Did you come across that copy of *A Streetcar Named Desire* I was looking for the other day?" Now he had found a box of crackers and was messily consuming them.

She had trouble picturing him as Stanley Kowalski. David was too smooth, too urbane. "No. If you find my library card, which you lost six weeks ago, you could always go to the library and take it out. We could copy the pages you need."

He was always auditioning for acting classes, although neither of them knew where the money to pay for them would come from should he ever be accepted. Scholarships were rarely granted for acting classes, since the failed actors who taught them had their own rent to pay.

David wiped cracker crumbs off his lips and chin and shouted, "Stella. Hey, Stella!"

Peggy laughed. "Keep quiet, Marlon."

At least David tried to be different. Nowadays everyone marched into auditions with copies of Sam Shepard plays under their arms, trying to be trendy, but David stuck with the twentieth-century classics he'd read in high school. Peggy wasn't quite sure he understood them, but at least he made the effort. She did sense, however, that he wanted to perfect the part of Stanley Kowalski, more because it was a famous, easily recognized role than because of any real appreciation of Tennessee Williams. At least he wasn't as bad as that air-brained New York newscaster who, on the day of the great playwright's death, referred to him as Tennessee Ernie Williams!

David worried her, she had to admit. On the surface he did (or at least used to do) all the things that struggling New York actors were supposed to do—he kept updating his photos, sent out résumés, read *Backstage* for news of roles opening up on and off Broadway, went to auditions (though lately he'd been slacking off)—but she wondered if underneath he was all that dedicated to the profession. He had a certain amount of talent, that she could tell from his performances in Off-Off-Broadway plays she'd managed to see him in, but he seemed more interested in attaining stardom than in perfecting his craft. Of course she understood that, living the way he did, constantly on the brink of poverty and worse, it would be hard for him not to desperately desire the more traditional kind of success aspired to by most career-oriented New Yorkers. Yet it bothered her that simply becoming a good, working actor wasn't at least as important.

David seemed to think he was destined for stardom because of something that had happened in his twenties, a brief interlude which he claimed was the closest he had come to "making it"—which wasn't very close. At twenty-three he had appeared in an Off-Off-Broadway production of a show by a Queens College acquaintance who years later became an Off-Broadway playwright of note. David swore that the man's most recently successful play, *Waves and Ridges,* had been an updating and revision of that play he'd appeared in back in Queens. The actor who played David's role in the revised version stayed in the part when the play moved to a bigger house on Broadway, and even kept the role in the successful film adaptation. He was now a fairly well known film star. David was convinced he had missed it by that much, that if he had stayed in touch with the playwright (who now wrote screenplays in Hollywood), he would have gotten the part in the revision and the kind of career he'd always envisioned.

But when pressed, David had admitted that the plots of the two plays were not really all that similar. The film star who'd appeared in the later version was a completely different type from David, who would probably not have been well cast in the rewritten role and wouldn't have gotten the part even if he and his college acquaintance had become good buddies. Yet, if it gave David some comfort or satisfaction to think of himself as having had a "brush with stardom," who was she to dissuade him?

Sometimes she thought all David really wanted to do was lie around living off her money until his big break suddenly materialized. Left to his own devices, he would probably not even get new pictures (which most of the time she paid for) or even go out on auditions. Perhaps he thought he would be discovered, like Lana Turner, in some drugstore.

His lean, sexy body, clad in tight dungarees that left little to the imagination, moved past the couch she was sitting on, and she thought if she must have a parasite, at least she had an attractive one.

She waited for him to come out of the bathroom so she could tell him to go down for the mail. When it was clear that he wasn't going to come out for quite a while—he spent at least ten minutes on his hair alone—she decided she had better trudge to the mailbox herself. It was down three flights of rickety stairs beside a wobbling banister.

For the second time since she'd awakened she made the descent, past bicycles and baby strollers leaning against the walls, coming to a puddle of urine on one of the landings like an appeasement to some angry tenement god. A moment later she was in the shabby, unlighted foyer.

She was gratified to see that her mailbox had not been broken into today. Thieves were always looking for checks, though how they planned to cash them was beyond her. She pulled out a small stack of bills, advertisements, a letter from her mother (no cash enclosed), and no checks. There was also a letter that had been forwarded from the office of the *East Village Vagrant*, a counterculture paper she had done some articles for. The paper was a weird combination of the trendy—anticipating the ravages of gentrification—and the political, leaning toward the left. One could only wonder what direction it would take once they were well into the nineties.

As she climbed the stairs, she took another peek at the curious letter. She would have assumed it was simply another advertisement except that it had been mailed to her, care of the newspaper. The return address read Barrows Industries, and the envelope itself was a pretty pink shade with a vague lavender fragrance. She knew it had to be from the Barrows Beauty Company, but she also hoped it might be a bit more personal. A kind of rush went all through her body, a sensation of excitement and anticipation mingled with a peculiar knot of anxiety. *Could it be?* . . . It had been years since they'd last seen each other.

By the time she got to her apartment she had opened the letter and read half of it.

"Anything for me?" David asked, as she walked in. He was on the sofa wearing a bright crimson shirt which contrasted nicely with his dark locks and the wavy curlicues of chest hair that showed below the collar.

"Nothing, honey. Just a lot of junk mail. Except for this."

"What is it?"

She finished reading it. "A press release from Barrows —you know, the cosmetics firm."

He laughed. " 'Barrows Means Beauty.' You sure use enough of that shit."

"I used to go to school with a girl whose father owned the company."

"Wow. She must have been loaded!"

Leave it to him to think of that. "Anyway, she probably read my last article in the *Vagrant* and decided to send me one of these notices through the paper. We lost touch a few years ago so she wouldn't know where I live."

David wasn't very interested. "What's it about?" he said.

She handed it to him and let him read it himself while she mulled it over. Barrows Industries was holding a press conference Monday morning at the Berkley Hotel on Fifth Avenue. They were to announce a revolutionary new product that would turn the whole cosmetics industry—not to mention the world—on its ears. She wondered what it was all about. Companies didn't usually hold press conferences just to show off a new shade of eyeliner.

"What do you think?" David asked when he was through reading.

Peggy shrugged. "Probably a new perfume or something. That's all the rage these days. Liz Taylor has her own scent. So does Cher. You know how they hype everything."

David grunted. "Hell, before you know it they'll be packaging bottles of 'Lassie.' "

She laughed. "Seriously, that's probably what it is. They got some movie star to lend their name to a new perfume. Sure, that's it. Why else would they have all this publicity?"

"You gonna go?"

"Yeah. Why not? There'll be lots of celebrities there. And it says there'll be a complimentary champagne brunch. Yeah, I think I will go. It would be nice to see Ronnie again. I'd give her a call and find out what it's about if I had her number. It was nice of her to see that I was invited. She *must* have been responsible. Of course, I am a member of the press, so to speak."

"Who's Ronnie?"

"Ronica Barrows. The girl I told you about. I knew her in college."

" 'Ronica'?"

"Short for Veronica, I suppose. Everyone just knew her as Ronnie or Ronica. She was beautiful."

"And rich."

"And her brother, Romeo. What a gorgeous guy!"

David swung around in his seat on the sofa and said, "Now, wait just a minute. Hold on. You mean to tell me that somewhere out there is a guy actually named *Romeo,* for crying out loud!"

"Romeo Barrows. And he looked like a Romeo, too. Dreamy."

"What did the guys on the lacrosse team call him, 'Skipper'?"

She smirked. "Everyone just called him Rom for short. Nobody made fun of him. He was too big and good-looking for that. And I think he did play lacrosse and basketball and all that stuff. He dated a lot of girls. Everyone had a crush on him."

"Romeo," he snorted. "I can just see the two of them now, Ronica and Romeo, two walking Ivory soap bars with twenty-carat teeth and charge cards at Bloomingdale's."

"There was no Bloomingdale's where we went to school," she retorted. "And neither of them was really like that. They were nice. Not what you'd expect. They had good manners, good breeding. Something special about them."

"Not slobs like us, huh?"

She decided not to answer him. "I'd like to see Ronica again. I think I will go Monday."

"Don't invite me, huh. Does it say you can bring a guest?"

"It's at eleven A.M., Davey; you won't be up."

"Shit, you bet I won't. You'll have to get a whiff of Lassie's new cologne without me."

"I'll manage."

He went into the bedroom to finish dressing. She took his spot on the couch, warm from his body heat, and stroked the armrest with her fingers, wallowing for a second in the feel, the smell, of him.

For a long time now she'd felt as if her life were on hold, as if everything were passing her by and there was little if anything she could do to halt it, to make it slow down and wait until she had it in order and achieved everything she wanted. For some time now she had waited to see a light at the end of the tunnel, some kind of sign that perhaps brighter days were just ahead.

She couldn't say why, but she had a feeling that this ambiguous press release was that omen, that it somehow promised the life of excitement, glamour, and fulfillment she had always dreamed of. She knew it didn't make any sense, but she was somehow certain that she was on the verge of major changes in her life and career. She just knew it.

She only hoped they wouldn't be changes for the worse.

CHAPTER FIVE

On Monday morning, Peggy took the IRT Lexington Avenue subway in plenty of time to reach the Berkley Hotel by eleven—assuming the train didn't break down en route. The subway car was comparatively deserted: a mother with a baby stroller and an older child in tow; a bewhiskered bum who stood in one corner and swayed in odd counterpoint to the motions of the train; two chattering black ladies who looked as if they were heading uptown for lunch and a movie. Peggy settled back in her seat and thought back to the last time she had seen her old friend Ronica Barrows.

It had been during Christmas week, she remembered. Four years ago? Five? She was still in her twenties, she was sure of that. Even by that time she and Ronica had started to drift apart. They literally bumped into each other in the snow outside Macy's, each doing last-minute Christmas shopping. Ronica had seemed glad to see her, yet distant and preoccupied at the same time. They'd agreed to rest their feet and get some hot chocolate at a nearby coffee shop.

She had sensed during the half hour they spent together that Ronica deeply needed to get something off her chest, to confide in someone. But perhaps the gap between them had already widened too much, and she found herself unable to open up to Peggy. There was no simple way to describe what had happened to them. They had always been from different worlds, separated by wealth, class, appearance. The miracle was they had ever become friends at all. Peggy viewed the dissolution of their relationship with equal parts sadness and relief; Ronica was a difficult person to keep up with, always on the go, and with plenty of money to go anywhere she wanted.

For months before that chance reunion they had hardly seen or spoken to one another. Ronica had gone to Europe, acquired a new apartment on the West Coast, traveled all over as a representative of her father's cosmetics firm. She could have modeled their products herself, but for a surprising shy streak that kept her out of the limelight, and even led her to go off to a small Vermont campus instead of a more fashionable, more prestigious university.

As Ronica immersed herself more and more in the social opportunities engendered by her background and position, she had less and less time for Peggy. Peggy was never bitter about it; she understood that Ronica had responsibilities and options that would never be available to her. It was only a matter of time before distance—social as well as geographic—drove them apart.

Although during that brief conversation over cocoa Peggy had sensed an opportunity to rekindle the closeness that had been lost to the passage of time, she held back. Perhaps too much time had gone by since the weekly outings, the thrice-a-week phone calls, the long, stimulating letters they sent each other during those months after graduation, when both had moved back to New York. It felt peculiar trying to get her friend to take her into her confidence, so she'd sat there and allowed the conversation to remain on a warm, amiable, but ultimately superficial level. Then their cups were empty, and they made empty promises to write or call. A few months later Peggy moved into her new apartment, met Davey, and didn't bother forwarding her new address and number to her old friend. It was over, but that was life.

Still, she was haunted by the look on Ronnie's face that night, a lost, frightened, lonely look. Thinking back, she wondered how she could have let the girl go away without asking—demanding—her to tell what was wrong. It was easy to see now that Ronnie had suggested they go to a restaurant just so she could unburden herself to someone she thought would be sympathetic and understanding. But then in the harsh coffee-shop light, among strangers, beneath the glare of the impatient waitress, she had been unable to proceed.

So lost was Peggy in her memories that she nearly missed her stop. She got off at Fifty-ninth Street, rode the escalator to street level, and headed three blocks west to Fifth Avenue. In a short while she was within sight of the handsome, formidable structure known as the Berkley. It was one of New York's oldest, and most expensive, hotels, squat and rectangular, with high shaded windows and a gray brick façade.

As it was still early, she killed some time staring wistfully into nearby shop windows, then after fifteen minutes headed directly for the hotel. She walked into the main entrance across from the park and headed for the elevators in back. The press release had said the conference would be held in ballroom B on the third floor.

She got off the elevator, stepped to the right past a sign announcing the conference, and soon reached the entrance to the proper ballroom. She noted that she was one of the first arrivals. As it was not yet eleven she debated going back downstairs and wandering through the shops on lobby level, but decided instead to sit quietly on a couch near the room's reception area and wait until more people came up. As she sat, she wondered what sort of reception she'd get from Ronica and why she had chosen this rather unorthodox way of renewing their acquaintance.

She supposed it would only be natural for Ronica to

hope Peggy would somehow be able to help publicize whatever Barrows was hyping this morning. Perhaps she'd mistakenly believed Peggy was on the staff of the *Vagrant* or had access to even trendier publications. Surely she must have realized there was a limit to what Peggy could do—free-lance writers were not in the advertising business after all.

Then again, perhaps there was no ulterior motive. Ronica had never been the type to exploit someone for personal or corporate publicity. She just wasn't interested in that. Even if Peggy suggested doing a write-up on her friend, Ronnie would most likely be more embarrassed by the idea than anything else. Of course, Peggy reminded herself, people did change.

People did change. It was due, in large part, to Ronica that Peggy had changed. If she had never met her, things might have been so very different. She thought back to 1974, the first semester of her freshman year at the University of Vermont in Burlington, the year she had first met Ronica Barrows, and the changes had begun . . .

Peggy was lying in her bed flipping through a movie magazine when her roommate, Joannie Anderson, swept into their room and hurled herself onto the bed against the opposite wall. "Shit! I am so stoned I'll never get my homework done!"

Peggy didn't really approve of her roommate's constant reliance on marijuana to get her through the day, but she kept her opinions to herself. Peggy had suffered enough being unpopular in high school and was not about to make the same mistake in college. She had deliberately chosen this Vermont university so that she could make a fresh start and avoid all the smug, hateful classmates she'd grown up with in the public school system in Queens, the ones who had long ago classified her as "dog shit" and would have nothing to do with her. Her parents would have been just as happy if she had gone to Queens College like the rest of them, but she promised to take

out a student loan, get a part-time job at the college to
offset expenses—anything so that they'd let her get away
from the scene of so many moments of disappointment,
disaster, and loneliness. She was a fat, pimply eighteen-
year-old, devoid of friends, who desperately needed fresh
territory in which to grow and blossom.

But so far it hadn't quite worked out that way. Free
from preconceptions, the girls in her section of the college dorm were generally kind and friendly, at least, if
not overly enthusiastic toward her presence. Peggy assumed the one they really wanted to get to know was
Ronica Barrows, daughter of a cosmetics magnate, the
one they called the Beauty Queen. She lived in the fourth
room down the hall. Of course, Peggy was also interested
in her, but knew from experience that girls like that
didn't bother with girls like Peggy Antonicci, so she kept
her distance and avoided the inevitable rebuff.

"Help me with science, Peggy, *please,*" Joannie was
groaning, spread across the bed in a supine position that
bordered on the vulgar. Some of the girls, including Joannie, liked Peggy because she was smart, helpful, and un-
likely to steal their dates away. Everyone seemed to agree
that Peggy was "sweet," a characteristic that seemed less
and less a compliment as the years went by.

Peggy was torn between agreeing to help her roommate and telling her truthfully that she really only felt
like sitting and reading, when someone entered the room
and completely altered the course of Peggy's college life.

Peggy had never seen Ronica Barrows quite this close
before. She was a bit shocked by what an anachronism
the girl was, but also startled by her pale, obvious beauty
and her height, well above average for a woman her age.
Ronica Barrows had clearly been brought up in a shel-
tered household, one untouched by modern times and the
TV news. In spite of her familial connection to fashion,
she was quite out of date, yet genuinely lovely as well,
able to bring off this fragile out-of-time quality without
appearing entirely ludicrous.

There she was, wearing a pretty pink dress and high heels, and exuding a sweet but heavy perfume. Her hair was styled and sprayed. She wore lipstick, eyeshadow, and face powder. Had she been devoid of good looks, personality, and money, she would undoubtedly have become a laughingstock. Luckily there were still enough girls on campus who secretly wished they could emulate her and who wanted urgently to befriend her.

Nevertheless, Ronica was doomed not to be taken seriously, the type one wanted to know for their entertainment value alone.

"Hi! Have either of you girls seen Laura, my roomie?"

Joannie thought Ronica was a Barbie doll and had told Peggy so on more than one occasion. "Why? Need to borrow some nail polish?"

If Ronica was aware the remark had been sarcastic, she didn't show it. "I just have to talk to her. If you see her, will you let me know?"

"Sure," Peggy said, smiling. Who cared if Ronica was a little old-fashioned? This was the type of girl Peggy had always dreamed of knowing, of _being_, as she was growing up, and she would not let this opportunity go by. Ronica seemed to have already developed a small circle of friends, mostly from square student government or homecoming committees, but there was always room for one more. Peggy went out of her way to do something she'd never bothered to do in high school: make the first move, reach out, start a conversation. She was determined college was going to be different.

"Ronica," she said, as Ronica was about to turn and leave in search of Laura. "I was just wondering. Do you think you'll try out for the drama club play?" It was Tennessee Williams's _The Night of the Iguana_.

"Don't worry, Peggy," Joannie said with a smirk. "You wouldn't be up for the same parts." Under her breath she added, "Ronica couldn't play anyone human."

A flash of hesitation, embarrassment, creased Ronica's

features. "Uh, I don't know, Peggy. I don't know if I'm any good as an actress."

"Who says you have to have talent?" Joannie said.

Peggy quickly said, "It might be fun." For lack of anything else to say, she added, "You look like an actress. I suppose everyone tells you that."

"Brother," Joannie muttered.

"Uh, people sometimes tell me that, yeah. I don't know why. I think I'd be too nervous to, y' know, get out in front of all those people on stage."

Why, this girl is actually shy, like me! Peggy thought. Aloud she said, "Yeah, me too. But still—maybe we should give it a try. Who knows? We might become big film stars or something." She held her hand behind her head and adopted a silly, theatrical pose.

Ronica laughed and did the same thing. "Yeah. Who knows? I *was* thinking about maybe trying out." She bit her lip momentarily. "Are you going to?"

"Yeah," Peggy said brightly.

"Well, maybe I'll see you there."

"Yeah, okay."

And with a flounce, Ronica was out of the room. Peggy thought she was sweet and easy to talk to, not stuck-up or cold or brittle as she'd expected. Joannie was staring at her disgustedly.

"Trying to suck up to the Beauty Queen, Peggy?"

"I was just being friendly."

"Hoping you can get your hands on one of the boys that always hang around her? Yuck. Jocks and straights, who wants them? She wouldn't let a freak get within ten miles of her, that one. If a guy's got long hair, forget it."

Peggy was about to mutter something in wimpish agreement, when she thought: I *don't* agree. *Why should I pretend I do? I'm a person with opinions that count.* She was not the mouse of high school days, too scared to speak out against anyone who might befriend her. They never befriended her anyway, so what did she have to lose by being honest now? Besides, Joannie could be awfully irritating at times.

"How do you know that?" Peggy asked. "Why don't you give Ronica a chance? Just because she's a little . . . out of it doesn't make her some kind of witch. She just needs time to adjust. For all you know she could wind up with a boyfriend who has hair down to his shoulders."

Joannie rolled over against the wall so that her back was to Peggy. "God, Peggy, maybe if you ask her real nice, she'll let you be her roommate next semester."

Peggy was hurt at first, frightened. But then she thought that that wouldn't really be such a bad thing after all.

CHAPTER SIX

A dozen people poured from the elevator, startling Peggy back to the present. A second elevator door opened before the first had closed and unleashed a new bunch of chattering arrivals. Before she knew it there were swarms of people gathering before the reception table outside the ballroom entrance.

Peggy got to her feet, pulled the press release out of her bag, and waited on the line that was forming. She looked around the hallway but saw no celebrities, no one she recognized or had ever worked with. Just ordinary people like herself who had come for the champagne brunch, a chance to slake their curiosity, and a change of pace from their run-of-the-mill, nine-to-five working patterns. Still, Peggy always felt inferior and out of place at glamorous functions, even when she was dolled up.

Inside the ballroom, Peggy saw that there was a dais at one end upon which a lectern and several folding chairs had been placed. Against the windows there were several long buffet tables containing all manner of tempting hot and cold dishes. Several huge coffee machines rose above the display of food like towers erected in the midst of an edible topography. The many aromas wafting through the air combined to form one intoxicatingly delicious fragrance. Already some people had filled their plates and were seating themselves at the many round tables situated here and there about the ballroom.

Peggy stood to one side for a bit, watching the other people, noting that very few of them had come by themselves as she had. Many of them seemed to already know one another, had arrived in groups of twos and threes, and were moving together to form little circles of even larger numbers. *Wonderful!* Peggy thought.

Peggy was not great at mixing. She figured the best she could get out of this was a good, free meal.

She got in the food line—she figured it was smart to get a plateful while it was still available, although most of the other early arrivals had settled for a cup of coffee. She wasn't sure how long they'd serve the brunch once the big announcement was made. Besides, she wanted to get a spot at a table before all the seats were taken.

She was waiting for a chef in a big floppy hat and white apron to spoon some scrambled eggs onto her plate when she spotted *him,* over in the corner of the ballroom, talking to two older men: the handsomest man in the room as he had always been back in college. Romeo Barrows. Even now, so many years later, he could still make her pulse race. He hadn't lost one iota of his appeal—if anything he had become better looking. He did not look very much older than he had in college. Certainly not anywhere near his age. What a gorgeous creature! With a timeless beauty like Dorian Gray.

Back in college, Romeo, like his sister Ronica, had eventually conformed to the mode of dress and hair that had been adopted by his peers at Burlington. He grew his hair long, switched from tailored suits to torn jeans and T-shirts, even sported a scraggly beard and mustache for a while. None of that had fully disguised his beauty, but Peggy had always been dismayed at what it had done to his appearance. Why look like other boys, she had felt like telling him, when he was not like other boys. Now she saw that he had gone back to the style he had once preferred, and which was so suitable to the nineties. The effect was, in a word, devastating. He looked like a movie star, political candidate, and Wall Street financier all rolled into one. He was magnificent.

Romeo had short blond hair which was combed straight back off his forehead and over to one side in a sleek, glamorous coiffure that would have looked ridiculous on a man with heavier features. His face was rounded, a bit long and narrow, with a strong chin, high cheekbones, a classic nose, and lips neither too full nor too thin. His small deep-set eyes were brown and penetrating beneath a high forehead and thick eyebrows. When his small round mouth opened in a galvanizing smile it revealed wide rows of perfect white teeth. Romeo was dressed in a light gray suit with a red tie with a diamond design. He had probably paid more for the tie than most men paid for their suits.

Peggy couldn't take her eyes off him. She had to be nudged into holding her plate out so that the heaping spoonful of scrambled eggs wouldn't drop onto the tablecloth. A man behind her spoke to her impatiently. Finally she snapped out of her trance and moved farther down the line for pancakes and sausage. But her mind was elsewhere, had in fact gone back in time to the day she had first been introduced to Romeo Barrows . . .

Peggy and Ronica walked slowly across campus to the afternoon rehearsal of *The Night of the Iguana,* chatting and giggling like sisters. Good sense had prevailed and Ronica had *not* been given the lead role of Maxine Faulk, but rather the part of the precocious teenager Charlotte Goodall who falls for the defrocked minister, Shannon. Peggy had gotten the even smaller part of the German tourist, Frau Fahrenkopf, but she did get to ask the hero if he made "pee pee all over the suitcases of the ladies from Texas." She had to admit she was hysterical saying that line. They were having a lot of fun and didn't have to be on call all the time like the lead actors did.

Peggy was ecstatic; there she was being part of a team,

making friends for the first time in her life. And she and
Ronica were getting to know each other really well. Because of the play there was a bond between them that did
not exist between the other girls who lived in their section
of the dorm.

"What do you think of Charlie?" Ronica asked Peggy
as they walked the footpath. Charlie was the young man
who played Reverend Shannon.

"He's kind of cute," Peggy said.

Peggy was just about to confess to Ronica which boy
on campus turned her on the most, when uncannily she
saw him step out from the science building and approach
from the opposite direction. She had seen him here and
there but had always been too embarrassed to ask anyone
who he was. She was about to lift her hand to tug on
Ronnie's sweater when Ronnie suddenly raised her own
arm to wave at the handsome stranger. Peggy's heart
sank: wouldn't you know the sexiest guy and the sexiest
girl at UVM had to know each other, and for all she
knew could even be lovers. But then she got a surprise.

"Hi, Rom!" Ronnie said as the gap between the girls
and the striding Adonis closed. When they were standing
side by side, Ronnie introduced Peggy to Romeo. "This is
my brother, Rom. And this is Peggy, a friend of mine.
We're in the play together."

"Nice to meet you, Peggy."

Peggy took his smooth outstretched hand and took in
his manly beauty with her own brand of shy intensity.
She finally knew what it meant to feel "weak in the
knees." He smelled like clean, fresh seawater—probably
a cologne with a "marine" scent—and had a patrician,
well-modulated voice. Now that she was close enough to
study him she saw the resemblance to his sister.

Afterward, when Peggy and Ronnie went on to the
auditorium, Peggy said, "I didn't know he was your
brother. I've been wondering who he was." She stopped
before she could tell Ronnie exactly how she felt about
her sibling. Seeing him close up, touching him, talking to

him had only made her infatuation grow stronger than ever.

"We don't get to see much of each other," Ronnie said. "He's a sophomore. Different majors, different courses, you know. He has his own friends. I sort of feel guilty that he's here."

"Why is that?"

"Well, he's a year older than me and he'd already started college on the West Coast. But when I told my parents I wanted to go to UVM they pretty much insisted Rom transfer." She laughed. "I'm not sure if they want him to look out for me, or if I'm supposed to help him with his studying. In California he spent more time on the beach than in classes. School has never really been that important to him, and his grades have never been that good. Neither have mine, for that matter."

Peggy felt like saying: *Oh, please, please Ronnie. Stay close—real close—to your brother. Make him part of our circle. Get him to try out for the next play.* She'd take a tiny part in the most boring play in the world if it meant she could get to know Rom better. The thought of not seeing, talking to him again for possibly weeks or months was more than she could bear.

That afternoon Peggy sat staring at the stage as she watched Ronnie play her big scene with Reverend Shannon over and over again. Ronnie was not very good, actually—she was too shy and reserved to give the role all the wild, childish sexiness it required. Instead of Ronnie and Charlie, however, Peggy kept seeing herself on stage with Romeo Barrows.

If she ever had a love scene with Romeo, Peggy knew, she would have absolutely no trouble coming on as strong as the part required.

But who was she kidding? The chance of her getting together with Romeo Barrows was as likely as the Christmas tree in Rockefeller Center uprooting itself and taking a mid-winter stroll up Fifth Avenue.

CHAPTER SEVEN_____

Things hadn't worked out quite the way she had planned, Peggy reminded herself. She crossed the room from the buffet to the nearest unoccupied table. She sat down at a spot not too far from the stage and tried to keep her eyes off Romeo while she nibbled on bacon and potatoes. Would he possibly remember her after all these years? They had never gotten to know each other very well. She was being silly, she knew. She was not a schoolgirl anymore, but a thirty-three-year-old woman.

Besides, thinking about the old days and all the pain they engendered filled her with infinite sadness. She had a guy, didn't she, a good-looking guy waiting faithfully for her at home? Wasn't Dave enough? Dave was real while Romeo had never been anything more than a fantasy. Yet the hard part of it was that during the short time she knew him she had sensed that he had underlying qualities that were more than a match for his surface beauty. Of course that made it worse. It was easy enough to fall out of love with a handsome heel, but a beautiful man who was warm and thoughtful? Those were the ones who really broke your heart.

She wondered where Ronica was. Had she changed much over the years? Peggy knew that she herself had not changed much and didn't know whether to be mortified or grateful. There had been some alterations, of course. She was not the dumpy little mouse of yesteryear. She was a confident, attractive woman of the nineties. At least that's what she told herself.

The food was delicious. Creamy eggs, perfectly toasted English muffins, delightfully tart sausages that snapped and exuded juice when bitten. She had only sampled a few of the items and her plate was packed to the edges. The coffee was piping hot and aromatic. As she bit into her buttered muffin, a few people came over to the table and began taking up the seats around her: two swarthy men with slick voices and expressions who were probably in the ad business; another woman on her own (brava!) who wore an expression that practically screamed "I'm tired, leave me alone" and was probably a writer for a tabloid or fashion rag; and an obvious, stereotypical reporter in rumpled clothing who spent more time writing busily in a notepad than eating from his overstuffed dinner plate. Two glamorous black women came over a few minutes later, and seemed very friendly. One turned to Peggy and asked if she knew what the big announcement was about.

"Beats me," Peggy replied, wishing she had thought of something more clever to say. "A new perfume, maybe?"

"That's what I was thinking," said the woman, who had a vague Jamaican accent and the most incredible cheekbones. A model perhaps? However, she was dressed in a severe black suit which indicated she was probably a businessperson.

Peggy thought she'd try out Davey's little joke on the ladies. "There's a rumor it's a new fragrance called 'Lassie.' "

The woman's eyebrows lifted. "Oh?" She didn't get the joke.

Before Peggy could explain, the woman turned to reply to something spoken by her equally attractive companion.

Then she saw, or rather heard, in the distance, the woman she'd come here to see. Peggy recognized the voice rising over the heads of the gluttonous assembly. When she heard Romeo's voice calling in reply she was certain.

She swiveled in her seat and tried to determine where the voices were coming from, but Romeo was no longer in the corner, and neither he nor his sister was yet on the dais. Finally she saw the two siblings standing to one side of the room, holding cups of coffee and calling to someone who stood in the hallway out of Peggy's line of sight. Ronica again seemed preoccupied and as busy as she had that Christmas. Peggy sensed this would not be an appropriate time to go over and say hello.

Then again, why else was she there? Why else had Ronica invited her? This might be the best time of all, before the press conference formally started and there were all kinds of questions and commotion. Yet the thought of leaving the table, calling attention to herself, and going up to Ronica only to catch her in an awkward moment or be dealt with abruptly made Peggy feel rather queasy. Or was it the food? She figured it would be better if Ronnie just spotted her and came over on her own, though she had no idea how long she might have to wait for that to happen.

Ronica stepped away from her brother and began to walk down the aisle on Peggy's left toward the dais. Peggy self-consciously turned her head and resumed eating. What if she called out or waved and Ronica didn't see her or just continued walking? She'd feel ridiculous. *Maybe Ronnie hadn't sent the invitation and didn't even expect—or want—Peggy to be there?*

She sensed that Ronnie had passed by and wondered if she had seen her. When she thought it was safe Peggy lifted her head and looked toward the front of the room. Ronica had stopped at the edge of the stairs leading to the dais and was engaging a squat, hairy man in conversation.

Peggy had never seen such a furry individual—hair poked out from the cuffs of his well-tailored suit, hair stuck out above his collar; his eyebrows turned upward absurdly at the far ends, giving him a vampiric demeanor. There was hair on the back of his hands, thick waves of it, and the spider's nest of discombobulated locks on top of his head was so grandiose and vulgar that it had to be a hairpiece. Then again, who would wear a hairpiece that looked as bad as that?

But her gaze did not stray toward this creature's countenance for too long; instead, Peggy found herself studying Ronica and being more taken with her beauty than ever. She had aged gracefully to say the least. She did not even look as if she were thirty yet, much younger in fact. She wore a black outfit, pearls, subdued but highly creative and effective makeup; an upswept hairstyle showed off her cheekbones and bright big green eyes. Her hair was now a reddish-blond instead of the honey-blond it had been in college, but there was something else different about her that Peggy could simply not put her finger on.

Ronica Barrows's features were delicate without being sharp or overly diminutive. She had a real nose, instead of those bobbed ones that were so popular in the early days of cosmetic surgery, those proboscises that looked as if some mad doctor had hacked too much off the end and pushed the nostrils several degrees too high in the air. Ronnie's nose was rounded and small and perfect. Peggy didn't know if her complexion was still naturally rosy beneath her powder as it used to be, but it looked no different than it had more than fifteen years ago when Peggy had first met her. Her head was a perfect oval, with a dainty chin, creamy cheeks, and moderately full, lightly glossed lips. Once again Peggy ached to think that one person could have such priceless beauty while so many others were physically bankrupt. If Ronnie hadn't been such a nice person, Peggy would have hated her.

But she didn't. She realized she loved her. And she thought back to the night during their freshman year when Ronnie proved worthy of that love, and turned into a friend not quite like any other, the night Peggy nearly died—and might have, if it hadn't been for Ronnie. It wasn't hard to sweep away the years. In some ways, Ronnie, standing there at the edge of the dais, looked not much different from the way she looked that night, at the final night's cast party for *The Night of the Iguana,* and Peggy could hardly keep from crying . . .

Peggy sat there on the ottoman in the corner of Professor and Mrs. Undermyer's living room, trying her level best to keep from crying. She hoped no one was watching her—but of course that was silly. Everyone was ignoring her as usual. She felt a flood of tears threatening to erupt any second and was determined to prevent that humiliation at least.

She should have known that she'd wind up like this. What made her think that Peggy Antonicci, fat, pimply loser, would be able to break away from her fate of pain and loneliness? How presumptuous she had been to think she could have real friends and find love like everyone else did. What made her think that, no matter what she did, no matter what happened, she would ever be anything but dumpy little Peggy Antonicci?

She thought she had successfully wrestled back an outpouring of tears, but to make doubly certain she lifted her glass of icy dregs to her lips and bent back her head, hiding behind the glass and pretending she was drinking what was once gin and tonic. She put the glass down when she felt in better control and looked around at everyone else having fun at the party, and wondered for the fiftieth time why it had to turn out like this.

Oh, she had had her moments; that was what made it worse. Fate had allowed her to go just so far before pulling her back to her miserable reality, like one of those iguanas tied to the verandah in Tennessee Williams's play that could go no farther than the end of its tether. She had cruelly been allowed to think she could have a normal life—and now this.

She looked over at one side of the room and saw Romeo and that girl, that unpleasant girl she had never seen before, making out like crazy, lips and tongues intertwined, practically burrowed into that big reclining chair like two orgiastic rabbits.

Well, she had been put in her place, all right. Nothing like a hard dose of reality to remind you what a drip and a dog you were. *What does he see in that girl? She isn't really that much prettier than I am.* But of course that didn't matter. The problem was, who would want to have Peggy Antonicci, who looked so funny and dumpy in her costume as the German tourist, for a girlfriend? Her reputation as a freak had preceded her. She didn't know how the kids in Bayside had managed to tell everyone up at UVM about her, but somehow they had. She might just as well have been back in Queens with the students who had tormented her all her life.

Someone pulled out from the crowd in the center of the room and came toward her. For a second Peggy thought it was someone who had taken pity on her and decided to talk to her, but it was only the costume mistress looking for an ashtray.

"You all right, Peggy?" she asked, almost as an afterthought, after stubbing out her cigarette.

Peggy managed a weak smile. "Fine. Just resting."

"Okay, honey."

Peggy felt bolstered a bit by the woman's attention. Why was it always grown-ups, older people, who asked how she was feeling? Why were people her own age never concerned? Her mother had told her more than once that she was mature for her age. Did her peers sense it and therefore avoid her? Was she doomed to be forever insecure and friendless?

Ronica, the friend she most admired, was sitting amid a circle of her other admirers at the opposite end of the room. Pretty, glamorous Ronica, still wearing the provocative outfit she had worn as the teenage girl vacationing at the Costa Verde Hotel, only she'd thrown a cloak

of some kind over her shoulders. Everyone had piled into
a couple of cars immediately following the final curtain—
they'd strike the set tomorrow—and driven the mile or so
to Director Undermyer's house. Most of the cast had
planned to remove their makeup and change into street
clothes in the Undermyers' bathroom, but some had decided to stay "in character" for the party. Peggy chose to
take off the unflattering outfit she wore as Frau
Fahrenkopf immediately, not that doing so had done her
much good.

She had lost track of how many gin and tonics she'd
had in an attempt to lose her inhibitions and feel more
like part of the crowd. She hadn't felt this left-out in
weeks. The girls at the dorm were friendly enough—
though they'd formed their own cliques while Peggy
hung out with the dramatics crowd—and at rehearsals
Peggy enjoyed talking to the crew and actors with small
parts. But tonight, with the leads and their boyfriends
and girlfriends, and parents and siblings, milling about,
Peggy felt overwhelmed by so many strangers, intimidated by people she had only spoken to briefly, if at all.
Everyone else was dancing and laughing and living it up,
and at first Peggy had been having fun. Though she could
not have reconstructed how it happened, she had somehow wound up here alone on the ottoman in the corner.
She looked around for a friendly, unoccupied face, some
laughing group she could join with ease, but everyone
seemed so involved, getting along so well without her. It
was as if she had utterly ceased to exist.

Twenty minutes ago she had seen Romeo standing to
one side of several couples who were dancing in the middle of the room. As he watched them his body moved
sinuously to the music. She had spoken to him briefly a
few times since she'd met him, and earlier he'd gone out
of his way to tell her how much he'd enjoyed her perfor-
mance. She figured he would not object if she were to go
over and ask him if he'd like to dance, just as friends; he
looked like he wanted to dance and it was not as if they

didn't know one another. Peggy was one of his sister's closest friends, in fact. Surely he'd be cool about it and say yes.

So, full of alcoholic courage, she got up, went over to him, tapped him on the shoulder, and said, "Would you like to dance?" She broke out into the widest and gayest, most nonchalant smile she could possibly manage. A second passed. *A lifetime.*

"Uh, maybe later," he said finally, a taut, uncomfortable look on his face.

"Okay," Peggy said, hoping no one had heard or noticed the mortifying exchange. Her face red with embarrassment, she made her way back to her corner. A moment later she saw that girl return from the ladies' room where she had apparently gone and lead Romeo out onto the dance floor.

Why hadn't she realized he would probably have a girlfriend? Someone as good-looking as Rom wouldn't spend his nights alone, for Pete's sake.

So she sat and sipped her gin and let the fear and paranoia and loneliness engulf her, let the music and the sound of conversation grow to deafening proportions, as the alcohol in her system exaggerated her feelings of isolation. She saw herself as a hideous troll pathetically taking up space in the Siberia of the Undermyer's living room, while her friend Ronica—glamorous Ronica, glorious Ronica—took center stage among her many male and female acolytes, and was made all the more charming because she seemed completely unaware of the warmth and sensuality she generated.

After a while, Peggy couldn't stand it anymore: Ronica's neglect, Romeo's passionate involvement with that girl in the recliner. She got up and left the house as surreptitiously as possible. At one in the morning she walked along the side of the narrow road that led back to the campus, hiding in bushes whenever a car would come along so that no one could catch sight of her in her misery. She was very drunk and had trouble maneuvering. It never occurred to her that many of the feelings she was feeling were not real.

In the dorm, which was half-empty because many of the students had gone home for the weekend, she found her section deserted and silent. She took a bottle of sleeping pills from the bathroom and took them into her room with her. She lay down on her bed, holding the bottle close to her breast. She cried passionately and pictured herself getting a glass of water, taking the pills. She had never felt so lonely, so desolate, so hopeless. *Freak, freak, freak.* She was about to go to the bathroom to get that glass of water when she heard someone walking down the outside hall. She realized with dismay that she had left her door wide open and whoever it was might have heard her sobbing.

Ronica came into the room. She was caught like an angel in a nimbus of light from the corridor. "Here you are!" she said. "Are you all right? I looked for you all over and figured you had left."

Did you care? Peggy felt like asking. She wiped her eyes and struggled to sit upright on the bed. "I—I was tired. I think I drank too much." Before she could stop herself, the alcohol stirred her to total honesty. "I felt so alone there. No one was talking to me." She gave a laugh that was more of a gurgle. "I've been sitting here crying. What a dope."

Ronica sat down beside her and held her. "Honey, you weren't alone. I was there. And Charlie and Susan and Burt. We all wondered where you had gone to."

"I was over in the corner where I belonged."

"What are you talking about?" She gave Peggy a look of tender exasperation. "All you had to do was come over and join us. After I found out you were gone I figured I might as well leave myself." She shook her head in mild reproach. "Charlie and Susan disappeared into a bedroom and Burt kept making passes. Where were you when I needed you, kid?"

Peggy couldn't get her English straight. "Not being

made passes at anyways." She burped. "Or something like that."

Ronnie laughed. "You *are* drunk, silly. That's all that's wrong with you. Boy, are you going to have a hangover."

And then Ronnie spotted the sleeping pills.

"What's this? For heaven's sake, Peggy, you weren't going to—?"

"I was thinking about it, yeah."

"But why, for heaven's sake. *Why?*"

"I told you. I was all alone there. And I just hate—there've been too many times when I was all alone, and I . . ." Even drunk she couldn't bring herself to tell her about Romeo, how she felt about him.

"Oh, honey, everybody's alone now and then. You think I don't feel alone sometimes?"

"Y—you?"

"When I first came here, don't you think I knew how everyone was laughing at me. I looked so weird and all. Everyone thought I was stupid and old-fashioned. I'm terrible in that play and don't think I don't know it. I felt so stupid running around on stage like that, trying to act sexy and feeling like such a jerk. Even at that party, I felt so out of it. Most of the time I just sat there and listened . . ."

"But I saw you. Everyone was gathered around you."

"You're so drunk you would have seen anything. Yeah, I was in a big group. They were talking about Ibsen and O'Neill and Strindberg and I felt so dumb because half the plays they talked about I'd never even heard of. Somebody said something about Chekhov and I said, "You mean the character on *Star Trek?*" I was just making a joke. I've heard of the *playwright* Chekhov, but everyone thought I was serious. I was only trying to contribute to the conversation. I heard someone turn to Mrs. Undermyer and say, 'Not too bright, that one, is she?' People were snickering. I felt so stupid." She looked down at her feet and her voice got lower. "Everyone thinks I'm stupid. Maybe they're right."

Peggy put her arm around Ronica and gave her an affectionate squeeze. "No, you're not. Just because you're not 'political' and don't want to smoke dope. A lot of girls are just jealous of you because you're pretty. They don't know you like I know you. You're really nice, Ronnie—and smart."

Ronnie smiled. Peggy held out the bottle of sleeping pills and said, "Want to use these?"

They both burst out laughing.

When they quieted, Ronnie said, "I guess neither of us commits suicide tonight, huh?"

"Nope. Boy, my first suicide attempt and I sure made a botch of it. It's almost as bad as when Kathy Foster on the third floor tried to slash her wrists with an electric razor!"

They burst out laughing again.

And that was the night they became the best of friends.

And there she was, her best friend in college, standing up there near the dais—almost a stranger. How could she have let that rift begin, widen? Peggy asked herself. They had been so close for so many years. How could they have let it go this far? There was so much more they could have shared, experienced together. Peggy resolved to talk to Ronica before she left the hotel. Hadn't that really been her main reason for attending?

A good-looking young man started testing the microphone, which resulted in most of the crowd putting down their forks and turning toward the dais. Ronica, Romeo, and the hairy man climbed the stairs and gathered behind the podium. Ronica took a step forward and spoke into the microphone.

"I'd like to thank everyone for coming today," she said. "My name is Ronica Barrows, and along with my brother, Romeo, I am the owner of Barrows Industries since our father passed away last year. You might be wondering just what is the astonishing discovery that we mentioned in our press release, and why we have chosen this unorthodox way of presenting it to the public. Makeup is makeup, isn't it? Well it is"—she paused dramatically—"except when it's something more."

Ronica had gotten over her college stage fright, all right. Aside from a slight sign of nervousness that dissipated almost immediately, she was extremely cool and professional.

"In a moment one of our scientists will explain to you what our new makeup product is all about. Let me first whet your appetites by saying that our product—new Beautifique Facesaver makeup—is virtually going to make all other cosmetics, both our own and those of rival companies, obsolete, and forever do away with the need for cosmetic and reconstructive surgery. Ladies and gentlemen, Barrows Industries is going to take you into the twenty-first century—today."

There was a murmur racing through the crowd and Peggy found herself as curious as everyone else in the room. Do away with cosmetic surgery? This was clearly not the announcement of some new perfume or line of lipsticks that she and almost everyone else had anticipated.

A woman in a lab coat whom Peggy had not noticed before was climbing the dais and being introduced to the assembly. "Ladies and gentlemen, our colleague and head of research and development for Barrows Industries, Dr. Betty Lincoln, will now tell you about the most amazing scientific achievement of the 1990s."

Peggy leaned forward to listen.

Dr. Betty Lincoln, though short and stocky, was quite attractive. She had long blond hair that glowed with a golden sheen from the overhead lights, and the blue lab outfit she wore could have come with a designer label. There was a strange quality about her skin, however, as if it were too smooth and clear for a woman her age—late thirties, early forties—or she had on a thick coat of makeup, though if that were the case it did not look quite as obvious as it could have. She had large green eyes, a long slender nose, and a mouth that was almost a cupid's bow. She wore a very fashionable pair of glasses that made her look like a chic, pretty parrot. Her careful phrasing could not quite disguise a kind of raw New York accent that Peggy detected.

"I want to tell you about our new product, Beautifique Facesaver makeup, which was developed under my supervision in our laboratories," she began. "But first, to put into proper perspective the amazing advance that this new cosmetic represents, I want, with your kind permission, to take you on a short, but important, survey of all the remarkable advances made in the field of makeup during the past few years."

As a speaker she was lousy: a flat, monotonous voice with no shadings or intonations whatsoever, but what she was saying was too intriguing to be ignored. Everyone's eyes were upon her.

"For instance, many of you know about the foam or mousse makeups that have recently been introduced, which provide a maximum of coverage with a minimum of heaviness and caking. These light-as-air makeups are more natural than those that were used in the past." She paused self-consciously as if she thought the audience would have trouble understanding what she'd just said.

"Then we have time-release makeups—makeups and perfumes that employ tiny microsponges to allow for maximum use and effectiveness. The scent you wear fades? You rub your wrists together and the fragrance reappears. If your lipstick fades, you just rub your lips together and the color instantly returns. Handy, no?"

She put her hands out on the lectern and leaned forward. "And then of course there are cosmetics that do a bit more than make us prettier or younger appearing. I'm talking about corrective cosmetics, which are used to hide scars, birthmarks, blemishes, even bruises or burned skin. These waterproof, long-wearing makeups cling to scar tissue, which can be so difficult to cover, and can be used to cover disfigurations even over large parts of the body.

"And, while this doesn't truly fall under the category of makeup, to keep things in perspective, as I said earlier, I should mention artificial skin, which combines collagen and GAG—that's glycosaminoglycan—to form a material that actually encourages the growth of normal, healthy skin cells all around it. This artificial skin has been proven more effective than skin grafts in treating burn victims. Nerve endings regenerate and a patient can feel all the sensations that he or she could with natural skin. Since 1979 when it was first used, artificial skin has been improved upon and is truly a modern miracle."

She stopped for a moment to cough into her hand, then continued. "And I should briefly mention cosmetic surgery, a long, painstaking, but usually effective process which can correct flaws, improve your appearance, reconstruct disfigured features, and simply turn back the clock. Until today, the cosmetics industry, in spite of the many advances I've already mentioned, has been quite separate and apart from cosmetic surgery. Makeup could conceal, improve, beautify, but it couldn't change. No matter how much makeup a person wore, the underlying features and flaws remained the same. Cosmetics offered hope for many people, but it was a transitory hope, an illusion—until today."

Peggy wouldn't have left the room now for anything, and she suspected everyone else felt the same.

"That gave Barrows Industries something to strive for with our makeup. Not illusion, not concealment, not a temporary metamorphosis, but a permanent change in a person's underlying appearance. Not concealment but *correction*. Without surgery. Without skin grafts or even artificial skin, although we have been following a similar concept—if a different technique—in our research.

"Artificial skin comes closest to effecting permanent change, in that it promotes the growth of healthy new tissue. But even it is limited in what it can do. It cannot change a person's bone structure, give them a bigger chin, a shorter nose, fuller lips, the way cosmetic surgery or collagen can. It's limited.

"But the new product we've developed, Beautifique Facesaver makeup—which goes under the generic name of porodyne—bypasses those limitations. Now we can permanently change the way a person looks, can change their features, the structure of their face—without surgery. How do we do it? How can a makeup do anything more than conceal or cover up? How can it induce permanent change? Well, let's just say that Facesaver is a makeup like none other. It goes on like a makeup, but it does so much more than any regular cosmetic. I am not exaggerating or overstating when I say that it will make most regular makeup, as well as cosmetic surgery, a thing of the past."

Her face took on an expression that was almost beatific. "Barrows Industries is here today to tell you that we are the wave of the future, the front line of a new world of unlimited beauty. For the first time in history a cosmetics company can truly give you—any man, any woman—the face you have always dreamed of."

At that the lights in the ballroom went out abruptly and people began chattering excitedly. A screen on the wall behind the dais came down out of the ceiling, and from the opposite end of the room a movie projector whirred into use. On the screen was a close-up of an unattractive middle-aged or perhaps elderly woman— late fifties, mid-sixties—with heavy features, a big broad nose, a stubby chin, pouchy eyes, and puffy cheeks. Her hair was worn in tight ringlets that did absolutely nothing for her, and she wore bifocals. The woman took off her glasses, opened her thick lips and spoke, giving the date the film was made and her name. Peggy was startled. The apparition on the screen said that she was Dr. Betty Lincoln! But it couldn't be. The voice was the same; same accent, raspiness, flatness to the tone. But the *face* . . . how could it be possible?

Then there came a second scene, showing the same woman who had just spoken to them from the dais. The features were all different from those in the first picture— a slender nose, thinner lips, the lines and wrinkles and pouches of fat beneath the eyes were all gone.

That could not be the same woman, Peggy thought. No makeup could have done that. She must have had surgery. But again the woman on the screen opened her mouth, gave a date—only a few weeks after the first pictures were taken—and identified herself as Dr. Betty Lincoln!

As the projector shut down and the lights came up, the woman anticipated the audience's reaction and said: "Yes, I am both of those women, my friends. And no, I did not—I repeat—I did *not* have any cosmetic surgery, and to prove it an independent team of polygraphers have

set up a lie detector while you were watching the screen."
Peggy then noticed two men standing by a chair and
table upon which sat several rectangular pieces of equipment and accessories—wires, graph paper, control box.
"They are going to ask me several questions and give you
their expert results and opinions."

The two men were unprepossessing in appearance but
efficient. They got Lincoln into a chair, wired her up, and
asked her questions in record time. Peggy thought to herself, *They're certainly putting on a good show if nothing
else.* But she was still not convinced.

One of the men asked a few test queries then got on to
the pertinent questions. "Are you the woman in both of
those scenes in the movie that has just been shown?"

"Yes."

"Have you ever had cosmetic or reconstructive surgery
of any kind?"

"No."

"You've never had a face lift, dermabrasion, a face
peel, or anything of that nature?"

"Never. Nothing. No."

The grilling continued: "Are you telling the truth
about this new makeup? Are you simply a hired spokes-
person? Do you believe in this new makeup? Have you
used this makeup and only this makeup to make these
extreme changes in your own face?"

They asked her a few more questions then huddled
over their machine to tabulate the results. A few minutes
later the shorter of the two men went up to Ronica and
whispered in her ear. Ronica invited him to the lectern,
introduced him, and directed him to address the audience.

It took a second for him to get used to the microphone
and adjust to the feedback.

"I can hereby testify that this witness, Dr. Betty Lincoln, answered these questions honestly and we are satisfied that she passed the lie detector test and gave only
truthful responses to our questions."

When the audience quieted down, Dr. Lincoln again took her position behind the lectern and smiled out at the audience. It was an oddly unnerving smile, but a triumphant one. "I tell the truth, my friends. I may not be asked to pose for *Playboy* magazine, but I look younger and better than I ever did before. Members of our staff are now handing out pamphlets upon which are printed those same before-and-after photos so you can study them up close at your leisure.

"I was the first person to test this product because I believed in it, because, like so many of us, I had always dreamed of a younger, more attractive appearance. I formulated this makeup with the help of other Barrows researchers, and I can attest to its purity, its safety, its effectiveness. I know how good it works and looks because I tried it." She beamed.

The next moment a young lady came forward carrying a plastic wash basin and a white facecloth. "I'm going to show you something else, my friends." Dr. Lincoln took the facecloth, dipped it in the basin, and began to scrub her face with it. "I'm really gonna use a little elbow grease," she said between strokes. "You see, except for a touch of lipstick and some eyeshadow, I'm not wearing any makeup. That's right—I had no surgery, I'm not wearing a lot of makeup." She held up the cloth which was only minimally streaked with some red and blue from her lips and eyes. "See there? And yet, I look a heck of a lot better than I did a few months ago. No makeup—at least no conventional makeup. No surgery. What happened?"

Peggy could tell the woman was making the most of her moment in the spotlight and having a ball. She was beginning to exhibit more personality and was even developing a sense of humor, as if she were some kind of stand-up comedienne. She was playing the audience now, whereas before she had only been lecturing it.

"I can tell most of you are confused as hell, right? Let's face it, you'd all like to make a few changes, wouldn't you? *Wouldn't you,* ladies, gentlemen? It may only be something minor, but—say, have you all gotten those pamphlets by now? Now take a look at those pictures, I mean *look* at them. Do you see the nose I had in the before picture? Hello, Karl Malden!" Peggy laughed, though the woman's nose had not been that bad. "How did I possibly get the slim petite nose you see before you without surgery? If I'm not wearing makeup, how can my nose look so different in size and shape? How did I do it, kids? You guessed it. Beautifique Facesaver."

The audience broke out into spontaneous cries of incredulity; no one was willing to believe this woman's astonishing claim. It simply did not make sense. Her features were simply too different. She held up her arms and finally succeeded in quieting the crowd. "Down, animals, down. I'm about to let you in on my secret." Peggy quickly glanced at Ronica and Romeo, who had shrunk to the side of the dais and looked quite apprehensive. For better or worse this was the good doctor's show from now on.

"I told you before about artificial skin, which is not a figment of my imagination, but something many of you have heard about, read about, even seen for yourselves. Well, let's say that Beautifique is a variation of artificial skin, but takes it a step further. Just as artificial skin can blend with real skin and promote healthy skin growth, so does our makeup blend with real skin and effect changes in it, even in the underlying bone and cartilage. Yes, *yes!* It can do it. I've seen it do it. I'm living proof it works. As amazing, as incredible, as unbelievable as it sounds, our makeup can promote change in a person's actual features *without surgery.* You want to know how it works?" She held her arms up and paused, looking about with undisguised glee at the people before her.

"Well, I'm not going to tell you. I'm not going to tell you because I would have to be crazy to give up the secrets of a patent-pending, million-dollar, earthshaking, revolutionary new formula like this. Barrows wants to make some money on this, y' know? Can you blame us?"

The audience responded with appreciative laughter; the woman was certainly refreshing, if that was the word. It was as if the change in her appearance had brought her such joy that it had also affected her personality, her way of looking at the world, making her, in fact, the perfect spokeswoman for this product. Peggy began to wonder if her monotone and nervousness at the beginning had all been an act.

"No, I can't give you the formula, but I can tell you a *little* something about how it works." She paused again as if she wanted to stretch out the suspense as far as she was able.

Peggy also wondered if the woman might take it too far. She was beginning to seem like a huckster now, a barker for a travelling medicine show trying to palm off bottles of miracle fluid on the unsuspecting rubes. Peggy wondered what Ronica thought about all this. Give some people just a little opportunity, she supposed, and they turned into monsters. Entertaining monsters, perhaps, but still monsters.

"You see," Lincoln continued, "first we put the makeup on a person's face. Say they want a nose with a different shape, like I did. Say they want to get rid of—not cover, not conceal—but *get rid of* a big port-wine stain or similar disfigurement. We apply the makeup. We apply it several times. We get the patients to think happy thoughts—that's important—to think happy thoughts just like Peter Pan." She paused and giggled theatrically. "And our makeup eventually merges with, transforms, the natural skin underneath, the skin and bone, if necessary—yes, the bone, my friends. Didn't I tell you this was no ordinary makeup? It transforms, literally metamorphoses the nose, the skin, the disfigurement into something healthy, wonderful, and attractive."

She increased her volume to drown out the rising din of disbelief and excitation. "Sounds simple? It isn't. I could be here all day explaining. Take my word for it, this crowd would never understand. But it works. This is not just a makeup. This is a revolution in cosmetics, a *revolution*. The plastic surgeons will be up in arms, and brother, I can't blame them. Because this is gonna make their jobs a whole lot easier, assuming any of them have jobs when we're through. You see, we mold this stuff around a person's face, any part of their face or body, and like a piece of clay touched by the gods, it comes to life.

"Want a smaller nose instead of a larger one? We put the makeup on just so and—let's just say it can shrink tissue, give you a smaller nose, smaller lips, or God help you, even smaller tits if you want them."

The crowd roared.

"This stuff can do anything. Face it, folks: today is history. You are witnessing history. And that's not all. We're prepared to stake our names and reputations on this stuff. We want to prove to you it works before it goes on the marketplace, before we open our planned chain of clinics across the country and people can come in and look the way they've always dreamed of looking without going under the knife, enduring weeks of bruises, unsightly bandages, missed appointments, and days of self-consciousness while they go through ugly recovery.

"And the best thing is, they'll look good *immediately*. And in a few weeks, once the makeup has fully taken effect, the change is *permanent*. They're not wearing makeup anymore. It's their skin, *their skin*. Do you people hear what I'm saying? Anyone can be beautiful without surgery. And at a fraction of the cost."

Most of the people in the room were talking excitedly and almost dementedly about the possibilities of this new product. Even Peggy's mind was awhirl at the thought of a Peggy Antonicci with a new nose and complexion with what seemed like little fuss and bother. But there was an angry contingent over in one corner whose hysteria threatened to drown out all the others. Peggy wondered if these might be plastic surgeons. If so, it was perverse of the Barrows Company to have invited them only to hear how a cosmetics firm was about to come out with something that was a more dire threat to their livelihood than if the world's population suddenly adopted a creed of self-acceptance overnight.

Dr. Lincoln had been bending down to talk to a bald man who had stepped up from a table in front to ask her a question. She stood up straight again and repeated in a louder voice, "Yes, this new product can grow hair. For what is hair but part of the organ we call skin?"

Dr. Lincoln noticed the uproar at the table in the corner. Like Peggy, she surmised the cause of the disturbance and thereby confirmed Peggy's suspicions. "Ah, you gentlemen must be the cosmetic surgeons we invited here today. We're particularly interested in your participation, gentlemen. If you'll calm down, I'll explain just what I mean."

A bearded man with rimless spectacles got to his feet and raised a fist. "Liar! Liar! This is some kind of trick! Those lie-detector men could have come from anywhere. This is nothing but a stupid publicity stunt." He threw down his napkin and stormed out of the room, nearly toppling a waiter.

Lincoln winked at the audience and said, "Too bad. We could have helped him with that receding chin and hairline."

The audience laughed again. She had them in the palm of her hand.

"We expect the surgeons to be outraged and frightened," Dr. Lincoln said. "There's virtually nothing they can do that we can't do better. But that's progress. I'll tell you—we invite any surgeons who want to participate to send us their toughest cases, just to see if we can handle it. They can monitor the patient, and our special 'make-over' will be done free of charge. If for any reason we don't succeed, we'll pay for the patient's surgery and also pay the surgeon double what he would charge."

She winked again and added, "I wonder how many of

you gentlemen will take us up on our challenge. If you really think as our departed friend does, that we're charlatans, liars, fakes, and fools, well, what have you got to lose? Talk to some of your patients, let them decide. Some of them would jump at the chance of getting all this done for free. Our makeup has been tested and is absolutely safe; we've submitted it to the Cosmetic and Drug Administration and approval is pending. We've nothing to hide. Beginning next week we'll be working our wonders on several specially selected test patients, including one or two celebrities we've already been in touch with. Additionally, we'll be asking a special panel of reporters and journalists to monitor every step of the process, perhaps undergo 'beautification' themselves, or interview the other participants. We want to be as open about all this as possible. My friends, we really can work miracles."

At that Dr. Lincoln walked off the stage with a very unladylike stride and went quickly out the side exit.

CHAPTER NINE _____

D r. Lincoln may have left the room physically, but the impact of her words was nearly as corporeal as she was. What followed her exit was pandemonium, with members of the press shouting out questions and taking pictures, while members of the audience argued loudly among themselves or shouted at the dais. The noise level intensified to a degree even higher than it had been previously. Ronica stepped back to the lectern and knocked loudly on the wood with a gavel. "Ladies! Gentlemen! One moment, please. One moment!"

When the audience finally quieted, Ronica said, "We will entertain questions from the audience and members of the press for a brief period. Please continue to enjoy our brunch—there's plenty of food and coffee left. Meanwhile, the waiters will be passing among you with glasses and small complimentary bottles of Dom Pérignon champagne so that you may join those of us up here in a toast to the new line of revolutionary products brought to you by Barrows Industries. In addition to our fabulous new Beautifique product, we'll be offering the usual line of cosmetics, creams, lipsticks, and eyeliner to enhance the new beautiful you created by our Facesaver makeup."

The questions that followed were generally on the same themes: How did the product work? What was it made of? How did it actually affect a person's bone structure? How was it discovered? What was the process by which it was made? Ronica fielded these questions expertly, managing to give absolutely no real answers while appearing to relay information. She kept insisting that the formula was secret and she was simply unable to reveal what was in it or exactly how it worked. "It's safe," she kept repeating. People wanted to know whether the makeup could remove crow's feet, varicose veins, aging spots; get rid of acne scars, unsightly cysts and wens?

Peggy wouldn't have dreamed of exposing herself so nakedly in front of others. She supposed it took a certain mad confidence to stand up in front of strangers and ask how to get rid of your wart.

Peggy spoke a little to the black woman she had talked to earlier, as well as several others at the table who were wondering just what this strange new makeup could be. Peggy found that she was actually having a good time. The waiter brought over their bottles of champagne and she poured herself a healthy glassful, as did some of the others at the table. Before long a spirited conversation was in progress, and included the two ad men and the woman who had seemed so remote before. Everyone was talking about how funny that Dr. Lincoln had been. Peggy and her black friend went back to the buffet for seconds, and Peggy brought back two servings of eggs Benedict, a sweet buttered corn muffin, more fried potatoes, a bit of fruit salad, and a hot bagel smothered with melting cream cheese. *So much for dieting,* she thought. She would definitely be skipping dinner tonight.

Peggy and the others at the table introduced themselves and talked animatedly while munching on the food and sipping champagne. Peggy would have felt tipsy had she not eaten so much brunch. She was really glad she had come, but was disappointed that she'd not yet had a chance to talk to Ronica. Every now and then, during a lull in the conversation, she'd look around and try to find her. Peggy wished she had simply gone up to her earlier and said hello, but now it was too late.

It was after one before people at her table and others began to disperse, heading back to offices or to appointments. Peggy reluctantly said good-bye to everyone and sat alone at her table finishing up the rest of the champagne. If it would not have looked vulgar, she would have gone up to the buffet for yet another plateful. Anyway, the waiters were beginning to take away the hot serving dishes. She finished the champagne in her glass, put it down in the middle of the table, and reached behind her for her bag. Getting to her feet, she took one last look around the emptying ballroom.

"Peggy!"

Peggy swung to her left and saw Ronica walking toward her, a big smile on her face. Peggy again felt that strange mix of apprehension and excitement.

"Oh, Ronnie! I was hoping I'd get to talk to you!"

The two greeted each other, their words overlapping until both had to stop and laugh. Peggy recovered first. "I got this invitation in the mail. I didn't know if you sent it or what, but I figured I'd run into you here. Say, I was sorry to hear that your father passed away."

"Thanks. We've finally adjusted to it, Rom and I. This is all kind of new to us—kind of overwhelming. Of course we have lawyers and other experts giving us advice, but running a big firm like Barrows isn't easy."

"I can imagine."

"That's basically why I didn't get in touch with you sooner," Ronica said. "I've been so busy, what with this new product and all."

"I know. We should never have let it go for so long, seeing each other again, I mean. Say, is this Beautifique for real? It sounds fabulous."

"It is, Peggy, it is. It really is a miracle. I'm so excited by it. Not just by the financial considerations, but the ability to help so many people. I'll be honest, Peggy, I've been thinking about you a lot lately. That's why I had a press release sent to you care of that paper, so you could come. Peggy, this makeup can do anything so easily."

Peggy felt a funny feeling in her chest. What exactly was Ronnie driving at?

Ronica looked her right in the eyes and said, "We want you, Peggy. We want you to be one of our test subjects.

"Peggy, you're going to undergo beautification."

CHAPTER TEN_____

Davey laughed so hard that he rolled off the sofa and writhed on the floor holding his sides. "A test subject for 'beautification'? *Beautification?*" Peggy didn't know whether to laugh with him or give him a good swift kick in the pants.

"Davey! *Davey!* Will you control yourself? I'm asking you for your opinion!"

Between gasps Davey managed to say, "It's crazy. She's crazy. You're crazy if you're going to let this broad smear some weird goo all over your face when you don't know what the hell is in it. You want my opinion? My opinion is *no.*"

Peggy was secretly relieved; she'd been reluctant to go along with Ronica's suggestion herself, even though Ronica claimed Facesaver had already been proven safe. It was all for the media, for publicity, or so she said.

Davey got to his feet and kissed her on the cheek. "Besides, I like you just the way you are, honey."

She took his hand and squeezed it. "Thanks."

Davey toddled off to the bathroom still giggling and muttering " 'Beautification,' Christ!"

Peggy's instincts told her to side with Davey. Ronica had certainly taken her by surprise. At first Peggy thought her old friend had commited a crime of abject tastelessness and insensitivity, but then she remembered:

I spent four years in college bemoaning my looks to Ron-ica, telling her what I thought, crying on her shoulder. She must have figured here was a chance to do me a favor and improve my appearance. I ought to be grateful.

Still she had been so hurt and startled at the ballroom that after telling Ronica she'd have to give it some thought, she told her she had an appointment to go to. Ronica had wanted her to stay and talk some more over a cup of coffee or more champagne, but Peggy felt she just had to get out of there. She did, however, make a date to go to Ronica's new apartment for dinner Wednesday night. Ronnie promised that she would explain the "beautification" process more fully then.

Peggy had walked for an hour up and down the streets around the Berkley Hotel, not seeing anyone, not hearing anyone, not sure if she should be sad and offended or full of bright hope and anticipation. Imagine—the possibility that she could be beautiful! Maybe not beautiful, but very attractive, the way she had always wanted to look. If what Ronica said was true, it was possible. Look at that woman doctor, how much she'd changed. She was not necessarily "beautiful," but the Facesaver makeup or miracle formula or whatever it was she'd used had turned a decidedly plain, even homely, thick-featured woman into one whose features were delicate and appealing. *If only she could have done something about that personality,* Peggy thought. *What a character!*

Could the Facesaver makeup do that for her? Even if the stuff were approved, mass-produced, and sold cheaply, it might still be too expensive for her, what with her limited budget, having to carry Davey half the time. This was a god-sent opportunity to have the whole pro-cess done for free. Yet, Davey was right. What if some-thing went wrong? Would Ronica allow anything awful to happen to a friend?

She was still confused now, hours later, sitting at her kitchen table. Davey was not a perfect man, but he did seem to have a good stock of basic common sense. If he said "Don't do it," maybe she should listen to him. Besides, he said he liked the way she looked now. Still, to be beautiful, glamorous, like Ronica! In the past Peggy had studied her own face from all angles in the mirror and had been convinced that with a little cosmetic surgery, just a touch here and there, she could really be a striking woman. Now this makeup sounded a lot better than surgery. And wouldn't it be wonderful to never have to cover up her acne scars with makeup again? To be rid of them forever? Yes, the more she thought about it, the more she leaned in favor of going ahead with the treatment.

But that's not what she said when David got out of the bathroom and sauntered over to the sofa. "Babe. I've been thinking."

"What, Davey?"

"Well, this 'beautification.' It sounded kinda silly at first, but . . ."

"But . . . ?"

"Well, maybe you oughta go ahead with it. I mean, when you think about it, this is really a golden opportunity your friend is handing you."

Peggy didn't like the sound of that. "What about that bit about you liking me the way I am? Don't you like the way I look?"

David held out his hands placatingly. "No, no, I mean it's a golden opportunity for you to really get somewhere with your writing. I mean, if it's true—and just suppose it is true—that this makeup can do everything they say it can, it won't only change the way everyone looks, it'll change our whole way of life. If this stuff is as cheap as they say, it will make everyone equal . . . based on looks." He looked for a second as if he weren't too crazy about that idea.

"People are turned off by the cost and bother of plastic surgery, but this is something else, something different and easier. Who knows? It may really turn out to be hot stuff. If that's the case, why shouldn't you be in on the ground floor? Everyone else will be writing about this makeup. There'll be articles in every paper and magazine, stories on every TV show. If you undergo this process yourself, you may be able to write about it from a perspective that's different from, and more intimate than, anybody else's. And if you're lucky, you may even be able to find out just what this makeup is made of and get a big jump on everyone."

Peggy had to admit that what he was saying made sense. Before she could reply Davey had thought of a new angle. "And did you ever think that maybe this Ronica will want you working for her? That she may want to hire you as a, what do they call it, copywriter or ad writer or whatever it is. She might put you to work writing publicity pamphlets or something like that for a fuckin' six-figure salary. Who knows?"

Peggy tried to picture herself working at Barrows. "That's not really my field. She could hire experienced copywriters for that kind of money."

"But you have an 'in' with her that they don't."

"I'm not a copywriter. I'm not a nine-to-fiver. I wouldn't like it."

"Not even for six figures?"

"It wouldn't pay *that* well." Before she could stop herself, she blurted out, "Besides, we both know you're only considering all the things I could buy for you if I made that kind of money."

David looked as if he were torn between acting hurt or throwing something at her. "You wouldn't exactly be suffering yourself."

"No, I guess not."

Now David's expression wasn't remotely indefinite. "Y'know, I get a little sick and tired of your bitchy cracks all the time. I'm not exactly thrilled about my low income and lousy career, either. It's tough enough having to play this game and be losing at it for so long without having you rubbing it in my face."

"I'm not rubbing it in your face, Davey."

"What would you call it?" He glared at her, nostrils flaring, eyes widened, as if he were doing his impression of a histrionic bull.

"It's just that—" She sighed with exasperation and brushed her hair back with her hand. "It's been two years since you moved in, and . . . it's so hard supporting two people most of the time on what little I make myself. There are such long stretches when we have nothing. If I could just believe that you were trying harder to get someplace . . ."

The bull bellowed. "Trying harder? *Trying harder?* Who tries harder than me, will you tell me? Who tries harder than me? Is it my fault if I'm not the son of a famous movie star? If my mother isn't a talent scout? If my brother doesn't work for CBS? You think you can get anywhere if you don't have connections? My aunts and uncles are all in textiles and fashion, not in the movie business. Do you think I'd be in this position if I had a relative who was a producer?"

They'd had this tiresome argument a thousand times before, and it never changed. Peggy didn't bother giving her usual response; she'd gotten up earlier than usual that day and she was too tired. She knew that if you didn't have connections or relatives, an easy passage into the kind of life or career you wanted, you had to accept it and simply put all your energy into working even harder. She'd reminded Davey time and again that she had had no relatives who were writers or editors or publishers, that she had simply written letter after letter, article after article, until she was getting assignments from some of the smaller papers and magazines and could use clips from those to make her way into the bigger periodicals. Hers was still a life with too many lean periods, but she managed to get by, and there was always hope of something better.

But he would only tell her that it was easier for writers than actors. Writers could always write, produce income-earning material, but actors could only starve or draw unemployment checks between engagements. She could understand his bitterness and would have felt sorry for him if only she didn't have the feeling that his initiative had plummeted in direct proportion to the amount of time he had been living with her.

Weary, she got up from the table and sat down on her knees by the couch, near him, as if in supplication. "When you moved in," she told him, "I was prepared, believe me I was. I knew what I was getting into, and I welcomed it. Or at least I thought I did. I knew the actor's life was a hard and penniless one. I knew it might be years before you made it, if you *ever* did, and I was willing to share your frustration and pain. I thought that we could have a good life, two 'starving artists,' struggling and sharing and making it together. But lately I've just had this feeling . . ."

"This feeling of what?"

"This feeling that you're not holding up your end of the bargain, this feeling that you don't care anymore. That as long as you have a roof over your head and enough food to eat, a little pocket change, you don't care about your career, or even about our life together. Oh sure, you'd love it if suddenly something good were to happen, you wouldn't turn it down, but you're not willing to fight for it, to go out and . . . I don't know, Davey. People like us have to make our own luck, at least as far as we're able to. I know a lot of it is up to chance, but at least you've got to *be there* in case your chance comes up, you've got to exploit every opportunity."

She moved off the floor and sat on the sofa, legs tucked under her, next to him. "It's not the money, it isn't. I just don't feel like you're a *partner* in this anymore, that you're out there *trying.* I feel more like your parent or guardian." Her head sank down and she scratched absently at a spot on her blouse.

When she got too close to the crux of their dilemma, Davey would always flip the subject a hundred and eighty degrees and turn it all back on her as if he hadn't heard a word she'd said. Tonight he did not disappoint her. "You're not doing so hot, either," he sneered. "How long has it been since you've had a really big assignment? What was it, that article on the Times Square renovation for *New York?* How many months ago was *that?* And who are you to talk about not exploiting opportunities? I'm the one who had to show you what a good opportunity this Ronica bitch was giving you."

Peggy sighed again. He could be such a child. "She's not a bitch, Davey. And besides, we're not talking about me right now." She paused a moment, then went full steam ahead, damn the consequences. "But if we were, I'd tell you about all the research I've done and queries I've submitted and clippings I've photocopied and people I've contacted. I admit it was a bad break when the editors who liked my work at *Vagrant* and *Citywide* got fired. But at least I'm trying to make up for it. There are things you haven't done that you could have done—"

He cut her off. "I've had to work at Hanrahan's, for Pete's sake. And until I get paid I can't afford new photos. And until I have new photos I can't send out my résumé."

She was having none of it. "Your old photos aren't that bad. You could have used them until you got new ones. Stop making excuses. There are auditions you've missed and people you haven't called and opportunities you've—"

"Shut up! Shut up! Shut up!" He jumped up and took a step backward. *"Bitch.* Stop telling me what I should do and take care of your own life. And hell, I think you *should* undergo beautification. And not just to write some crummy article. But because you're not all that good-looking, lady, and you should be damn grateful somebody like me even looks at you."

He pulled a heavy jacket out of the closet and stormed down the hallway toward the door to the outside corridor. She heard the door slam behind him.

His words would have hurt her more had they not

been spoken in anger. She sat there trying to hold back tears, wondering if she really felt like crying, if it would do any good, or if it was better to let the tears out and expunge the poison they carried. She let go, allowed herself to cry, and wondered what exactly it was that she was crying for. Her confusion over Davey? His remarks? Their life together, their penury? Her looks and the insecurity they engendered? Ronica's offer? The fact that an offer had been made, or needed to be made? Was it the sudden loneliness of the room, the chill air coming in through the open window? Anything and everything. She wanted Davey in her life but she didn't know if what they had was any good for either of them.

She did know that she couldn't stand the thought of being alone in the world again.

When Peggy was blue she put on the VCR. The VCR was the only really new thing in the apartment. When she had troubles with Davey she liked to play romantic films about mismatched couples whose love triumphed over dissatisfaction and loneliness. Tonight she chose *Sawdust and Tinsel,* a truly lovely Ingmar Bergman film from the fifties about a fat, impoverished traveling circus owner, his young lover, and their attempts to escape each other and their drab existence. At the film's bittersweet conclusion they are reunited, not really happy, but held together by a bond that is stronger than either had imagined.

She told herself that she and Davey were like that couple, but they really weren't. If they were better or worse off she couldn't say. She had herself a good sob, used up half a package of tissues, and then decided to play some *I Love Lucy* reruns to snap her out of her funk.

The Ricardos and their friends, the Mertzes, had rented a dilapidated cabin for the night which was so close to the train tracks that every time a train went by the bed would rock itself from one end of the room to the other. The expressions on Fred's and Ethel's faces were priceless. By the time the gang had resumed their interrupted journey to California, met Bill Holden, and stolen John Wayne's footprints from in front of Grauman's Chinese theater, Peggy was in a much better mood. It was only ten o'clock and Davey would hopefully be at work until midnight. She decided to call her mother.

Her mother was a sweet but irritatingly obtuse and preoccupied woman in her early sixties. Peggy's father was a kind, if humorless, man of sixty-eight who had worked as a plumber until retirement. A few years ago they had moved to a small house in New Jersey where both were unutterably bored with life and each other. Peggy was reluctant to call her parents because her mother would complain about everything and her father would complain about mother. Mom wanted to go out, do something, see somebody, while Dad was content—if that was the word—to sit on the back porch reading novels. Peggy sometimes thought the two would be happier if Mother ran off with an aging rhumba dancer and Dad opened up a small used-book store in Bayonne.

After the usual litany of complaints, Peggy was finally able to tell her mother about the press conference and Ronica's offer. "What do you think I should do? Mom? Should I go ahead and have it done?"

Her mother never answered a question directly, nor immediately after it had been put to her. She said, "A cosmetic that can do all that, my goodness. I've been wondering if I should do something about all these wrinkles. God, I look like some hag. And you say this makeup can do all that? Why, it's just wonderful. What took them so long to make it? Dear, do you think I could use a face-lift?"

"No, Mother. I think you look fine the way you are. But what about—"

"Well, of course that all depends on what it is you want done. This woman—Ronica, did I ever meet her?—says she'll beautify you, but what exactly does she mean? I've always thought you were very pretty, darling. Just what is it you want her to do?"

"Of course you met her. Ronica, *Ronnie*. She was one of my best friends. You remember her?"

"If they wanted to do something about those big hips of yours, maybe, but not the bust, not the bust. You have a fine bust, dear."

"Mother, we're talking about the face, *the face*. Should I have anything done to my face?"

"She was a nice girl if she's the one I'm thinking of. You brought very few friends home from college. There was that extremely attractive girl with the nice manners I always liked. Was that Ronica? We never saw her very often."

"Yes, that was Ronica. But Mother—?"

"Why, I don't think you should do anything to your face. You have a lovely face." Then in a softer voice, "What is it you think they could do?"

"I don't know, Mother. I don't know. What do you think needs to be done? My nose is too big—don't tell me it isn't—I know it's too big. I have a big Italian nose."

"A very pretty girl that Ronica. I remember—"

"Mom, what about my nose!"

"I don't think it's right to fool around with nature. All this stuff they're doing these days—new animals and bugs and makeups. Why, it's all going to come crashing down on us someday."

"Is that a yes or no, Mom? Should I or shouldn't I get this done?"

"Your nose is lovely. A little large, perhaps, but it fits your face. I say leave nature alone."

"A minute ago you were thinking about getting a face-lift."

"That's just a few wrinkles, dear, not a whole nose. Nature doesn't mind if you get rid of a few wrinkles."

"Mom, I have to go to the bathroom."

When her mother thought Peggy was going to hang up she would always quickly get to the point. "I've always liked your face, but of course I'm your mother. Why don't you tell Ronica you're a little nervous about trying the process, but that you'd like to do a story on it, and would she let you observe some of the patients as they undergo treatment. You could always decide later if you wanted to get something done, when you were sure it was safe. I like your old nose, but if you'd be happier with a new one, then, darling, I'm all for it."

"Thanks, Mom." Her mother always came through for her, at least in normal situations. But "beautification" was not exactly normal.

Peggy, she wondered, *what* are *you going to do?*

CHAPTER ELEVEN_____

Ronica Barrows lived in a corner building in Manhattan's East Sixties that looked as if it had been built
only a few months ago, all gleaming glass and steel and
mirrors. Peggy gave her name to the doorman, and he
directed her to the elevator. As the car ascended she
checked how she looked in her compact. Not bad.

She knew she could never compete with Ronnie's expensive clothes so she had chosen something elegant but
simple; a lovely blue dress that flattened her belly a bit
and made her seem taller. She had set her hair in an
upswept style, a small curl hanging over one eye, and put
on earrings her mother had given her for Christmas. Her
makeup was heavier than usual, but she was determined
to show Ronnie that she was not in such desperate need
of "beautification." She thought she really looked rather
luscious tonight—for Peggy Antonicci, at least.

She got out on the thirty-fifth floor and found herself
not in a hallway, but some kind of antechamber. There
were only two doors. *Two apartments to each floor—God,
how some people live!* She rang the doorbell of the door
marked "A," but before she could remove her finger from
the button the door was opening.

It was Ronica herself who answered. She looked positively smashing. She had let her hair down to her shoulders, put on a white jeweled barrette, and poured herself

into a tight black full-length evening gown. She wore
pearl earrings and a pearl necklace which were probably
genuine. She gave Peggy a hug and welcomed her
warmly. "Just in time. I hope you're hungry."

"Did you ever know me when I wasn't hungry?"

A saturnine maid came over and took Peggy's overcoat
—which Ronnie quaintly called a "wrap"—and the two
women left the hallway and entered the living room. Peggy's eyes almost popped in amazement.

Ronica had never been poor. Her various apartments
in New York had never been hovels, but none of them
had been as luxurious as this. She had always tried to live
off her own income—with a little help from her trust
fund—but now her resources as co-owner of Barrows
were obviously stupendous.

You could see the entire city from a window which
took up nearly one whole wall. The white shag rug
seemed to be several inches thick, and the furnishings
incredibly tasteful and expensive. Peggy could see a hallway to the right that apparently led into a very large
kitchen. The maid disappeared in that direction while
Ronnie led her guest to a couch as big as a small automo-
bile and sat her down in front of a beautiful marble-and-
glass coffee table. "We'll have drinks first, all right?"
Ronica said.

"Fine," Peggy said, feeling overwhelmed. Was this really Ronnie, her old friend? Gone was the gawky drama
club member of '74, the girl who had felt uncomfortable
being sexy on stage in *The Night of the Iguana*. Peggy
could not imagine this woman having trouble vamping
Reverend Shannon or anyone else for that matter.

"Now we can have time to talk," Ronnie said. "Everything was so hectic on Monday." When she spoke Ronnie
did exude some of the warmth and friendliness of yesteryear. Peggy surmised that Ronnie might be as nervous as
she was, not quite comfortable with someone she hadn't
spoken to in several years. But even before the drinks
were served, Peggy felt the ice breaking and knew she

could look forward to an enjoyable evening. They were working on their second martinis when Ronica brought up the subject of men.

"Tell me, Peggy, are you seeing anyone?"

"I'm living with someone."

Ronnie's mouth opened in a glossy O. "Peggy Antonicci is living with someone!"

"Yep, can you believe it?" Peggy had always been the "good Catholic girl" in college, one of the last of her friends to support free choice for abortions or experiment with marijuana. But on one thing she had never wavered: she might sleep with a man before marriage, which she did, but she would never, absolutely never, let a man live with her without benefit of clergy. It had been her one sacrosanct rule. She hadn't realized how out of date she was until she called to tell her mother the bad news, three months after David moved in, and her mother just sighed and said, "That's the way of the world, I guess. Honey, is he Catholic?"

"Who is he?" Ronica asked.

"He's an actor named David Kravitz. He's done some theater work, bit parts in commercials, soaps. The usual."

"Oh, that's nice. Where did you meet him?"

"I interviewed the director of a play he was in for the *News*. He noticed me when I was backstage and remembered me a few nights later when I was at a club opening in Soho. He came up, introduced himself. It turned out we had a few mutual friends. I saw him a couple of times after that and we started dating. Last year, when he lost, uh, moved out of his apartment, I asked him if he wanted to move into mine, and well, that's that."

"Congratulations! I miss having a man in my life. What is David like?"

Peggy would rather have asked Ronnie why someone so beautiful should be unattached, but she answered her question instead. "He's in his late thirties, medium height, good-looking. He has kind of curly black hair and a nice face, a slender build."

"Do you ever think you'll get married?"

Peggy thought a moment. "I don't know. We're still . . . getting used to each other, I guess. I can see why so many people prefer to live with each other before they get married. It gives you a chance to see if you're compatible. We've been together nearly two years now."

"Two years? You must be compatible."

Peggy wanted to tell her the truth. In the old days she would have confessed all her fears and doubts and confusions, but it no longer seemed appropriate, the closeness wasn't quite there. "Yes, I guess you could say we're compatible. What about you? Any men in your life?"

Ronica lifted her glass and took a sip of her martini before answering. "A few. Nobody special. There's been nobody since Dennis."

"Dennis?"

"He's a guy I was involved with a few years ago. It's been a while since I broke up with him. In fact, remember the last time I saw you? Christmas week, outside Macy's?"

"Of course."

"Well, that was the night. The night I broke up with him. I was coming from his place when I ran into you."

"I sensed something was wrong that night. Why didn't you tell me?"

"I wanted to tell you, but I guess it was too painful to discuss then. Now it's a different story. We were really a hot item for a while, Dennis and I, talking marriage and everything."

"And there's been nobody since him? Ronnie, you should have your pick of men."

Ronica smiled. "You were always a big booster, Peggy. I've thought about you a lot these past few years. You always listened to my problems. I guess I didn't want to bother you with them anymore. You had your own problems."

"That's part of friendship. You listened to me and built me up whenever I was down. If you've got a problem, let me know."

"Same here. I want you to give me your address and phone number before you leave. I don't want us to lose touch again."

Peggy agreed. They got off the sofa and went to a raised level of the living room where a table was set with china plates, silver cutlery, and big Waterford goblets. There was a low, tiled wall separating this dining section from the main area which was piled high with a variety of plants and at one end held a large aquarium. Past the table by the window there was a porcelain cherub out of whose mouth gushed a stream of water that collected in a basin beneath the statue. The window was decorated with long orange draperies, which the maid closed as Peggy and Ronica seated themselves.

As the older woman served the meal—a crunchy Waldorf salad, thick, spicy tomato soup, beef Stroganoff with buttered noodles—the two women caught up on each other's lives, and the years just seemed to melt away. Peggy told Ronnie about her writing career, her parents, other men she had known. Ronnie told Peggy about her widowed father's cancer and death, the places she'd traveled to in the ensuing years, the complicated battle for control of Barrows Industries, the disappointing men she'd met and discarded. It wasn't until they had reached dessert—a chocolate soufflé with almond ice cream and hot cappuccino—that "The Subject" was broached: Facesaver makeup and Peggy's "beautification."

"So, have you thought about my offer, Peggy? Would you like to go ahead with it?"

"Well, Ronnie, that's one thing I wanted to talk to you about." She paused and tried to affect an open, positive look. "I'm sure the makeup is safe."

"Oh it is! Dr. Lincoln has assured me. Why, you've seen what it did for her!"

"Yes, it was wonderful, but it's just that—"

"What is it, Peggy?"

"Well, I know I was always complaining in college about the way I looked. And I know you did an awful lot for me, giving me advice on what to wear and how to style my hair, and my makeup. If it hadn't been for you, for your concern—"

"Did I tell you how nice you look tonight?"

"Yes, you did, thank you. But you see, well, that's just it. I've grown kind of comfortable with my looks now. Or maybe I just have more self-esteem than I used to have. I mean, I know I could stand some improvement, and I know there are still plenty of times when I'll get depressed about my appearance, but basically I'm happy, or at least satisfied."

She stopped treading softly around the issue and the words came out in a rush. "Oh, Ronnie, I know I'm no beauty, but I just don't feel *ugly* anymore. I've often thought about having some minor surgery, making a few adjustments here and there, but I'm not sure I want to make major changes right now."

Ronica gave her a concerned, earnest look. "You won't have to do anything major. And this isn't surgery, it isn't anything like it. It's actually a rather simple process. The best thing is, if you don't like the way you look afterward, we can do the process all over again until we have exactly the result that you want. You will literally look the way you've always seen yourself—as perfect as you can be."

Peggy hoped that Ronica wasn't going to launch into a sales pitch for Beautifique for her benefit. "I know, I know, it sounds terrific. But I can't help it. Maybe it's the Puritan streak in me. I just don't really like the idea of fooling around with Mother Nature. I know it's all become very commonplace—implants, transplants, face-lifts, liposuctions—but I guess it just scares me."

Ronica reached out and patted Peggy on the hand. "I understand. A lot of people feel that way. And I'm glad you've become accustomed to the way you look."

Accustomed? Peggy thought. She made it sound as if Peggy were a brave, latter-day Quasimodo.

Ronica continued: "But it's a shame that anyone should deny herself the beauty that's now possible for her to have because of a little unwarranted apprehension."

Was there a touch of condescension in Ronica's voice? Peggy was beginning to get a little miffed. "Ronnie, I'm not exactly hideous, you know?"

Ronica looked stricken, alarmed at being misunderstood. "Oh Peggy, I know that. I didn't mean to hurt your feelings. I've always thought you had a lovely face. But with just a few minor improvements you could be gorgeous, really gorgeous, that's all. Wouldn't you like that? Why not be gorgeous if you can?"

Peggy ran her fork across the smears of chocolate left on her dessert plate and sighed heavily. "Ronica, I'd love to do a write-up on the makeup. I'm not associated with the *Vagrant* anymore, but I'm certain I could sell a piece to another major paper or magazine. I'd love to be part of all this, to interview you, and Dr. Lincoln, and the test patients you're going to be beautifying. But as for doing it myself—"

Suddenly a new thought came into her mind and even she had to admit it was brilliant. "Well, how could I be *objective* if I was beautified myself? I mean, on the surface it seems like a good idea: journalist subjects herself to beautification and writes about it. That might be fine for a paid advertising insert in *People* magazine, but it wouldn't do for a major article about the process in any serious publication." She was making this up as she went along, but Ronica just might buy it. "I'd lose my objectivity, don't you see? I couldn't look at things from an unbiased viewpoint. It would be a 'personal experience' piece with a limited market instead of an objective overview. If this makeup is as good and as safe as you say it is, you've got nothing to worry about. Let me query a few magazines, tell them you and your associates are willing to be interviewed."

"I can't give away any secrets, Peggy, this formula is—"

"You won't have to give me any formulas. Just background data. I can follow each patient's progress, interview them, too. We can help each other out, Ronnie. I'll be giving your makeup positive publicity, and I'll get a juicy magazine assignment out of it."

Peggy was surprised at how quickly Ronica countered her. She was sharp. "Won't they say you've already lost your objectivity simply because you're a friend of mine?"

"I don't have to tell them everything, do I? Seriously, this won't be a fluff piece, Ronnie. I'll go into both the pros and cons of this process, with total honesty. As for my friendship with you, that gives me an in that a lot of my competitors won't have." She shrugged. "What do you think? You know I'll be fair and give you every reasonable advantage. If this makeup is as wonderful as you say, why wouldn't I want to praise it? In return you can get me on the inside, direct me to the right people to talk to, get me those interviews and quotes I'll need. We'll be an unbeatable combination."

Ronica didn't seem entirely convinced. "I thought it would be preferable for you to write about the process while undergoing it, but if you think this would be better . . ."

"I do. But let's just say at some future point I did decide to undergo beautification for myself. What exactly would it do for me? Which of my features would be changed?" She braced herself for the answer, not entirely sure she should have asked the question.

"Well, we'd restructure, oh, just a little bit. The chin, the nose." She tilted her head so she could see Peggy's face from a different angle. "The lines under the eyes, the fatty deposits on the cheeks. We could fix all that. We could raise the cheekbones, too, give you that sexy sculptured look that models have."

"With makeup? You'd raise my cheekbones with makeup?"

"I'm telling you, Peggy, this isn't some silly cold cream we're talking about."

"But *how* does it raise cheekbones? How could it?"

Ronica sat back and sighed as if she wanted to lay her cards on the table. "Y'know, it's funny. At first even I assumed that it didn't actually raise the cheekbones so much as it reshaped the skin on top so that it looked as if you had high cheekbones."

Before she could continue, Peggy said, "Any good makeup artist in the movies could do that."

"Yes, but when the makeup artist in the movies takes the makeup off, you look the same way you always did. When our makeup does its work, you're *permanently* changed and you don't have to wear any more makeup to look that way. But to get back to what I was saying before, Dr. Lincoln tells me that our makeup can actually change and affect bone structure by reshaping the bone itself."

"But *how?*"

"I don't understand it myself, Peggy. Dr. Lincoln could tell you more about it. I'm not the scientific expert around here and to tell you the truth it even confuses me. Just try to look at it this way. Suppose a makeup artist came in with all his tools and paints to give you an entirely different appearance. Suppose he made you look like . . . Elizabeth Taylor. I mean *exactly* like Elizabeth Taylor. The same features, skin tone, beauty spot. Only it was all just makeup. Now suppose you left that makeup on for several weeks. You walked around looking like Elizabeth Taylor—"

"Not exactly a fate worse than death."

"And then, when the several weeks were up, you went to remove the makeup, only it wasn't makeup anymore. Somehow the makeup and your skin had *merged,* the makeup had *become* skin, and you really did look—permanently—like Elizabeth Taylor."

"You mean—"

"That's how it works."

It sounded like something out of *The Twilight Zone*. She had a peculiar vision of *hundreds* of women walking around looking exactly like Elizabeth Taylor. Pretty confusing. Especially for Liz. "But *how?* How can makeup turn into skin?"

Ronica sipped her cappuccino. "Dr. Lincoln will tell you—part of it, at least. We have to be careful. No other company has this formula and we're not about to let it leak out. *No one's* going to get too much information. But at least she can explain a little more of the process so that it will be more understandable."

"I hope."

Ronica signaled for the maid and the woman poured them more cappuccino. "After you've written your article, when you think you're ready, we'll make those adjustments I was talking about."

"Who would actually do the work on my face?"

"For now, Dr. Lincoln or one of her assistants. When we've opened up clinics across the country, we'll hire trainees—makeup specialists, cosmeticians, dermatologists—men and women who can adapt their own skills to our particular needs. It won't take much to train them. The simplicity of this is what is really astounding."

"How much will it cost?"

"I'm not going to charge you anything. Our regular clientele? Let's say it depends on how much has to be done. Certainly less than half of what cosmetic surgery would cost. Maybe only a fifth or a quarter. The ingredients aren't all that expensive."

Peggy was bothered by the possibly questionable ethics involved in her accepting free treatment, even if it was in the future. She'd have to give it all a lot of thought later. She changed the subject. "And I heard Dr. Lincoln say this stuff could even grow hair. By the way, where did you find Dr. Lincoln? She's quite a character."

Ronica had to smile. "I know. She's usually so stern and proper. I think the day of the press conference, she was a little nervous. She's not used to speaking in front of large groups of people. So she had a little champagne, or took something, or both, and it finally had its effect on her. She certainly was funny. For a moment I was afraid she'd go too far, say something stupid, but she really had that crowd on her side."

"Yes."

"And the formula *can* grow hair. Better than minoxidil. Better than transplants. Hair is skin, just like our nails are skin. We expect to make billions of dollars on that aspect alone."

"I can imagine. But how will it be done? You mean this makeup artist we were talking about will put a wig on some bald guy's head, and after a few weeks the wig will come to life?"

Ronica laughed so hard she nearly choked. "It's a little more complicated than that, Peggy, but—"

"Ronica! I think it's only just now hitting me how incredible this is!"

"Yes, it—" She was interrupted by the sound of a loud buzzer. Ronica turned in her chair and called to the maid. "Hilda, will you find out who that is, please?"

"Yes, ma'am."

"It's the lobby calling," Ronica explained. "I wasn't expecting anyone." She asked Peggy if she wanted more cappuccino or dessert, but Peggy refused.

"Watching my waistline," Peggy said.

Hilda called from the foyer. "It's your brother, Miss Barrows."

"Rom! Tell them to send him up, please."

"Yes, ma'am."

Rom!

Peggy froze in her seat.

CHAPTER TWELVE

Rom. *Romeo.*

Peggy felt all the breath in her body rush out and could have sworn she was actually getting dizzy. What was he doing here? Seeing him at a distance at the Berkley was one thing, but having him in the same room, alone with her and Ronica, talking to him, sitting at the same table. . . . What would she think of him after all this time?

She had trouble concentrating on the conversation while they waited for Romeo to arrive on the thirty-fifth floor. Finally the door buzzer sounded, and Ronica went off to answer it. Peggy sat there alone at the table, watching Hilda remove the dishes, and trembling. Romeo had such presence that it was as if the very atoms he displaced upon entering created a molecular chain reaction that showered Peggy's body with waves of excitement. She heard Ronica greeting and kissing her brother, heard their footsteps in the living room, climbing up the steps to the dining area, and then . . .

"Well, hello, Peggy," Rom said. "Long time no see."

Peggy stood up self-consciously and took his hand. "Nice to see you, Rom. How are you? Your sister's been telling me all about Beautifique. You look wonderful." Her mouth wouldn't stop working, and if he had responded to any of her remarks she hadn't heard him.

"We just had a lovely dinner; too bad you missed it. Is it getting cold outside? You look wonderful."

Finally Peggy wound down. Now that her small talk was out of the way, Rom could reveal the reason why he had come. "I hope I'm not intruding," he said to Peggy. "I didn't know my sister had company." He turned to Ronica. "I thought we'd go over the candidates so we could make a definite decision by tomorrow. I don't like putting it off."

Ronica explained to Peggy what this was about. "We're trying to narrow down the initial patients for the makeup to no more than half a dozen." She turned to her brother. "Peggy's going to be doing a story on us, so she might as well be in on this. Let's have after-dinner drinks in the living room and relax."

As they made their way back to the elephantine sofa, and Hilda gathered together an assortment of liqueurs for them to choose from, Rom asked Peggy: "Are you going to be 'beautified'?"

God. She put her hand to her neck and struck a campy, sexy pose. "I think I'm beautiful enough, thank you."

Rom didn't laugh. "I mean . . . didn't Ronnie . . . ?"

"We discussed it, Rom," Ronica said. "Peggy has decided it would destroy her objectivity if she were to be one of our test subjects. She can always have it done later."

Peggy had a sudden urge to scream at them: *Look, you two pretty airheads. Beauty is all well and good—but what about* character, *what about inner qualities such as compassion, intelligence, honesty? Isn't any of that important anymore?* Instead she found herself sitting awkwardly between the two of them on the sofa, a wrinkled brown potato in the middle of two glistening Fabergé eggs.

Rom opened his briefcase and flipped several folders onto the coffee table. "We need test subjects that are difficult and dramatic enough to suit our purposes. We also have to consider the media value of the participants, how much publicity we can get out of them. And on a more personal level, how patient these people will be; the process doesn't work overnight. We need people who will be easy to work with. What we don't want is someone who expects immediate results, and then screams 'foul' to the press before we've even had a chance to complete the treatment."

His nearness was unsettling. Though she nodded at regular intervals, Peggy had trouble paying attention to what he was saying.

"We'll need a replacement for Peggy," Ronica reminded her brother.

"Well—she was your candidate, Ronnie. Can you think of anyone else offhand?"

"Give me a while. Let's go over what you've got."

Her candidate. Peggy wasn't sure she liked the sound of that. Was Ronnie just being compassionate, offering her a chance to look the way she'd always wanted to, at no charge, or had she merely assumed her old friend would be easily manageable and far too grateful to write anything negative?

She shoved her suspicious thoughts to a back burner for the time being and tried to listen more carefully to what they were saying. She didn't feel any need to take notes at this point. Apparently each of several people connected to the Barrows Beauty Company had recommended one or more candidates to be a test patient for the benefit of the media as part of their opening publicity campaign. In addition several plastic surgeons had agreed to send patients to Barrows if only in the hopes of proving that the makeup was a fraud. Peggy wondered how any ethical doctor could recommend that a patient try some unproven, possibly dangerous, new technique. She assumed they simply told their poorer patients about the process (what little they knew of it), said that it would be free of charge, and let them decide for themselves.

"I don't think we'll need more than one or two of the cosmetic surgeons' candidates to prove our point," Romeo said. "They did not send us very easy cases, believe me."

Ronica smirked. "We didn't think they would." She picked up the phone at one end of the table. "Let me call Victor. He should be in on this. If he's not busy, he could be here in ten minutes. You're right, we might as well get this over with as soon as possible. The sooner we get started the better. It won't hurt Peggy to know just which individuals we'll be working with."

The man Ronica was calling couldn't make it until later. For the next half hour they discussed, accepted, and rejected several candidates. Now and then Peggy added her two cents worth, though she felt none of this was really her business. When Ronnie and Rom had come up with a final list of applicants to submit to "Victor" for approval, however, Peggy did jot down the names on a notepad. Some of them she had heard of:

Cecily Crenshaw, a model that Romeo had recommended, wanted adjustments made to her already lovely face without the danger of unsightly scars or the prospect of weeks of healing during which she would be unable to work. (Peggy hoped she wasn't Romeo's lover.)

Emily Stuart was a wealthy ex-publisher in her sixties who wanted to look years younger. This "Victor" person had suggested her as a patient.

Matthew Douglas had been recommended by one of the disapproving surgeons who'd attended the conference at the Berkley. According to the report, Douglas had been an up-and-coming male model until a car accident and the resulting facial scars brought his promising career to a halt. He had very little money and could not really afford the kind of cosmetic surgery he would need. Peggy suspected the surgeon was only too happy to hand him over to the "quacks."

Ralph Tarramonte was a well-known playboy and producer in his fifties, who apparently wanted to do something about his jowls and age lines, not to mention a receding hairline and oversized jaw. He had apparently become friendly with the transformed Betty Lincoln, as he had been recommended by her.

Yolanda Vasquez was another patient submitted for approval by a plastic surgeon. She was an impoverished Hispanic woman who had been caught in a burning tenement. Her husband and three children had been killed. Much of her body was burned, and she was in constant agony. She could only look forward to weeks of skin grafts and multiple operations, possibly the application of artificial skin. Vasquez had agreed to undergo the Barrows process against her doctor's better judgment; he had felt obligated to tell her about it.

These five people would offer all the drama, pathos, joy —and publicity—that Ronica and Romeo Barrows could possibly have wanted.

It was getting late. Peggy thanked Ronica for the dinner and the opportunity to cover the story. She even dared to give Rom a swift kiss on the cheek, promising to get back in touch within a day or two to see how things were developing. She felt a little giddy from the food, the liquor, Romeo's presence and the possibilities she hardly dared think of.

As she stepped out into the street she saw a man hurrying toward her. It was that obscenely hairy creature she had seen speaking to the Barrows siblings at the conference. He must be Victor, she thought. Next time she'd ask Ronica about him.

He did not look at her as he passed by and entered the lobby of the building where Ronica lived. He walked like a tiny, human steamroller: head straight, neck rigid, arms moving up and down like pistons in a brief arc at his side, feet shuttling across the pavement as if he were assisted by millions of invisible legs. That's what he reminded Peggy of, a centipede, a big hairy bug that would trap you and eat you if you dared reach out and touch the sticky, fibrous strands of his spiderweblike hair. He filled her with misgivings that she passed off as xenophobia, but which lingered until long after she had entered the subway and begun to make her way back home.

CHAPTER THIRTEEN_____

Romeo left his sister's apartment at midnight. In the elevator he did a little jig at the wonderful feeling wealth and power were giving him, and at the thought that the Barrows fortune would soon be increasing. Romeo was not a particularly greedy man, but neither did he believe in the parsimony practiced for so many years by his father.

Romeo was a tasteful gentleman, however; he did not believe in ostentatious displays of wealth. He took taxis instead of hiring a limo and driver, which he could easily have done. He didn't buy restaurants or buildings or endow hospitals with the provision they build a wing in his honor. He enjoyed his privacy. His sister took care of charitable contributions from the estate, which he heartily approved of.

If he did overindulge in one thing, it was clothing. He had an appreciation for fine apparel: good suits, sweaters, a variety of trendy hats. He also indulged his latest girlfriend, Cecily Crenshaw, with expensive jewelry, stoles, small objets d'art.

As for Cecily, he could hardly wait to tell her the good news. She had been chosen to be one of Beautifique's first test subjects. Not only would her appearance become even more perfect, but she would get loads of free publicity even as she helped publicize the product. Everything was working out beautifully.

Romeo hailed a cab on the corner and directed the driver to head for Cecily's apartment downtown. He sat back, loosened his tie, and watched the traffic outside, feeling that after many years of being merely one of the millions of people who inhabited this city, he was now one of the people who owned it.

For years after college graduation, the unambitious and not very academic Romeo had tried to make it on his own—with a little help, in the form of loans, from a patient daddy. First he took over a failing publishing firm, one that produced confession mags and skin rags—and sank it into bankruptcy within a year. His next project was as an independent movie producer, a vocation for which he was particularly unsuited as he had little real interest in the business (aside from meeting starlets) and no skill in ferreting out location sites, dealing with testy associates, or securing financing. He didn't produce a single picture.

After that he backed a rock band, which dispersed, tried to take over a newspaper (the *East Village Vagrant),* which eluded him, and even considered starting his own cosmetics firm geared toward outré males or teenyboppers. None of these projects worked out; but then he didn't really care. If he really got into trouble, his dad would bail him out, for his father, rather than being angered at Romeo's failure to take an interest in the family business, was secretly proud of Romeo's attempts to become a self-made millionaire. This was borne out when Romeo inherited one half of the business. He had always known it would come to him someday, ending his troubles.

If he was entirely honest with himself, Romeo would admit that he felt like a Young God. A Young God who still looked great at thirty-five.

And he was genuinely excited by the possibilities of Facesaver, not only by its financial possibilities, but the very real possibility of providing help to so many people. He thought of that old friend of Ronnie's for the first time since he'd left his sister's apartment—Peggy whatsername. He bet with a little application of Beautifique she wouldn't be half bad. He had always thought she'd had a crush on him back in college, but tonight she simply seemed preoccupied.

Romeo arrived at Cecily's apartment, paid the driver, and buzzed his lady friend from the lobby. Five minutes later she was greeting him at her door, kissing him on the mouth so passionately it was as if she wanted to suck out all the oxygen not only in his lungs but circulating in his bloodstream.

Pulling out of the kiss, Cecily took Romeo's hand (she never called him "Rom") and led him over to her sofa. Her apartment was small but handsomely appointed. Cecily's tastes tended toward the masculine: wood floors, dark colors, plaids instead of pastels. "They're going to do it?" she said. "Make those improvements?"

He kissed her on the nose. It was one of the things she wanted to change; she felt it was too bulbous. "Yes, honey. Probably next week."

"That's wonderful. I know it seems frivolous of me, but I want to be absolutely perfect."

He kissed her on the brow. "Don't worry. You will be."

"And you're sure it's safe?"

"Positive."

"And no one will know I'm undergoing surgery? I can walk around looking normal all the time?"

"I told you—it *isn't* surgery. And yes, you'll look normal, better than before, while the makeup you're wearing is doing its magic. And then *voilà*—no more makeup. It gets absorbed into the skin underneath and changes it until you're perfect."

"It sounds too good to be true."

She pulled out of his arms and went over to the mirror hanging in her foyer. There was a light above this mirror which she switched on, the kind of light normally used to illuminate classic paintings. She twisted her face this way and that, touched her skin. "Perfect . . . Absolutely perfect . . . I always hated this chin. People tell me I'm beautiful but I don't believe it."

Cecily was perhaps more charming and lovely in appearance than out-and-out beautiful. She had a fresh, lightly freckled quality (usually she covered the freckles with makeup) like a hybrid of a tomboy and a sexpot who was equally at home on a farm or in the city. When not working, she tended to wear virginal clothing: white pantsuits, white blouses, white sweaters. Her features were delicate: small eyes, small bones, small nose, small mouth. Her lips were perhaps a touch too thin but that didn't bother her so much.

She went back to the couch and cuddled up against Romeo. "I have these nightmares where I wake up and my nose looks like Pinocchio's and my chin like Margaret Hamilton's in *The Wizard of Oz.*"

Romeo threw back his head and laughed. "You'll never have to worry about that." Romeo knew that what really scared Cecily was waking up in the morning with even a small pimple, or—horror of horrors—an unsightly rash. She seemed plagued by an assortment of very minor, benign skin growths occasionally appearing on her body out of (most people's) sight, but luckily nothing ever erupted on her face.

"Are you sure this will work? Are you sure it's safe? Are you sure it will do exactly what I want it to?"

"Yes yes yes yes yes," he said, still smiling.

His smile faded when she added: "Because if it doesn't, Romeo, if it fucks up my face in any way, I swear I'll kill you."

He wanted to ask her if she was serious, but he could tell from the expression on her face that she was.

CHAPTER FOURTEEN_____

"**G**ive me the fifteen hundred now or I go to the police!"

Scott pounded on the desk in Emily's library with his fist. "Do you want that, old lady, huh? Do you want me to go to the police? Wait till they find out what you've been doing—wait till they learn what a pervert you are!"

Emily Stuart put her hands up and covered her ears. She didn't want to hear any more of this. She couldn't hear any more of this. It was driving her crazy.

"Stop it, Scottie. Stop it! Will you calm down? Calm down and we'll talk about it. I won't say a word until you're quiet!"

"Bitch!" Scott said, banging the desk one more time for good measure. He turned his back on his aunt and folded his arms across his chest.

"Fifteen hundred dollars is a lot of money, Scottie. I can't give you that kind of money unless you tell me what it's for."

"It's none of your goddamn business what it's for."

"Scottie, don't talk to me that way."

"I want that money."

"No, no, no! I won't give you the money until you tell me why you need it."

Scottie turned around to face her, his attractive face twisted into an ugly mask of frustration and anger. "I don't have to tell you a damn thing, old lady. But I *could* go tell the police. You tell everyone I'm nineteen years old, but we both know I'm not. We both know I'm only seventeen; a minor. You've been fucking a minor, old lady. Your own nephew. You've been *molesting* me. That makes you two kinds of pervert, and unless you give me the money I'll go to the police and tell 'em all about you."

She knew he wasn't really serious in his threat, but those hateful words, his hysterical manner, were frightening her. "Scottie. Please calm down. Sit down and we'll talk about it."

"There's nothing to talk about. I want my money."

"Fifteen hundred dollars?"

"You can afford it."

"Is it drugs, Scottie? Have you been taking drugs? Do you owe people money?"

"None of your business."

It was so odd. Scott looked his youngest and most helpless when he was threatening her. It was during these ugly moments that she was reminded what a child he really was, and she chided herself for ever bringing their relationship to a level for which he was so unprepared. Still, she wouldn't give him up.

"Have you ever thought of seeing a psychiatrist, lady? Having sex with children. You pervert."

When he was younger, fifteen or so, when it started, he didn't "know" what they were doing. She blamed television for his enlightenment: Oprah Winfrey and Phil Donahue, those exploiters who dragged every subject out into the scrutiny of cameras and the public. It was not like that. She was not a pervert. They were not related by blood; it was far from incest. And at fifteen, he had been more man than most men were at forty. Yet she supposed if society excoriated men who slept with adolescents, there was no reason why people should view her actions with any less censure.

"Shut up, Scottie," she said quietly when his temper tantrum had run itself out. She had still not given him the money he wanted, and she realized that she still held power over him. If he ever did decide to go to the police or to tell Oprah or Phil all about them on national television, he knew his life would become as horrible as hers would become. When her sister and brother-in-law died several years ago she had taken the boy in, but had never legally adopted him. He was not in her will. If she went to jail, he would become a ward of the state, or be sent to some foster home where life would be infinitely less elegant than it was here. True, in a year, at eighteen, he'd be out on his own. But without Emily's money to buttress him, he'd probably end up selling himself on Forty-second Street.

"I'll give you the money on one condition." She spoke softly now, her cultured voice revealing traces of a British accent.

"What is that, old lady?"

"First you apologize for those remarks. I don't deserve them. I don't want to hear them."

"Why should I—?"

"You want your money, don't you? Next, I want you to take off all your clothes."

Scottie flipped her a finger. "I'm not in the mood, old —Aunt Emily."

"I don't care." She took out her checkbook and reached for a pen. "I'm writing the check now. A check for fifteen hundred dollars. That's a lot of money for a boy your age. And you'll have it, every penny. If you just shut up and do those two things. Apologize, and remove your clothes."

Scottie looked at her sheepishly, then at the check. "I apologize."

"And now?"

He started stripping. He had a smooth, slender body, supple young limbs. Arms, legs, and pubis were ablaze with soft down glowing in the light from the lamp. His hair was dark blond, worn long, parted in the middle and nicely styled. He had a rounded nose, deep blue eyes, lips that were red and wet and delicious. Emily sometimes wondered if in a former life she'd been a pederast, perhaps one of the Greeks who died in bloody battle whispering the name of the boy he loved. She *hungered* for young men so. Were women, old women, supposed to feel this way?

She stood up, holding the check in her wrinkled paw. She was an old woman, but she was stronger than her feeble appearance suggested. She had once been pretty, that was still obvious, at least to other adults. She had pretty, brownish-gray hair, worn the way she had worn it for thirty years. Her once-lovely skin was marred by too many wrinkles; her prominent upper teeth lifted her lip up in a peculiar permanent curl or scowl. She wore clothes that were too young for her; today it was orange pants with a frilly white blouse.

She had always loved sex; lived for sex. She had chosen her three husbands for their bedmanship. She had associated with her inferiors because of their erotic ability. At sixty-two, she had few friends—she had little interest in platonic relationships. All she had was this mongrel in front of her, this wretched, ill-mannered, ungrateful, spoiled, but beautiful boy who was the issue of her ignoramus sister and a semi-retarded clothing clerk who had done her, Scott, and the world a favor by merrily driving across a highway divider after attending a turkey-necked cousin's wedding.

"Scott," she said. "It's time for me to have my fun. Lie down."

Scottie wouldn't treat her so badly if she was young, she thought afterward. Victor had told her his company's new cosmetic could literally work miracles. He had promised to call as soon as he was certain she had been accepted by the others. She would not just look ten or twenty years younger, Victor said, but possibly thirty or forty.

The phone rang.

It was Victor.

Emily smiled.

CHAPTER FIFTEEN_____

Just one second.

Just one second and your whole life changes.

Everything that once was, is no more. Everything that *is,* is without meaning.

Matthew Douglas's philosophy.

He sat on his bed in a Hell's Kitchen apartment that was hardly bigger than a furnished room in a fleabag hotel. He had had to move out of his nice East Side condo when the accident happened, and his career came to an end.

Just one second. Just one lousy second.

Matthew Douglas had short-cropped brown hair, blue eyes, and a broad, handsome face that had once made him look like a poster boy for Annapolis. He found his type was coming back into fashion just as he began his career as a model. An old girlfriend of his had first suggested he try modeling, and had put him in touch with some people. Every month or so he got a letter from her containing scribbles that seemed just as insincere as the cerise lip prints she left at the bottom. He never saw her anymore.

Things were going great—back then. And then the accident. A car rammed into the taxicab that Matthew was riding in. Or was it the other way around? He hadn't been paying attention, his head was full of other things, the things twenty-five-year-olds' heads are full of when they are happy and successful and have every reason to hope the future will be even better.

A large piece of glass had nearly cleaved his face in two.

Doctors patched him up in emergency. They were trying to save his life, stop the bleeding, hold his face together; they had no time to worry about how he'd look tomorrow for the cameras. A skilled cosmetic surgeon tried to minimize some of the damage but had simply been called in too late. The scar was a jagged line, running from the center of his forehead, across his nose, down nearly to the tip of his chin. It was more than enough to end his modeling career.

And the bills, the bills. The whole case was tied up in litigation; it would be months before he could collect any damages. Meanwhile, he had borrowed as much from friends and family as he could, applied for benefits, everything. He'd changed his life-style radically. A friend moved temporarily to L.A. and suggested Matt sublet his apartment, a dark, close, and shadowy place, even when all the lights were on. There was no kitchen to speak of and the bathroom was down the outside hall. Matt lived on canned food which he heated on a two-burner hot plate. In cooler weather, he would leave perishable goods on the windowsill. There was only one large window in the room and Matthew pulled ugly heavy brown curtains across it so that people could not look in at him from upper stories of the building across the way. The bedsprings squeaked, and the mattress was filthy. Periodically he saw roaches—not just the small German roaches, but the very large American type that people often mistook for water bugs—crawling around the floor, antennae wiggling.

Last week his surgeon, who had scarcely begun a series of collagen and dermabrasion treatments, and who he suspected was wondering how this scarred man would ever be able to pay his bill, had told him about the magi-

cal new process a cosmetics firm had claimed to develop.
"I know men don't like to wear makeup, but this stuff is
supposed to be incredible. Now, I'm not recommending
this to you, but they *say* it'll be done free of charge
and. . . ."

There was no need to continue. The doctor had made
it clear that there was a limit to what surgery could do.

Although the rest of his face had not been affected,
Matthew was convinced the two halves on either side of
the scar did not match. As a child he had read comic
books and his favorite superhero was Batman; his favorite Bat-villain, Two-Face, the district attorney who was
hit by acid and wound up with half of his face looking as
handsome as ever and the other half hideously disfigured.
That's what Matthew called himself now—Two-Face.
And Two-Face would do anything to look whole again.

He agreed to meet with these people at Barrows. They
talked to him, studied him, took photographs, and told
him, somewhat indirectly, what their makeup could do.
They even said that it would not just conceal his scar, but
heal it, make it turn into fine, healthy flesh again. When
they said that, he knew he had to become one of their test
subjects. He didn't care if there was a risk; he was willing
to take any chance.

Maddeningly, they had said they would get back to
him. All those interviews when he first started modeling
—everyone would "get back to him." Didn't they understand that this was not just a job, that they held his life in
their hands?

Matthew sat on his bed and held a small round mirror
in front of his face. He hardly recognized himself. He had
lost weight; his face had gotten thinner—it was gaunt and
pale, with hollow eyes and cheeks. There was three days'
growth on his beard, and his hair was long and tangled.
His left index finger traced the scar, following its winding
path from forehead to chin. Couldn't he at least make its
stark white color match the color of the rest of his skin?
He'd tried to conceal the scar with special scar tissue

makeup, but he'd had to apply so much of it that his face looked almost as abnormal with it on as it did without it.

Two-Face, he thought. *I'm Two-Face.* He dropped the mirror on the floor and started to cry.

And then the phone rang.

CHAPTER SIXTEEN

Ralph Tarramonte hoisted his flabby body into the circular bed in his Fifth Avenue town house and held up the champagne bottle. "Ready for more champagne, girls?"

The two naked women who were squealing and writhing in the bed with him held out their plastic glasses and cried "More! Yes, more!"

Tarramonte poured the champagne, getting nearly as much on the girls and the bedsheet as in the glasses. "Here we go! Here we go! Champagne! Champagne for everyone!"

It was a cheap brand but the girls didn't notice. They were practically identical twins: both in their mid-twenties, both quite stupid, with bouncy blond hair, big tits, and large front teeth that made them resemble chipmunks. Tarramonte had been ravishing the duo—each would be paid one thousand dollars for several hours' work—since seven that evening. Tarramonte set his glass down on the night table and went to work nibbling on the breast of the girl who was nearest him. He had mounted each of the ladies once tonight. He hoped to double that figure before the night was over.

The room was riotously tasteless. Red satin sheets, mirrors on the ceiling and the walls, low red lights, various objets d'art, usually of an erotic nature, scattered around the chamber. Tarramonte was last of the old-time lover boys, embroiled in a sixties fantasy that did not take women's lib or AIDS into account. He had divorced his three wives the moment they got too old to interest him. The older he got, the younger he wanted his women.

He was tired of paying for them, though. He pretended it didn't bother him, but it did. Twenty, thirty years ago he'd been fairly attractive, but now he was losing his hair, getting fat, developing jowls. He decided if he was going to do something to make himself younger, he might as well do something about his lantern jaw, too. It was the only feature that had troubled him since childhood. He didn't understand how this makeup Betty Lincoln told him about could fix his jaw or grow hair, but if she recommended it, he was only too happy to try it.

The two girls pushed Ralph down onto his back, and started stroking and kissing him everywhere. He felt his limp dick begin to harden again. But his mind wasn't really on sex. He was thinking how nice it might be to go to bed with a young, beautiful woman who really *wanted* him again.

Of course, Ralph had enough money that he did not have to get free treatment from anyone, certainly not in exchange for allowing himself to be part of early publicity for the process. He had some reservations about letting himself be so brutally exposed before others, the press and media. Still, something about being in the forefront, one of the first people after Betty to go through "beautification," appealed to the maverick side of his ego.

Besides, he absolutely hated the thought of surgery— just imagining knives slicing his flesh, cutting away strips of skin, all that blood running down, made him queasy. This way sounded so much . . . cleaner. And he didn't want to wait until all the results were in; those overly cautious Cosmetic and Drug people might decide the process wasn't safe because it caused cancer in one out of ten thousand or so laboratory rats. No sir, he didn't want

to wait and find out that Barrows wasn't allowed to do it
anymore.

One of the girls succeeded in making him come again,
using lips and teeth and tongue in a way he had formerly
thought impossible.

Suddenly the phone rang.

It was Betty Lincoln.

"Ralph. Ralph. . . . I'm coming over."

"Uh, what? Now?"

"Right now. I have wonderful news. I just heard from
Victor."

"Heard what?"

"They're going ahead with you. They want you to become one of the first. Isn't that wonderful, darling?"

Damn! He must be psychic. "Say, that is wonderful!
Y'know, I was just thinking about it."

"I'm bringing a bottle of champagne. I want us to celebrate together. Soon you'll be even handsomer, darling.
You'll look as wonderful as I do."

What could he say to that but "Great!"?

Ralph said good-bye and hung up. He got busy paying
the girls, hustling them out of the apartment, and showering and changing. He didn't want to turn off Betty Lincoln at this point, not before he was through using her.
He knew she had much stronger feelings for him than he
had for her.

He had met Betty through Judson Barrows, his old
college classmate, when Betty was appointed head of the
research department. Judson had held a dinner in her
honor. Ralph offered to drive her home afterward, and
wowed her with tales of the movie business, the pictures
he'd produced, the stars he'd met, how he'd tried to help
Romeo in the business but the kid just didn't have the
right stuff. At that time he had thought Betty was one of
the homeliest women in the world, but Ralph was one of
those men who got excited, aroused, at the idea of someone really *wanting* him. Betty really wanted him. They

made love that night and many nights after, even though she was hardly his type.

A few months later a new Betty showed up at his door. The voice was the same, but he hardly recognized her. She was good-looking all of a sudden, younger, still not quite the type he wanted but a hell of a lot better than before. He found himself using her in a pinch far more frequently than he previously had. The woman also seemed transformed in the bedroom, as if her newfound attractiveness brought out the animal in her, as if confidence worked as an aphrodisiac and she finally felt worthy of loving him to the hilt. She was an insatiable, almost savage woman in the boudoir.

He had just finished changing into a suit when the doorbell rang. He answered the door, and Betty rushed in.

She kissed him hard on the mouth then backed up. She pulled a bottle of champagne out of a paper bag. "Get some glasses, darling," she said, "and meet me in the bedroom."

Ralph could only stand and watch her with amusement as she ran down the hall shedding her clothes. It would take a herculean effort, but he knew he must try and satisfy her.

When he was young and handsome again, then he could tell her where she could go.

CHAPTER SEVENTEEN_____

Yolanda Vasquez thought it was raining outside, but she couldn't be certain. Sometimes she thought it was raining, but it was really only the crinkling of her bandages. Sometimes she thought it was raining and it was only the soft sneakered steps of the nurses making their rounds or the squeal of the wheels of the carts and stretchers that brought food or carried patients from place to place. The flush of the toilet sounded like rain, as did the rustle of her bedsheets and blankets, the crackle of someone opening a package of needles or cotton-swab sticks or even unwrapping a candy bar.

She always thought it was raining.

She thought it was raining because she hoped the rain would wash away her agony, the pinpricks of fiery pain throughout her burned limbs, face, and torso, the dead but gnawing sensation she felt on her flesh and in her heart. She was sure that a nice cooling rain, a soothing rain, a wet, cold deluge would absorb the heat and put out the fire, bathe her in a wonderful, numbing frigidity.

But it was not raining. It had not been raining the night she lost her family, either. The night someone put too many plugs in an extension cord, or left something flammable too close to the stove, or knocked over an incense candle on the wood floor in a drug-induced frenzy. She didn't know how the fire started; she only knew it killed her husband and children. Roberto was forty-three, six years older than Yolanda. Their children, Ernesto, Maria, and Roberto Jr., had been eight years, five years, and six months, respectively. She'd never hear or see any of them again, except in nightmares.

Mostly she dreamt of the fire, when she wasn't dreaming of rain. If only there had been rain to put the fire out. She saw flashes of what had happened that night. The way they were just sitting down to dinner in the crammed two-room apartment when they smelled smoke and heard someone shouting. A neighbor knocked on the door and told them a fire had erupted three stories below them; they should get out, rush for the roof. There was no fire escape on this side of the building.

Trying not to panic, Yolanda went and got the baby. Roberto gathered the other two children and they went out into the hall. People from the third and fourth stories —below them, but above the fire, which had spread rapidly—were piling up the staircase. Roberto and Yolanda were separated. The smoke was terrible. Soon Yolanda couldn't see. She tried to hold on to a banister. She had assumed that at least Roberto and the youngsters were ahead of her, racing up the stairs to the roof and precious air, but apparently they had come down in search of her and gone past her into the confusion of smoke and racing bodies. Roberto had probably told the older children to continue running to the roof, but they must have disobeyed, too scared for Mommy, anxious to make certain she, too, was safe.

Oh God, they died because they loved me.

And somehow, thinking the others were safe, Yolanda nearly made it to the roof. She would have made it had there not been an explosion. She thought someone had bumped into her but it was actually a collapsing wall that hit her. The baby dropped right out of her arms. Hysterical, she bent down through the smoke, wood, and plaster to try to find him. Someone did bump into her this time; many people were stepping on her. She tried to shove them aside before they hurt Roberto Jr. When her hands came up all bloody she prayed it was her blood and not his.

Firefighters had climbed up the stairs in the building next door, which was a couple of stories lower than the one Yolanda lived in. They gained access to the hallway from a window, and began dragging out people who'd been overcome by smoke inhalation. By the time they got to Yolanda, the fire had got to her. She was alive but so badly burned she hardly looked human.

She was rushed to the burn ward at Roosevelt Hospital. When she was finally conscious her only living relative, Aunt Concepción, told her her family was dead. The worst thing was, her aunt wanted to hold her, and she wanted to be held, but because of the bandages and the pain, they had to grieve and console each other while separated by several feet. How badly Yolanda needed human contact; how badly she needed her husband and her children.

Yolanda passed her days and nights in endless misery. She would have prayed but something now inside her made her feel that it was futile. She slept as much as possible, and welcomed the comparative respite from her tormented thoughts. She did not think about tomorrow, what she would do, what she would look like—she hoped she would die. She thought only about Roberto and the children, replayed in her mind those last minutes, and tried to figure out what she might have done to save them. Should she have handled it differently, given the baby to a neighbor and gone back to make sure they were out? Would she have saved their lives or simply died with them? She saw herself moving through the smoke with confidence and assurance, grabbing her husband and children by the hand and leading them, guiding them, up the stairs to where there was hope and salvation. If only things had been different; if only she could have another chance.

After a while doctors came and told her about skin

grafts, the extent of damage, and so on. They spoke in low voices and seemed to be sitting behind an invisible curtain that separated them from her anguish. A surgeon associated with the hospital came and told her—strictly off the record—that he had heard about a new process that was being developed; something that was even better than artificial skin. Did they have such things? The treatment was new, and comparatively untested. It would be free of charge. He could not recommend it, but . . . there was the pain, and cost, and discomfort of skin grafts to consider. In a lower voice: would she be interested?

Aunt Concepción guided her. "You're still young. You could be beautiful again. Roberto would not have wanted you to suffer so."

She said yes, but her heart wasn't in it.

Who cared if anything went wrong? she told herself. *Nothing could possibly be worse than this.*

Could it?

CHAPTER EIGHTEEN_____

As she sat in the classroom at the Barrows clinic and listened to Dr. Lincoln drone on about the human body's largest organ, skin, Peggy thought, *I feel as if I were back in high school.* It wasn't that what the doctor was saying wasn't interesting, but her delivery was not nearly as spirited as it had been at the press conference. And to make matters worse, Peggy wasn't used to being up so early in the day. She chanced a surreptitious glance at her wristwatch. Not yet eleven o'clock, and the doctor had only been at it for ten minutes.

Try as she might to pay attention, Peggy found her mind wandering. She saw herself arriving at the uptown clinic a little after nine o'clock, having another cup of coffee, thank God, with Ronica while they waited for the other "select journalists" Ronica had chosen to come. Obviously Ronica was not making this an "exclusive" for Peggy. One by one these men and women were ushered into the cafeteria and introduced. There was a smartly dressed, if unprepossessing, fellow with a big head from the *Times;* a chubby, jolly sort of female with rimless spectacles from *U.S. News and World Report;* a downright homely young man with the face of a basset hound from *Playboy;* and a tall, thin fortyish-trying-to-be-thirtyish gal in a pantsuit from *Medicalstyles.*

After querying five other publications, Peggy had man-

aged to get an assignment from *Woman Today* magazine.
If this worked out, she'd soon have several thousand dollars in her bank account and a nice big byline in a prominent, distinguished periodical. What made it even nicer
was that Peggy could approach the subject from a different slant than in the usual woman's magazine, which
would merely look at it from the "how wonderful, we'll
look younger and attract more men" standpoint.

Peggy wanted to go into the ramifications of this
makeup, both the positive and negative possibilities, what
all this would lead to. Thousands of people walking about
looking *just like* their favorite celebrities—God! Ten
thousand Vanna Whites and Elvis Presleys! Then there
was the very real possibility that criminals on the run
could easily change their faces virtually overnight. And
perhaps worst of all, would there emerge from all this a
hollow, uniform beauty that was utterly without meaning? Would the very concept of beauty disappear as it
became commonplace? She expected any day now the
Barrows ad men would come up with the slogan "Changing the Face of the World," if they hadn't already.

The journalists were taken on a tour of the facilities.
The Barrows clinic was located in a converted town
house in the east sixties, three stories high and almost a
perfect square in structure. It was an old building, dating
back to the mid 1800s, and according to Ronica had once
been owned by, among others, exiled Spanish royalty and
a famous silent-movie star. Outside, it was a handsome if
imposing edifice of white stone, bay windows, and ornate
grillwork. Inside, it was appointed like an exclusive men's
club that had been taken over by the wives. Feminine
elaborations superseded a basically masculine decor:
carpeted corridors, light creamy walls, windows hung
with thick velvet drapes, and old-fashioned mahogany
furniture. One could imagine old fogies in suits, smoking
cigars and sitting about reading the papers while hushed
butlers in tails carried in trays of brandy snifters. To the
right of the large foyer was a library that had been turned

into administrative offices. Across the hall the old living room served as a lounge. Down the hall there was the cafeteria, formerly a kitchen, some storerooms, and a classroom. The other rooms on the first floor were laboratories.

The group was taken up the large front stairs and briefly shown the treatment rooms on the second floor. These were partitioned chambers that resembled large beauty parlor cubicles. Each cubicle held a chair, several mirrors, including a large one on the wall, a sink and drawer for instruments, a small rounded metal table, and a tabletop refrigerator. There were about twenty of these chambers on the floor. The rest of the space comprised an employee lounge, a patient's resting area, several rooms with cots, a conference room, and bathroom facilities.

The third floor contained larger rooms for those patients who wanted to remain in the clinic until the process was completed, or whose cases required more extensive treatment. These rooms resembled the chambers of an old-style guest house or hotel: large beds with heavy brown backboards; thick wool coverlets and massive pillows; huge, old-fashioned wardrobes in one corner; frilly curtains; a small sink with mirror in another corner; cream-colored wallpaper; thick, if slightly tattered, carpeting.

Some of Peggy's fellow free-lancers took photographs as they were shown the building, but Peggy had been told the clinic would give her whatever she needed in the way of illustrations later on.

The tour ended in the classroom on the first floor, where the crudely delightful Dr. Lincoln waited for them. Today she did not seem as bubbly as she had been at the press conference; rather, she seemed determined to impress upon them the seriousness of what they were doing at the clinic. Ronica introduced her to each journalist. When it was Peggy's turn to shake Dr. Lincoln's hand, she was surprised at how strong a grip she had.

The other thing that surprised her, up close, was how weird the woman looked.

Yes, she was attractive—far more attractive than she used to be, judging by the "before" picture in the pamphlet—but it was a peculiar attractiveness, as if the various features on her face did not match. Those cupid's-bow lips would have been better on someone with a smaller face. The nose did not quite go with the lips. It was as if someone had wiped her face clean of features, taken a mouth from one face, a nose from another, and so on, and plopped them down where her own nose, mouth, and other parts had been. The result was not ugly or even unpleasant, just strange.

Peggy reminded herself, however, that she had not got that impression the first time she saw the doctor. This new impression was undoubtedly influenced by the knowledge that the woman had undergone some mysterious treatment. Perhaps if she had not known this, she wouldn't have noticed anything irregular about her face.

"Dr. Lincoln is going to talk to you all for about half an hour," Ronica said. Like Peggy, the other journalists stirred in confusion. "We feel it's important that you have some background knowledge before you write anything about this process."

"Relax." Dr. Lincoln smiled. "I promise there won't be a test."

At least she hadn't entirely lost her sense of humor, Peggy thought as she and the others took their seats in the classroom.

Dr. Lincoln began: "I want to talk to you about the skin. If I give you a short lesson in skin, you will better appreciate what it is we do at this clinic. For it is the skin that we manipulate."

The man from the *Times* raised his hand. Peggy stifled a giggle. "Can't we ask some questions first, before you give the . . . umm . . . lecture?"

Dr. Lincoln's expression did not change. "Go ahead."

"All right, I'll get right to the point. How do we know

that your 'before' picture in the pamphlet wasn't faked? How do we know you didn't just put on theatrical makeup for that photograph to cover your face and make yourself look . . . well, ugly."

Peggy felt incredibly stupid; such an obvious deception had never even occurred to her. That would certainly explain a lot of things.

The doctor looked quickly at Ronica, who was sitting near the window. "Such suspicion so early in the day. Well, why not? That's what they're here for, right, Ms. Barrows?" She winked at Ronica. "Okay, sir, I'll answer your question. All you have to do is look in the morgue of your own newspaper, or in any scientific journal of a few years ago, and you'd see my picture, my face, as it was. There's only one Betty Lincoln. If the homely woman of yesterday and the more attractive woman you see before you are one and the same person—and she is— the only conclusion you can reach is that I _did_ change. Don't take my word for it, any of you. A little investigation, which, after all, is part of your job, should give you all the proof you need. I'm even willing to have my fingerprints compared with ones that have been on file for years. Nobody's trying to pull a fast one, believe me."

Dr. Lincoln added that there had been tests made first on animals, then on other members of her research team, but though all of the results were positive, none were quite as dramatic as hers. "I saved the best for myself."

The _Times_ man seemed satisfied with her answer, but Peggy's mind was working. If, as Ronica said, this makeup could literally make you look like Elizabeth Taylor—or anybody—why hadn't Dr. Lincoln chosen to make herself over into a real beauty, say, a Brooke Shields type at nineteen, or someone like Emma Samms? Perhaps there was a limit to what the makeup could do. Or perhaps the patients were limited by their own viewpoints. Probably Dr. Lincoln _thought_ she was beautiful, and had retained enough of her old features so as not to completely disorient herself. Beauty was in the eye of the beholder, after all, and it must be disconcerting enough to wake up one morning and have an altered countenance without looking like a complete stranger on top of it.

"Now, where were we? Back to the skin, my friends."

Before long Dr. Lincoln was back to her old self, her voice reciting facts and figures in that unenthusiastic, monotonous drone with which she had spoken initially at the Berkley. It was obvious that her long and illustrious career had not included teaching. According to Barrows news releases she had made a name for herself as both a biochemist and a biologist, not in the halls of academia. In spite of Peggy's fatigue, snatches of the "lesson" came through her morning fogginess.

"Skin, as I said, is the largest organ of the human body, and includes our flesh, our hair, our nails, and even certain of our glands. Spread out flat, the skin of an adult male might cover twenty square feet or more."

Gross, Peggy thought, imagining a slab of human skin spread out across the floor of the classroom like a rug or tarpaulin.

"The epidermis is the outermost layer of the skin and is no thicker than, say, a sheet of paper. The epidermis's first two layers, 'horny' and 'granular,' are made up of a total of about forty rows of dying cells. Then there is the spinous layer, which has approximately a half dozen rows of living cells. These have spinelike projections, by which the cells make contact with each other. The final layer, the basal layer, is a single row of living basal cells which continuously divide and form other cells which eventually form the upper layers I've already mentioned."

She pulled a diagram down from above the blackboard and pointed at it. "The basal layer is extremely important, ladies and gentlemen, as this is the layer of the epidermis most affected by our process. We can stimulate this layer to create more cells whenever and wherever they're needed. By manipulating certain areas of the basal layer covering the face, for instance, we can create healthy new tissue, fill in scars and pits, and lighten or darken the skin's pigmentation by manipulating the production of melanin. This is the brown pigment produced by basal cells called melanocytes. In addition we can control the keratinocytes, which produce keratin, a substance that makes skin more durable and prevents fluids from moving through it."

The man from *Playboy* stuck his pencil in the air. "How is all this done?"

"Patience, sir, patience. I can't explain without giving you the necessary background."

The young man persisted. "We've all had Biology 101, Dr. Lincoln."

She winked. "Indulge me.

"Below the epidermis is the dermis layer—blood vessels, nerve endings, connective tissue. There are projections on the surface of the dermis called papillae which fit into corresponding holes on the undersurface of the epidermis. These projections have nerve endings which make them extremely sensitive to touch, particularly in your palms and fingertips. Below the dermis is what we call subcutaneous tissue, which is similar to the dermis but also has cells that store fat. Fat protects our body from injury and stores body heat.

"The dermis, by the way, is many, many times as thick as the epidermis, and subcutaneous tissue is much thicker than both the epidermis and dermis combined. Since both the dermis and subcutaneous tissue, the largest section of our skin, contain blood vessels, there's a new complication now. Here I must highlight an important difference between 'beautification' and cosmetic surgery."

She put down the pointer and put her hands in the pockets of her smock. "In surgery, the doctor must take great care working around and with the blood vessels, reconnecting these minute strands, constantly cauterizing the wounds he keeps making. What is surgery but the making and mending of wounds? With our process there are never any wounds, no cutting; no blood vessels are touched. The changes occur around these vessels. There is no danger of bleeding or scarring. The tissue is changed, not damaged. You can see what an advantage it is."

The woman from *Medicalstyles,* who sat next to Peggy, leaned over and said, "This sounds more and more like science fiction." Peggy nodded in agreement.

Dr. Lincoln plunged into a long discussion as to how their makeup—though it no longer seemed accurate to refer to it as a makeup—would change a person's features and even affect the bone structure. But Peggy wasn't fooled. She realized the woman was pulling the same trick Ronnie had at the press conference: giving out a lot of data without really saying much about how the process actually worked.

"For heaven's sake," the man from the *Times* finally said. "Just what is this stuff, Doctor? I'm not asking for a list of its ingredients or a copy of the chemical formula—just tell us what it is! I just don't have a story yet; none of us do, unless you just want us to reprint your before and after pictures, which frankly don't prove anything. How exactly did this miracle cosmetic work its magic on your face? The qualities you've given to it make it sound like hoodoo."

Dr. Lincoln quickly looked over at Ronica again. Ronica looked tense, but said nothing. "We're reluctant to give out too much information about the process," Lincoln said slowly. "And if you really think you have no story, you won't feel that way after you've met our test patients, seen what the makeup will do for them."

"You say this makeup turns into . . . living tissue, that it stimulates the growth of living tissue?"

"Artificial skin does the same thing," Dr. Lincoln replied, "and you have no trouble accepting that. Why can't you accept that we've taken it a giant step further? The makeup is not artificial skin, but it can do all that artificial skin can do and much, much more. I don't expect you to believe me now. But wait until our treatments begin. When you see for yourself—"

The woman from *Medicalstyles* spoke up. "But we still won't know how the process works or what the makeup *is?*"

"But even better, dear, you'll see it at work, see it applied, see it 'work its magic' as the gentleman put it. All I'll tell you for now is that it's safe, it works, and it's foolproof."

"Nix on the advertisements, please," the *Playboy* writer suggested.

Dr. Lincoln gave him a dirty look. "The makeup is comprised of *natural* ingredients, not synthetically produced chemicals, or acids. We have found something in nature, just as the creators of artificial skin used collagen, the protein that skin is mostly comprised of."

"They got the collagen for their artificial skin from cowhide," the *U.S. News* lady reported in a voice that was loud and raspy. "Are you telling us that the basic ingredients for your makeup are also taken from some animal?"

Peggy felt intimidated. These people did their homework.

Ronica got to her feet and stepped over to Dr. Lincoln's side so quickly that Peggy swore she left afterimages. "I really must apologize to all of you. You must know that the cosmetics industry is a highly competitive business, and though Dr. Lincoln would like to tell you more, she's prohibited by contract from talking too much about the process."

The *Playboy* writer muttered, "Then what are we doing here?"

"You own the company, Miss Barrows," the *Medicalstyles* woman said testily. "Can't you allow her to tell us more about this makeup?"

Dr. Lincoln spoke up before Ronica could reply. "It's okay, I can at least tell them if they're going in the right direction." She addressed the lady from *U.S. News and*

World Report. "You're on the right track," she said. "Our cosmetic is similar to artificial skin in that it is basically derived from a natural, organic animal product. Any more than that I can't say. Please bear with us. Be patient and we'll reveal more to you. This process is truly revolutionary."

Dr. Lincoln folded her arms across her chest. "But there is one other thing I should prepare you for. It may sound farfetched—"

"Compared to what?" The *Playboy* writer snickered.

Dr. Lincoln ignored him. "—but there is precedent. I'm sure all of you have heard the theory that one's mental perspective affects one's health. They say that recovery in cancer patients is more likely if the patient has an optimistic attitude. Then there's holistic medicine and biofeedback, all of which put great emphasis on the mind's role in healing.

"Well, we believe that our process can also be greatly abetted by a positive attitude, the patient's willingness to transform, his or her *need* to look better and different. How well the process works depends on how hard our patients work with us, mentally speaking, to bring about the proper transform—"

"Wait a minute," the man from the *Times* said. "Here we go with that hoodoo again. Is it the makeup—the process itself—or the patients who are responsible for the sweeping cosmetic changes you're promising? Now you're going off in a completely different direction. Does this stuff work or doesn't it? A patient's attitude doesn't have anything to do with it. How could it? Your mental state doesn't determine whether a cold cream works or not, or whether a suntan lotion keeps you from burning. Why should it determine whether or not your process will do what you say it will?"

Dr. Lincoln was obviously trying hard not to bristle. "I am merely suggesting that, just as a proper attitude, plenty of rest and relaxation, and healthy thoughts influence recovery from an illness or surgery, the same is true here. Our cosmetic doesn't work overnight. It will work faster for some people than others. To tell you why the patient's attitude is so important would tell you more about the process than I am able to at this time, but I'm sure we'd all agree that how we feel emotionally at any given point has a lot to do with how we feel *physically*. Nobody knows quite why this happens, but we'd be wrong to completely ignore this phenomenon, this psychic element. Whatever you want to call it, it's a major part of the treatment, and if you don't believe me you'll just have to wait and see. I really don't think there's anything more I can say."

The "psychic element." Peggy didn't like the sound of that. What was a patient supposed to do—send out thoughts *ordering* the "makeup" to change their features for them? It was too weird for her. She was glad she had not agreed to become a patient. Not until she knew a *lot* more about this. She had always been distressed by the new line of thought that blamed the patient for his or her illness, and based the prognosis solely on the patient's mental state. This smacked too much of that kind of thinking.

The conference was over; the group began to break up. Ronica told everyone she would soon be in touch with them, that the patients would begin treatment the following week and that everyone was invited to see the makeup applied. The *Times* reporter asked if he could drop in anytime to see how the patients were doing.

"We have to take their feelings into account," Ronica said. "They'll be staying here the first few days so that we can monitor them and they may not always be in the mood for reporters. I'm afraid you can see them only at prearranged intervals."

That did not sit well with the *Playboy* writer. "Is this process dangerous?" he asked gruffly. "Do you anticipate problems?"

Dr. Lincoln shook her head vigorously. "No, no. Not at all. But they might have apprehensions. That would only be normal. They'd prefer to be here where we can keep watch over them. The process is painless but it does make the skin feel funny, tingle sometimes. We want the patients to stay here, only at first, more for psychological reasons than anything else."

When the other journalists had gone, and Dr. Lincoln speeded away to wherever she went during the day, Peggy asked Ronica if she had time for another cup of coffee.

"I can't," Ronica told her. "I have an appointment across town in fifteen minutes. We're already going over possible ad campaigns. I'll give you a call next week. We'll have lunch or something." Her fingers flapped in the air. "Look, I've gotta rush. I have a change of clothes upstairs . . ." She headed for the large main staircase off the foyer.

"Okay, Ronnie," Peggy said. "We'll be in touch." She waved good-bye to her old friend's back. Ronica turned sideways for a second so she could give Peggy one last flap in return.

It was then, seeing the woman's body in profile, that Peggy realized what was different about Ronnie that she just hadn't been able to put her finger on before. Her breasts! Ronica had bigger breasts! Not Dolly Parton's size, nor even Jane Russell's, but much larger than before, too large to be attributable to a padded bra. Ronica had not been flat-chested, but her breasts had always been small compared to Peggy's. *Did she have silicone implants?* Peggy wondered.

One thing was certain, Peggy knew, and that was that you didn't get big breasts from any makeup, no matter how miraculous.

Or did you?

CHAPTER NINETEEN

Two and a half hours later Peggy had a lot more on her mind than Ronica's breasts or her wonderful new makeup. Her whole world had come crashing down around her and nothing seemed to matter anymore. The artificial structure of love and happiness she had built around herself for her sanity's sake was crumbling and she could do nothing to hold it together.

It all started half an hour after leaving the Barrows clinic, when Peggy went to a midtown restaurant to have lunch with an old friend of hers. Evelyn Miller was an extremely amiable person whom Peggy had known for several years, since Evelyn had edited a popular fashion magazine that Peggy had written several pieces for. They'd had lunch to discuss future assignments and taken an instant liking to each other. A good, strong friendship had resulted.

If Ronica represented the beautiful woman Peggy wanted to resemble, Evelyn was the sophisticated, un-tamed creature she wanted to be. She was scandalous in what she said about people and the racy subjects she talked about. Evelyn had taken Peggy to places she would never have dreamed of going herself; in fact, Peggy probably would not have gone to the club opening where she first met David unless Evelyn had talked her into it.

Now Evelyn worked for a public relations firm. "It pays better," she explained.

Evelyn looked wonderful. She had cut her hair, lost fifteen pounds, and was wearing a stylish suit that was a knockout. Evelyn was not a terribly pretty woman. She had thin, sharp features and was rather bony, but she was always well groomed and in the height of fashion, managing to appear sexy without really being so. It was definitely a case of personality conquering all.

"So, what's new with your life, Peggy?" Evelyn asked as they glanced through the menus. They tried to have lunch together at least every couple of weeks. "And what has Davey boy been up to?"

The way Evelyn asked the question made it clear how Evelyn felt about David and had felt about him for some time now. It hadn't always been the case. She had heartily approved of the man the first time she met him. But that was over two years ago, when Peggy and David had only been dating. Evelyn had thought it was a mistake to let him move in. Still, she had had dinner with him and Peggy, gone out to clubs and shows on double dates with them, so she couldn't have objected that much. But lately she resisted any suggestion of doing anything involving David.

"Davey's not up to much. Things are pretty much the same as ever."

Recently Evelyn had seemed a little bit tense when she had lunch with Peggy, as if she were holding back something that she was secretly dying to let out. Today Peggy's awareness of this was particularly acute, or else Evelyn was especially nervous about something. "Has David been working lately?" she asked.

"You mean acting jobs?"

"I mean anything."

Peggy paused. She always used to tell Evelyn the truth, but lately she'd been refraining, as if afraid Evelyn might give her a long-suffering look and say "I told you so."

What had changed her? Still there were times you needed to get things off your chest and this was one of them.

"Well, a couple of weeks ago he did some bartending and he filled in for one guy a couple of nights ago. But he hasn't done much else. As for acting . . ." She sighed. "I admit, Evelyn, I'm worried. He seems to have lost all of his initiative. He just wants to lie around and whine all the time. I really do love him, but . . ."

"Peggy, can I ask you a pretty serious question and get an honest answer?"

"I guess. What is it?"

"Does David love you?"

"Yes. I think he does."

"Are you sure he's not just using you?"

Peggy figured that if this wasn't a good time to get a lot of things out into the open she didn't know when would be. "Evelyn, what happened? Why are you so down on Davey lately? You used to like him, I know you did. In fact, when we first met him I think you liked him more than I did."

Evelyn nodded. "Yes, that's true. I thought he was cute, that he had personality. Let's face it, he was charming. But that's all fine for a one-night stand, someone you fuck on occasion or party with. But I'm not sure that's enough for a serious relationship. Peggy, David had 'leech' written all over him and you're the only one who couldn't see it. I never expected you to let him move in. You were so excited by it I didn't have the heart to *really* tell you what I thought. I should have been much more insistent. If I was any kind of friend, I'd have talked you out of it, but I didn't want to interfere. When a year went by I thought, 'Maybe they're working it out, maybe I was wrong.' Peggy, I couldn't have been happier. I knew how lonely you were, how you thought David was such a great catch." She paused to light a cigarette.

Peggy was determined to make Evelyn see the situation as it was. "Evelyn, a lot of people don't like Davey or think he's no good for me. But no one can really understand the core of a relationship like the two people involved. There're things about Davey—gentle things, exciting things—you may not know about."

Evelyn gave Peggy one of her let's-be-serious looks. "He's a good-looking guy who knows how to do it. C'mon, Peggy—is it really more than that? It's nice to have a pair of hot buns waiting for you when you get home. It's better than a cat or a sheepdog. But you're selling yourself short if you think that David Kravitz is the best you can do. He's not good enough for you."

"Where is all this coming from, Evelyn? When did you start to feel this way about David? Besides, I didn't have many other prospects, remember? No one was knocking down my door—"

Evelyn interrupted with surprising vehemence. "And no one will as long as you have that leech living with you."

Peggy couldn't understand the anger she saw in her friend's face, heard in her voice. What was it all about? Their drinks arrived and they sipped them in silence, each pausing to collect her thoughts. Evelyn spoke first.

"Look, Peggy. I'm not trying to hurt you. We've been friends for a long time. But damn it, I hate to see you being abused. There's just some things I have got to tell you."

She put down her cigarette and leaned in closer. "I know we both thought Davey Kravitz was kind of romantic when we first met him; the handsome actor, the struggling artist. He was different, he was exciting. I think we both believed that he was this noble fellow suffering for his art, a guy whose only crime was being poor, someone who would justify all our faith in him, all your support—including financial support—by working his tail off to get someplace and then repaying you, loving you. If things didn't work out for him careerwise, it wouldn't be his fault—at least he'd tried. Most of the struggling actors and writers and singers in this city—the ones who don't work, who are too full of pride to get day jobs, who live off spouses and families and lovers—most of them fall into that category. And I can accept that.

"But David falls into another category. He wants overnight success, and he doesn't want to work for it. He's attractive, he's got talent, but he's not *that* talented or good-looking. He's getting older, losing his hair, getting a paunch. He walks around in that pseudomacho way of his, as if he's covering up his artistic, sensitive side out of embarrassment. He's nearly forty. He knows if he doesn't make it soon he never will. And he probably won't. He's given up, Peggy, and he doesn't give a shit. If he can't make a living acting, he'll do the next best thing—he'll live off you. That was his goal in the first place. He doesn't bother going to auditions, or keeping up his contacts, because he never really had the dedication or the basic ambition. He just wants to leech off you or whoever else is stupid enough to let him."

"I've never heard you talk this way, Evelyn. Something must have happened to make you be so—"

"Stop making him out to be a tragic hero, Peggy. David's not a nice guy who just needs a lucky break. There are a lot of guys like that out there, but Davey isn't one of them. He's a parasitic sleazeball. If I told you half the things I know about him—"

"Tell me. Tell me what you know. And who told you."

Evelyn put her drink down and folded her hands over her face. "Peggy, I didn't want it to come to this. I take no pleasure in it."

"Tell me. I can handle it. I swear."

"Oh, Peggy. If you have to hear it, at least I'd rather you hear it from me." She took a last drag on her cigarette and crushed it in the ashtray. "I've known David Kravitz for quite a while. He was doing the bar scene back when I was, years ago. We knew each other by sight if not by name. I'd heard a lot of stories, but didn't know if they were true or not. Frankly, we did it together years before that night you met him."

"Okay. I can handle that."

"There's more. It's worse. Since he moved in with you I've run into a lot of people who knew David pretty well. I've double-checked things because I know how much he means to you . . ."

"What is it, Evelyn? Tell me."

Evelyn wiggled and shifted in her seat as if in preparation and said, "It seems that David has about half a dozen gullible women on the string; he sleeps with them and they give him loose change. He's a small-time hustler, Peggy. And worse—this is what I recently found out and really made me nervous—he deals drugs on the side, whenever he can't get money from you or some other sucker. He could care less about acting. He's a loser looking for a lucky score, that's all. Everyone who knows Davey knows it. You're so blinded with admiration that you can't even see him for what he is."

"Evelyn! Why are you saying this? People are lying about him!"

The waiter came over, sensed the tension in the air, and beat a hasty retreat.

"They're not lying. Ask around like I did. Anyone will tell you. None of this is a big secret. That 'workshop' he was going to last year—it was where he got his drugs. The 'audition' that ran late the night he showed up late for my birthday party in March? He was fucking Michelle Green. Remember her? Peggy, I'm sorry, but she told me all about it. The night I really began to despise David was the night I held a party for your birthday at Larabee's. You know why he came late that night? Because he was in bed with some other woman. Robbie Myers even saw David kissing this broad outside the restaurant when she dropped him off and said he bragged about it and swore him to secrecy. There've been others, lots of others. Everyone could see it, for God's sake, except you."

She kept talking but Peggy could hardly hear her. "Some of us supposed you had an open relationship or something, but I didn't think you'd ever go for that. I was amazed you'd even live with anybody. And there's a limit, after all. He seems to delight in doing things behind your back. He's such a sleazeball. Barry Greller told me Davey . . ."

Davey did this, Davey did that. The list went on and on until Peggy couldn't listen any longer. It seemed David Kravitz was one of the most notorious men in town. And she knew it was true, all true; Evelyn wouldn't really lie. Nothing, actually, was that big a surprise.

Oh God, you never do escape your past after all, she thought. Once you've been branded, the mark never goes away. Just when you think you're finally happy you realize it's all a lie. What made her think that a sexy guy like David Kravitz would actually love or desire her? It was the apartment he wanted, the base of operations, her handouts. When he was through with her, when someone better, someone dumber, came along, Davey would leave her just like that. He only went with her instead of a prettier, wealthier sucker because he was getting older and wasn't quite the handsome stud he used to be; he had to take the dregs. She could see it all now. Everything was so clear.

And yet, and yet . . .

"I don't feel much like having lunch, Evelyn," Peggy said in an emotionless voice.

"Honey. I'm sorry. But you had to know sometime. Why don't you stay and talk about it? Please, Peggy, let's work this out. Now that you know, you can go on with your life."

Go on with her life? What life? She didn't want to talk; she only wanted to go somewhere and cry. *Was it really necessary for you to tell me, Evelyn? Couldn't you have let me go on in blissful ignorance?* But she couldn't move; she just couldn't move.

Evelyn ordered two turkey clubs for them. When the food came, Evelyn consoled her and told her what she should do while Peggy chewed listlessly and automatically. She couldn't have said what she was eating.

When she finally got home she was much too demoralized, depressed, and exhausted to get into an argument with Davey. That would come later. Davey was sitting on the sofa—his favorite spot—watching television. She walked past him, went into the bedroom, and crawled into bed.

He came in and started complaining again. It seemed his obnoxious cousin Frank had bought one of those adjustable beds and been interviewed for a TV commercial. Soon his ugly face would be splattered across the airwaves. Already he was telling everyone what a TV star he'd be while "actor" Davey was still a nobody after all these years.

She was in no mood to hear him whine about his "career." Angered by her lack of attention, he went into a jealous and pointless snit over Romeo and Ronica Barrows, telling her if she had more self-esteem she wouldn't be so attracted to such mindless yuppies because she thought they were better than she was.

It went on and on. He began to sound like her father, who had always told her she didn't aim high enough. "If you're gonna use these people, why not make the most of it?" Davey said. "Why write just an article? Why not a book? Get a book deal out of it, babe. Get an agent and get yourself some money. One hundred thousand bucks or something. Think what we could do with one hundred thousand bucks."

Yeah. Think what you *could do,* she thought.

She was seeing him in an entirely different light. She could clearly see all the little flaws she had never cared about or paid attention to before because she was a woman in love: the bald patch on the back of his head that was getting bigger; the belly that was swelling from beers he bought with other women's and drug addicts' money. The way he put on that macho act when he spoke and gestured, as if he were a preppy doing an impression of a stevedore. And as for those tender moments, the protestations of love and devotion, the gentle touches and kind words—well, he was, had been, an actor, after all.

Finally, she spoke. "I can't take anymore, David. No more, please. It is now the beginning of November. I'll give you two months—two months and no more—to find a new place to live. After that, I don't care what happens to you. Move in with one of your other woman friends. Michelle Green, maybe."

David was thunderstruck. For the first time in a long time he was speechless.

"I want you out of here—and out of my life—by the end of the year."

In the basement of the Barrows Clinic on Sixty-third Street Ronica was having heated words with Dr. Lincoln. The hums, gurgles, and drips made by machinery, tubes, and the occupants of assorted tanks and cages made a bizarre backdrop to their conversation. In spite of the age of the yellow, chipped walls with their water stains and niches, the lab—like the smaller ones down the hall and upstairs—were outfitted with the latest equipment and safeguards.

"I told you, Betty, until we *prove* exactly what its capabilities are, we all agreed that the less known about the makeup the better."

"Oh, keep your girdle on, sister," the doctor snapped. She was standing at a long table adjusting a microscope. "I didn't tell those reporters much of anything. Besides, this makeup, no matter where it comes from, is perfectly safe. Do you see anything wrong with my face?"

"That's not the point. You know how people are. We want this product to have a positive image. If people knew where it came from, they'd be disgusted."

"They'll have to know sooner or later. The CDA will have to examine it."

Ronica looked uncertain as she said, "Victor can take

care of the CDA. Once everyone knows how wonderful this makeup is, when we have write-ups in every publication in the country, when the clinics are open and we have to turn the crowds away, then we can tell everyone where it comes from. We're working with an extremely radical process here, Betty. The American people aren't quick to take up new things, you know that."

Betty laughed. "Are you kidding? Put shit in glass jars and stick a label on it and half the country would buy it."

Ronica was always dismayed by the doctor's crudeness. "Never mind. We're just not going to take any chances. Not until we're sure we've got people hooked. Once they see how well it works, *then* they won't care if we make the stuff from peanut butter."

Betty turned away from the microscope. "All right, all right. You can count on me." The doctor moved toward the center row of the lab, between several big glass tanks inside which large grayish-red things were shuffling.

Ronica was halfway to the exit from the lab when she turned back. "Betty?"

Dr. Lincoln looked up. "Yes."

Ronica walked over to the doctor's side. "My breasts —they've been itching. Badly. You don't think anything's gone wrong?"

Lincoln tsked. "It's just a natural reaction to the process, I should think. Entirely normal, I imagine. It's all in your head. Ronica, do you want me to take a look?"

"Yes."

They walked into a small office cubicle in one corner of the lab and Dr. Lincoln closed the door. Ronica moved closer to the older woman and started to undo her blouse. "I'm sure it's nothing," the doctor said.

But as she bent her head to investigate she didn't look happy.

PART THREE
Metamorphoses

CHAPTER TWENTY_____

It had been nearly a month since Peggy's last trip to the Barrows Clinic on East Sixty-third Street. In spite of Ronica's promise that she and the other journalists would be present when the miracle makeup was applied to at least one special patient, Peggy hadn't seen even one of those people being treated. Ronica explained that she wanted to preserve their sense of privacy and diminish the feeling that they were guinea pigs. But surely the grateful impoverished ones who were getting treatment for free would be only too happy to cooperate in any way possible.

Meanwhile, the writers from the *Times* and *U.S. News* dropped out; they were not after scoops nor did they care about beating the competition. When and if this process was proven to be effective and reliable, they would do full write-ups on it in their respective publications. But for now they would not put up with all the secrecy, not to mention Ronica's insistence that they could only view and talk with the patients at prearranged times and while other reporters were present.

Like Peggy, however, the writers from *Playboy* and *Medicalstyles* were freelancers on assignment who needed the money and were determined to see it through. Even if the whole process were a fraud, they figured it might still make a good story. On the other hand, Peggy, with a

sense of loyalty, hoped that her friend wasn't overesti-
mating the capabilities of her product.

At least, during a second trip to the clinic, they had
been introduced to the patients before treatment began,
so they could see exactly what needed to be done to them.
The only one who really seemed in serious need was Yolanda Vasquez, who lay in her bed in her room at the end
of the third-floor hall swathed in bandages. Emily Stuart
and Ralph Tarramonte seemed only to want to get rid of
wrinkles, and Cecily Crenshaw, with her negligible im-
perfections, was a mere slave to her vanity. Matthew
Douglas was still attractive even with that rather nasty
scar, but she could see how his modeling career had been
destroyed by it. For that reason, he seemed a needy case,
though not as needy as Yolanda. But could makeup, no
matter how miraculous, really help any of these people?

Peggy had had an opportunity to ask these patients
how they felt about themselves and the prospect of being
"beautified," but her time was limited. She berated herself for not having had the foresight to contact them before they were admitted to the clinic. That was her
problem—she lacked initiative and boldness, and her career was suffering because of it.

Ronica greeted Peggy, George Burke from *Playboy*,
and Jennifer Lindsey from *Medicalstyles* in the drawing
room/lounge at a quarter after eleven. "I just have time
before lunch to take you up to see our patients," she
bubbled. "They've made some great strides already. Wait
till you see. They've had their second treatment already."

"Too bad we couldn't have seen it," Burke said irrita-
bly. "You know, Ms. Barrows, this secrecy is getting to
be tiresome."

Ronica looked as if she were about to say something
rude, but instead she met his eyes calmly and said, "This
is still a patent-pending process, Mr. Burke, and our formula is confidential." She seemed to relax a bit and
added, "On the other hand, I know how frustrating this
has been for you, and I appreciate your patience. But you

must understand that if the men and women who are being treated at the clinic don't want to be observed during treatment, we have to respect their wishes."

"That's bullshit," Jennifer said. "They were willing to let us look at their 'flaws' beforehand. Why should they be so skittish about us watching the makeup being applied? I think this whole thing is fishy. I'd like to see at least one of them getting treatment. I'm not asking to analyze your makeup under a microscope so I can sell the formula to the highest bidder, for heaven's sake. Is it so much to ask just to watch?"

Reluctantly, Ronica finally relented. "All right, all right. Matthew Douglas is still being worked on in room 2A. Let's go up there and you can see for yourselves that we've nothing to hide."

They marched up the grand staircase and walked down the second-floor corridor until they reached the treatment cubicle where Matthew Douglas sat. His face was being worked on by Dr. Lincoln herself. Ronica separated herself from the others, and stepped into the chamber to stand beside the older woman. She whispered a few words. To Peggy it was obvious that it had probably been Dr. Lincoln all along who had objected to the treatment being observed, and not Ronica or the patients. There was a furious expression on Lincoln's face and she glared at the three journalists as if wishing they'd expire on the spot. But Ronica, to her credit, held her ground and said, rather fiercely, "I don't see why they can't watch. I'm letting them, and that's that!"

Dr. Lincoln muttered under her breath, "Damn it! You were the one who . . ." but went grudgingly back to work.

Peggy, George, and Jennifer crowded around the chair in which Matthew Douglas reclined. A light had been pulled down and placed over his face, illuminating every pore. Peggy was amazed to see how much better his scar looked today. There were still traces of the line splitting his face, but the scar was much narrower than before, and not as deep or white.

Peggy imagined if you applied enough of any kind of makeup to a scar it would have that same effect. It didn't mean the underlying skin itself was actually healing. If only she could have run her fingers over the scar to see if it felt like flesh or like makeup.

Douglas himself seemed quite aloof and distant, but she suspected that it was a pose. The whole situation must have been uncomfortable for him. But surely the improvement in his face would cause his morale to rise. He was very good-looking. She sensed his scar gave him an only recently developing vulnerability and humility without which, ironically, he would probably seem less attractive.

Dr. Lincoln had apparently decided that if she must endure the presence of the journalists, she had a perfect right to go into an act of her own. She began speaking to them as she worked. "This, my friends, is the makeup you've been hearing so much about."

There was a pale white canister on a metal table to her right, and she dipped her fingers into it as she had been doing periodically. The stuff she dug out was a flesh-colored substance that appeared to be greasy and rather dense. She rubbed it over the scar and smoothed it into the skin around the injury.

"The whole process is simple, uncomplicated, and perfectly painless. This is how it works. You just repeatedly apply the makeup to the scar, filling it in, smoothing down the edges, covering it up completely. First, the makeup is mere camouflage, a makeup only in the everyday sense of the word. But then"—the fingers dipped, came up with more fleshy grease—"the makeup begins to work its magic."

With her free hand, she pointed to Matthew's chin. "I haven't touched this part of his face today. Repeat, I haven't applied any makeup. The scar looks better because it *is* better. It's healing, slowly disappearing. All because of the makeup I applied last week. Just a few more applications and Mr. Douglas will look just the way he used to. No more scar. Just perfect, unblemished skin.

"In the meantime, we carefully rub our makeup into his scar, being careful not to put on too much or create an unwanted effect." She picked up a small scalpellike instrument and began to plane away some of the excess makeup from his nose. "So you see, I'm part doctor and part makeup artist. We'll be training a great many people to do just what I'm doing here today to work in our clinics across the country."

"You've got big plans," George Burke said with a touch of cynicism.

"Is there anything wrong with that?" the doctor asked.

Burke smirked, but said nothing.

They watched for a few minutes longer as the doctor completed the job, rubbing some of the "makeup" into the rest of his face. Now Matthew Douglas looked completely normal. But it was still largely, as Dr. Lincoln put it, camouflage. Still, if the makeup was really doing what she claimed it could do, it *was* nothing short of miraculous.

Dr. Lincoln spoke directly to Matthew Douglas for the first time since Peggy and the others had appeared. "Now, remember what I told you, Matthew. Think positively. I want you to wait here a few moments and think only of your scar, of treating your scar, getting rid of it. *Visualize* this. Concentrate on healthy flesh, healthy cells. Picture yourself whole and perfect again. I cannot stress the importance of this. *Picture yourself perfect.* Do you understand?"

"Yes, Doctor. Whatever you say." It was as if he were unconvinced by this part of the treatment but would do whatever the doctor told him if it would get results.

Peggy knew how Dr. Lincoln felt about the power of positive thought, but she still didn't see what difference it made if Matthew Douglas sat there "picturing" himself perfect for half an hour or not. Wouldn't the makeup work in any case? It almost seemed supernatural.

Having had the journalists forced upon her, Dr. Lincoln now appeared to enjoy their presence and was eager to explain more about her work, though she would not defend or explain her power-of-suggestion hypothesis any further. Additionally, she forbade the writers to interview Matthew while he had to "picture himself perfect." She took them to see the other patients, all of whom were resting after treatment in their rooms upstairs, though most did not remain on the premises full-time.

All of the other patients were in better condition than they had been previously, though it was difficult to tell with Cecily Crenshaw, who had been so attractive to begin with that you would probably have to carefully compare before and after photos under a magnifying glass to see the difference in her nose and chin. Dr. Lincoln explained that the makeup had a "shrinking" effect and would be able to reduce the cells and make particular facial features smaller than they were before. Cecily's face did seem lovelier, somehow, but Peggy imagined that it could just be in her mind because she had expected it to happen.

Cecily was picking at a fruit salad and chatting on the phone. When she saw the doctor she hung up, lay back on her bed, and told everyone she wanted to take a nap. There'd be no talking to her today. Peggy didn't mind. The woman seemed self-absorbed and unpleasant.

Tarramonte and Stuart—who were either sleeping or "visualizing"—looked much younger than they had a couple of weeks ago. Tarramonte's upper forehead was lumpy where makeup had been spread over the receding hairline to supposedly stimulate new hair growth. Dr. Lincoln even pointed out that Tarramonte's heavy lantern jaw was smoother and slimmer than before.

"Yes, at first it was just an illusion created by the artful application of makeup, building up the other parts of the face to reduce the heaviness of the jaw. But now, it's slowly changing."

Tarramonte lay on the bed, apparently thinking positive thoughts, in such a stiff position—as if they'd just taken his body out of a freezer—that it was almost comical. "How are you feeling?" Dr. Lincoln asked him.

"O-okay, I guess."

Before Dr. Lincoln could hustle the others out of his room, he added: "My jaw hurts like hell, Doctor."

Although she bent over his bed and whispered, Peggy could hear her. "I told you to expect that. It's nothing to worry about. The makeup is affecting the bone, transforming it the way I've told you to visualize it. I'll have the nurse bring you some more painkillers. In the meantime, do as I've told you: see yourself in your mind as you'll be, as you've always wanted to look. Handsome. Young. *Beautiful.*"

"All right—all right, Betty, uh, Doctor."

Peggy thought that Tarramonte and Mrs. Stuart seemed rather pathetic in spite of their wealth and the limitless opportunities it offered them.

Outside, in the hall, Burke spoke first. "I thought you said this process was painless."

"When treating the skin, yes, but Mr. Tarramonte's treatment requires the shifting and shaping of bone itself. It hurts no more than a bad headache, but some people are not used to pain. We'll give him a pain suppressant and he'll be fine."

Burke turned to Peggy and Jennifer. "Headache, huh?"

The doctor turned back to Burke and said sharply, "Don't look for trouble where there isn't any, Mr. Burke. Our makeup will be able to help a great many people. Maybe even you someday. Please remember that."

For a moment Burke didn't know what to say. Then he replied, "I just expect total honesty if not total disclosure, all right?"

Lincoln nodded. "Agreed. Shall we continue?"

The most dramatic change had occurred in Yolanda Vasquez, who was sitting up in bed, mostly unbandaged, smiling and sipping a cup of mild herbal tea. She still looked awful, but at least the skin had lost much of its blackened, raw, infected quality. There was a layer of pale red tissue growing where before there had been only dead flesh. As she had the first time she met her, Peggy felt a strong concern and sympathy for this sweet, disoriented woman who had lost her husband and children.

"Yolanda's treatment is, of course, the most extensive, and will take the longest to complete. But our prognosis is a good one. Our makeup is reacting with her burned skin just as we knew it would. Like artificial skin it is stimulating new growth of healthy cells while covering up the worst aspects of her condition. After another application she may be able to walk about looking no worse than if she'd had a mild sunburn. Another application, and the skin will be healthy and pink. And it will keep on getting better and better. We're very proud of our accomplishment here."

"Any pain?" Burke asked the patient.

Yolanda shrugged. "It tingles and itches sometimes. That's just the feeling coming back, I guess. I feel—I don't know—hopeful, happy, for the first time since the fire." There were tears in her eyes as she looked up at Betty Lincoln. "Thank you, Doctor."

Back out in the hall, Lincoln continued. "There's been a great deal of discord among certain surgeons as to our so-called 'exploitation' of Yolanda Vasquez, our 'using' her to further our own ends. You saw what condition that girl was in when she was brought here, and what condition she's in now, so you can judge for yourselves. Are we 'exploiting' her or helping her?"

The doctor smiled, said good-bye to Peggy and the others, and walked down the hall.

Peggy had to admit: they put on a good show in this place.

* * *

"So what do you think of this whole business?" Jennifer Lindsey said, as she split open a packet of sugar and poured it into her coffee. They were sitting in a coffee shop two blocks down from the clinic to compare notes. George Burke had rushed off for another appointment.

Peggy put down her donut and said, "I don't know. On one hand it really does seem like a miracle. On the other hand, there's something so peculiar about it I can't help but have my doubts."

"Me, too. All this 'visualizing' and 'picturizing' . . ."

"Maybe that's just a psychological thing, to help relieve the patient's anxiety. It may have nothing to do with the treatment itself."

"Yes, but the things they claim this stuff can do! Changing that guy's whole jaw, for instance, affecting the bone. I know this stuff is really more than a makeup, but it seems incredible that it can actually make bones move under your skin. Brrr. The whole thing gives me the creeps."

"Maybe it doesn't make the bones move so much as it reshapes them, makes them larger or smaller according to what's needed."

"But how can a makeup, which is applied externally, go all the way down to someone's bones? I mean, I know it sinks into the skin, into the muscles and vessels, but can it actually work its way through all that and reach, *change,* the bone?"

"Apparently it can."

"Well, if it can do that, what can't it do? I mean, this stuff might cure cancer or AIDS. I'm not being facetious, Peggy. If it can change a person's skin and bones, which are made up of cells, after all, why can't it change other kinds of cells, cancer cells or I don't know what. I mean, it could be of much more beneficial use than as a makeup to help Cecily Crenshaw get rid of her pimples."

Peggy laughed. "Seriously, I don't think this thing could cure cancer. Dr. Lincoln would have told us. Besides, changing skin and bone is a lot different from getting rid of cancer cells. I imagine the makeup could be used to get rid of skin diseases, maybe skin cancers. But anything else? Something as complicated and internalized as AIDS? I don't think so."

Jennifer wiped some crumbs off her mouth. "You're right. I got carried away for a minute. You should be writing for *Medicalstyles*. You sound more practical than me."

"Nobody's ever accused me of being practical."

"Still, I'd love to know what's in that makeup."

"Wouldn't we all? But they're not telling."

"You say you knew Ronica Barrows in college? You can't get her to talk, old friends and all that?"

"Afraid not."

"You know when I told her I didn't want to sell her formula to the highest bidder?"

"Yeah?"

She lowered her voice and looked around surreptitiously, but in a theatrical way that was clearly just for show. "Well, that doesn't mean I wouldn't like to get my hands on some of it."

"I don't see how you could do that. When they're not using the makeup I'm sure it's kept under lock and key. I think I saw guards in the building, too. And the labs are probably locked after hours. Say, you're not thinking of breaking in there, are you?" She winked to let the woman know she was joking.

Jennifer wore an ambiguous expression. "No, not breaking in. But who knows? Maybe something will occur to me."

Peggy sipped her coffee and watched Jennifer for a moment as the other woman chewed her donut and stared off into space.

CHAPTER TWENTY-ONE_____

When Dr. Lincoln went to Ralph Tarramonte's room to check on her beloved, the nurse told her that he had left the clinic an hour ago.

It was permissible; only Yolanda Vasquez was in such serious condition that she was required to stay at the clinic. Cecily Crenshaw's adjustments were minor and she only came in on her days of treatment. Matthew Douglas and Emily Stuart, however, had moved into the clinic for the duration, the former because his room at the Barrows clinic was undoubtedly more appealing than his sleazy Hell's Kitchen digs, and the latter because she had a hypochondriacal need to have nurses, doctors, and assorted attendants on hand at all hours.

Ralph didn't have to stay at the clinic, although his facial restructuring was more delicate than any of the others', and Lincoln wanted to monitor him. She did not insist upon his staying because it would have curtailed their erotic activities for several weeks, and that she simply could not abide. The makeup was starting to effect changes in Ralph's already attractive features—tightening his cheeks, smoothing away wrinkles—and she found herself wanting him more and more each day. As long as he came in each week for treatment and several follow-up examinations it would be all right. There was little they could do for patients in between visits.

"Did you give him a bottle of those pain capsules I recommended?" Dr. Lincoln asked the nurse.

"Yes, Doctor."

"Fine."

He had probably gone home, bored with lying around his room "visualizing" his handsome new face. It was more important than he realized, but she supposed the time he had stayed there had been long enough. She rushed down the hall to the dressing room where she kept her street clothes. She changed quickly, applied some conventional makeup, and brushed her hair. Minutes later she dashed out of the building and hailed a cab.

Ralph Tarramonte would have been surprised to learn that Dr. Lincoln was perfectly aware of his hired love-partners. But that was part of what she found attractive in the man. Now that she was pretty she wanted a man who could appreciate the female body, who knew what he liked in women and who liked women with a passion. Tarramonte was made-to-order. She welcomed his having sex with younger women. She would rather he get it out of his system, instead of winding up resenting her and always wishing she was twenty. She knew how often he had sex by checking to see how many packages of condoms were left in his drawer. At least the sleaze was smart enough to protect himself, and her, from sexually transmitted diseases.

There were times when she wondered if she was going utterly crazy, developing this desperate need for sex after so many years of doing without it. It had become one of the driving forces in her life and at times it threatened to overwhelm her. But she was not about to give it—to give Ralph—up. She would sooner cut off her right arm. Let the man screw all the bimbos he wanted; she would be the one to marry him.

Ralph could take care of her in her declining years, and he had plenty of money to back whatever research project she tackled after Beautifique was officially launched. Of course, with her percentage of the profits, she'd be wealthy enough on her own. It all seemed like a dream.

She arrived at Ralph's town house, used the key he had given her, and as expected, found him home watching a football game, his hand on his chin. (She hated football. With all these cable stations it seemed there wasn't one hour of any day when the sport wasn't being played somewhere.) She turned off the set—to which he did not react—and began a striptease in front of the couch where he sat. Usually he was ready to go before she was.

"What's the matter, Ralph? Don't you wanna fuck?"

Ralph shook his head from side to side and said in a miserable voice: "It hurts like hell. My jaw hurts like hell."

She came to a stop. "Didn't you take those painkillers?"

"I took as many as I could without killing myself. What did you do to me, Betty? What the hell did you do to me? It *hurts.*"

He was actually crying.

He could be one of those people who can't stand the slightest pain, she thought, but Betty had no reason to believe he was that bad. Perhaps the pain really was excruciating. Even the painkillers wouldn't work. But it didn't make any sense—that hadn't happened with her, and she had required changes in the bone every bit as extensive as what Ralph required. That's what made the whole "operation" so attractive—its comparative painlessness.

"*Will* it away, honey," she told him, sitting down half-naked at his side. "Just don't think about it. Occupy yourself with something else. *Visualize* how handsome you'll—"

"Oh, shut up with that already. I've *been* 'visualizing.' And why do you think I turned the football game on? To try to keep my mind off the pain. But it hurts, damn it, it hurts."

She reached out and touched his cheek. He reacted

violently, knocking her hand away and cursing. "Get off me, you bitch! Look what ya done to me."

She was appalled and angered by his accusations. "Done to you! You look better than you have in your life! And you'll get better and better looking every day." Her attitude suddenly mellowed. "Stop being such a goddamn crybaby and kiss me already. That will take your mind off things." She grabbed his hand and held it against her naked breast.

"Are you crazy? I think you're crazy! Thinking about sex at a time like this. Who can think about sex? I tell you my face feels like it's falling apart!"

That's when it finally hit her: Ralph Tarramonte *not* thinking about sex?

He really was in trouble.

They were in trouble. All of them.

Something was going wrong.

CHAPTER TWENTY-TWO _____

When Emily Stuart woke up, Scottie was standing by her bed, holding a present wrapped up in cheery green and red wrapping paper. She smiled. What could it be? A book? Scottie knew how she loved to read. A corsage, perhaps, though the package was not the right shape. A box of candy? Yes, that was probably it. Candy always cheered her. Still, the shape was peculiar. . . . *Leave it to Scottie to be creative.*

"How ya doin', ya old bag," Scottie said in his inimitable manner when he saw that her eyes were open. "For a minute I thought you were dead."

"Don't get your hopes up," she said. She wished he'd bend down so she could kiss him, but he kept his distance. "Is that a present for me? Why Scottie, I'm astonished."

"Yeah. It's for you." He handed it to her and she tore off the wrapping.

It was a mirror. A large oval mirror with a pink plastic backing and slender handle. The cheap kind you could buy in the five and dime for a buck and a half.

"Well, you certainly didn't spend much of the fifteen hundred dollars I gave you on this."

As usual, Scottie flew into one of his mini-rages. He did so at the slightest provocation. "You don't want it, old lady, give it to me and I'll throw it out the window!"

"Calm down, Scottie. I was only kidding. I can use it."

"Figured they wouldn't have too many mirrors in this place. Wouldn't want you old people scaring yourselves to death."

She ignored him and studied her face in the mirror. There really had been a marked improvement. And this was only the beginning.

"Scottie, how—how do you think I look? Be honest."

"Okay. For an old lady. But be serious—they can't make you look as young as me, can they?"

"No."

"So what good is it? Everyone will *still* think you're my grandmother."

She sat very still for a moment. "Yes, Scottie."

Scottie. Her beloved. Her joy. Her curse. Scottie, who always brought her crashing down to earth and made everything she did for him seem so futile.

The nurse, whose name was Mitzi Myencott, had just come from the lounge. She had caught the last few minutes of her favorite soap on the old TV they kept there for when things were slow and boring, which was often. She loved *Snow Valley,* and had watched it since she was a young girl. She would have given anything to meet a man who looked like Drake Hardesty, who played Brian Westcott. Drake was her ideal man; he did things to her that no other actor or boyfriend could do. She wanted to cry when she thought that she might spend her whole life without making love to a man like Hardesty.

She was still thinking about Hardesty when she went in to check on that model, Matthew Douglas, who was good-looking but not in Hardesty's class. Douglas seemed to take a lot of naps, but there wasn't much else to do, she supposed; the patients didn't even have TVs in their rooms. Sure enough, he had turned out the light by the bed and gone to sleep. She spent a few minutes collecting his dinner dishes and tidying up the room. The few nurses who worked in the clinic had to do everything. She stepped closer to the bed, just to make sure he was breathing; you never knew.

She had to bite her lip to keep from crying out. That wasn't Matthew Douglas on the bed; it was Drake Hardesty!

She stood there, her heart pounding, and tried to calm herself. She was afraid to open the curtains or turn on the light for a closer look because it might wake him. It couldn't be Drake—she was imagining things. The shadows falling across the man's face had played a trick on her, that was all. Everyone knew she had Hardesty on the brain. Still, that just didn't look like Matthew Douglas on the bed. Not quite Drake Hardesty, but more like Drake than Douglas. Perhaps they had moved another patient in here without telling her. A patient who resembled Hardesty. Yes, that was it.

She went out to the nurses' station to find out what was going on.

"Olga, who is that in room thirty-seven?"

"Matthew Douglas."

"Are you sure?"

"Sure I'm sure."

Mitzi explained the problem. The two women went back to the room and turned on the light.

It was Matthew Douglas. He looked a little different than before, but that makeup was supposed to make changes, so she assumed it was nothing to worry about.

Olga smirked and gave her an affectionate pat on the shoulder. "Stop watching those soap operas, Mitzi," she said. "They're making you see things."

Mitzi wouldn't stop watching the soaps, she thought, but she just might have her eyes checked tomorrow. Or go see a good psychiatrist.

It was nearly eight o'clock by the time Ronica got back to her apartment. Romeo had insisted on going over advertising strategies with their consultants until a firm campaign had been mapped out. While eating her reheated dinner, she pondered all the things that had been happening lately.

The money they all hoped to make was of less interest to her than the scientific advances they'd be offering to people in need everywhere. She already had more money than she knew what to do with. If it was up to her, she'd just offer this service to anyone free of charge, but of course that was unrealistic. It would take large sums of cash to keep manufacturing the makeup, to set up the clinics, pay all the employees, let people around the country know just what the makeup could do.

But none of them were really facing up to the fact that they had no idea how people would react once they knew just *where* the makeup came from. That was the one negative aspect that seemed insurmountable. If the CDA refused to approve the product, all their hopes would be dashed, not to mention those of all the people who'd go untreated when beauty could so easily have been theirs. Romeo had said not to worry about the CDA, that he was sure Victor could take care of them, but she felt certain they would prove a greater adversary than the general medical profession and cosmetic surgeons combined.

She finished dinner, brushed her teeth, changed into her nightie, and dismissed the maid. She was flipping through a fashion magazine when the door from the hallway suddenly opened and a man stepped into the living room where she was sitting.

He was in his early forties and was very tall, over six feet two, slender but well built. He was amazingly ugly. The face was long, and had a large lumplike nose, thick lips, heavy brows, and a receding chin. The eyes were large and rarely blinked. The skin color was a mottled gray. His hair was close to the scalp, a wiry mash of tightly curled strands which resembled steel wool.

"Ronnie," he said. His voice was gravelly, deep, European in flavor.

Ronnie got up from the couch and ran over to the

visitor, who still held the keys to her apartment dangling in his hand. They embraced, kissed, fondled each other. The man removed Ronica's nightie with a swiftness and surety that came from many years' practice. When she was naked, she bent before him as if offering homage. He picked her up roughly by her hair and thrust his full wet lips against her thinner unresisting ones.

When he was through, Ronica pulled back, stared at him for a moment, and then put her hands down hard on his shoulders. She pushed him down, down to his knees, and tightened her lips, smeared with his saliva, into a cruel, thin line of scorn and contempt.

"You piece of shit," she said. "You're ugly. You're gross. You disgust me."

The man on the floor shivered, trembled at the words. "Yes, yes, I know."

"I hate you, you piece of shit."

"I don't deserve you," he said.

"You're nothing but shit to me."

"Yes, yes, I know."

The phone rang.

"Damn," the man said, picking himself up from the floor. "Just when it was getting good."

Ronica turned her back on him and went over to the phone. "I didn't expect to see you again, Dennis." She picked up the phone and turned to face him. "But I'm glad you're here. I think."

That had been strange, really strange, she thought. After all these years he abruptly walked into her life again —who did he bribe to get her keys? she wondered—and they started right off as if nothing had ever happened. "Yes?" she said into the phone.

It was Romeo, and he was hysterical. Her brother had always been calm and in control, but now he was so overwrought he could barely talk. "Romeo, get hold of yourself. *What's wrong?*"

"Spots, tumors, eruptions, all over . . ."

"All over where? Who? What are you talking about?"

"Cecily! *Cecily!*"

"What happened to her? Calm down and just tell me what happened."

"Cecily—Cecily's . . . I tried to get Dr. Lincoln but she's not home. God help us, Cecily's . . . you have to come, Ronnie. You have to come!"

"I'm on my way."

She hung up the phone and began gathering her clothes. She dropped the nightie on her bed and changed into street wear.

Dennis had just walked back into her life and already she was walking out on him. Part of the things she had said to him a moment ago had not been entirely nostalgic playacting, but in spite of her misgivings she was still happy he'd returned to her.

"I have to go out," she said.

"Go out. But why? After all the trouble I went to . . . Darling, you can't go out. Not now."

"Yes I can."

"Why?"

"Because the shit has hit the fan, Dennis. The shit has hit the fan. And I don't have time for playing your little games right now. My brother needs me. You kept me waiting years; you can wait an hour or so longer."

On her way out she slammed the door and left him standing there, homely, openmouthed, and utterly astonished.

I can't believe I got this far, Jennifer Lindsey told herself. Creeping down the stairs to the basement of the Barrows Clinic, she was almost disappointed by how easy it had been, even though the whole time she'd kept telling herself she was crazy. She wasn't the Girl from U.N.C.L.E.; she was a writer for established medical journals and should have been above sneaking about like some kind of cat burglar.

She had deliberately left a notepad—some fake notes hastily scribbled on the first few pages—in the clinic's lounge. After saying good-bye to Peggy Antonicci, and resting at her apartment for several hours, she'd gone back to the clinic and asked if she could retrieve the pad. She had figured someone would get it for her, but the preoccupied lady at the front desk merely waved her through. Ronica Barrows and Dr. Lincoln were not around and the whole first floor seemed deserted. She had suspected that the night crew would be small—and less watchful.

Retrieving the notepad, she made her way from the lounge into the hallway and down to the labs without being spotted. Two fat security men were playing cards in a small room to the right, but she was careful about making any noise and didn't disturb them. She hid the notepad in her bag so that if anyone asked what she was doing there, she could claim she'd thought the pad might have been mislaid elsewhere during a tour of the building.

There was nothing of great interest in the labs; nothing that seemed out of the ordinary or any different from chem lab in high school. There were several locked refrigerators in which they probably stored the makeup. Perhaps she could find a canister with that makeup in it, and just swipe it. No, that would be a certified criminal action, and she had no desire to get arrested. *Medicalstyles* didn't pay enough for that.

Back out in the hallway she noticed a door at the very end marked KEEP OUT/AUTHORIZED PERSONNEL ONLY. Funny, they hadn't taken them in there as part of that tour. *For goodness' sake,* she thought, *they might as well have a big red arrow pointing toward it, saying "This is where the good stuff is."*

The door was not locked, which indicated someone was downstairs. Heedlessly, she threw open the door, stepped inside the narrow wooden stairwell, and descended. The walls were made of rough white stone and there was a musty, unpleasant smell in the air. She heard humming noises, the click-clack of machinery, or were they distant footsteps? At the bottom of the stairs was a narrow corridor that led in two directions. The ceiling was lined with bright fluorescent lights but shadows on the edges made it all the more ominous.

She soon came to a metal door with a large window in it. Another lab, brightly lit except at the corners. She took a deep breath, swore, opened the door, and stepped through.

The room was full of several large, long tanks and the air was full of gurgling noises. The smell was much more intense in here—a harsh, multilayered aroma that nearly made her gag. On the nearest table a cigarette was still burning in an ashtray. She wouldn't have much time.

Quickly, Jennifer went over to the nearest tank and bent over for a better look at what was inside.

Oh my God! What was going on in this place? Giving in to curiosity and temptation, she pulled up the glass lid.

Something in the tank moved. Jennifer screamed.

It was the last thing she would ever do.

CHAPTER TWENTY-THREE_____

To say things were grim in Peggy's apartment would be an understatement.

Since she had given David her ultimatum over a month ago, the two had hardly spoken a word to one another. David spent very little time in the apartment, except to sleep. In the beginning he usually came in drunk late at night, and clambered into her bed and tried to make love to her. She was lucky he was not a violent person. When she refused his attentions, he would break down and weep, telling her he loved her, that he wanted to stay with her, that she didn't understand. He swore he had only sold grass a few times; nothing heavy like crack or cocaine. It was quite pathetic, really. She told him he'd have to be content with sleeping on the couch from now on.

She didn't think it had quite sunk in for David that her attitude toward him had drastically altered. He was torn between believing she would eventually give in, beg him to stay, and desperately scrambling to hook into somebody else who would put up with him. Apparently after all this time he had not found another sucker who would offer him bed and board. Time was running out, but Peggy didn't care. She would try to be as humane about the whole thing as possible, but she wanted David Kravitz out of her life.

Now she sat in the living room reading the newspaper. David was in the bathroom, showering. In half an hour she would have to leave for her appointment at the Barrows clinic. Ronica had promised her some time ago that today she could come in and do follow-up interviews with the patients; see for herself how the treatment was progressing.

David came out of the bathroom wrapped in a towel. He was whistling some sixties rock tune. He got dressed quickly, and disappeared into her bedroom. She knew that he rummaged around looking for money, but she was careful to hide it in places he'd never think to look. He came out of the bedroom holding up a photo album she kept in her night-table drawer. Luckily there was no money in there. He would try anything, it seemed. Now it was the "nostalgic" approach.

"Say, any pictures of us in here, babe? I've never gone through this before."

She tried to ignore him, but he sat down beside her on the couch and opened the book.

"What have we here? Say—childhood pictures. Let's see what you looked like as a baby, huh?"

"David. Please put the book away."

"Why, honey? I'm interested in your life, your past. The fact that I'm moving out of here and out of your love life doesn't mean we can't stay friends, does it?"

Yes, it does mean that. "Please, David. Give me the album. There's nothing in there that would interest you."

He flipped through the pages. "Baby pictures, confirmation pictures, high school graduation. Your whole life's in here. What do you mean, I wouldn't be interested? Did you put any pictures of us in here? The ones from the party or the trip to Atlantic City?"

"They're in there, yes. But you've already seen them."

He had flipped back to the beginning of the album. "I haven't seen this. Cute little Peggy as a baby. Where are pictures of you as a child, though, when you were older, y'know?" He broke out into a bemused smile. "Hey, who's this little boy with your parents? Don't tell me you have a brother you've never even told me about."

She froze. "No. I don't have a brother." Then she regretted saying anything. "I mean—give me the book, David."

"Why can't I look at it, huh?"

"Just give it to me." There were some things about herself that she did not want David Kravitz or anyone to know.

"Say, how come there are no pictures of you as a little girl? There's just this boy in every photograph. Who was he? Did you have a brother who died?"

"No." She leaned over and tried to wrestle the photo album out of his hand. "Give me the book. That's enough."

"Say, what's with you? What's wrong with my showing a little interest in your life?"

"You have no interest in my life, just in my apartment."

David tried to affect a hurt, misunderstood look. He was not very good at it. "We've been all over that, Peggy. You've got me all wrong. Don't worry—I'll get out of here as soon as I can. But I just don't want you believing a lot of nasty rumors spread by silly bitches who are jealous of what we have together."

"We have nothing together. We never did."

"You're gonna get lonely on those cold winter nights."

She snorted. Where did he get his dialogue? Certainly not from Tennessee Williams or Eugene O'Neill. "I'll manage somehow, David. I don't want to talk about it. I said you could stay here until December thirty-first. Now be grateful for that. I don't hate you, I don't despise you. I just don't want you living here anymore. I think this relationship was a mistake. Now be a man about it— accept it—and move on. Please. As soon as possible." She was thinking: *Now that he's seen those pictures, he really* must *go. I will not go through what I endured in grade school ever again.*

He leaned back in his seat and exhaled dramatically. "I still think you're acting crazy. But I'm not the type to beg for anything."

Oh no? she thought.

He got to his feet. "Just remember. When I'm gone, I'm *gone*. I won't ever come back. Believe it."

I do, I do. Just go, just go.

He was about to go into the bathroom again—probably to check his bald spot, Peggy thought—when he turned around and advanced toward her with a sly, sleazy smile on his face. "You know what your problem is, babe? You know what your whole problem is? You don't like yourself. You've got no self-esteem."

Here we go again, Peggy thought. *Can't he ever change the record?*

"That's why you're so crazy for this Ronica broad. She's everything you wish you were. She's got everything you wish you had. And this Romeo fag you're so hung up on?—he's probably fucking his sister."

She could have asked David why Romeo would be interested in his sister if he was gay, but what was the point? Like a lot of insecure men, David was full of moronic sexist and homophobic attitudes that made little sense.

"That's the only reason you like the Barrows kiddies, 'cause you hate yourself. You hate yourself 'cause you're not pretty. 'Cause you don't look like Ronica. So you worship the bitch. Worship her good looks and her hot pussy, don't you, huh? You're jealous. And miserable—"

He was building up to a stormy tirade and Peggy wanted no part of it. She got up, walked past him, and went into her bedroom, shutting the door behind her. A moment later she heard the hall door slam. He had gone out. Damn it! Why did he have to see those pictures?

She had just left her bedroom when the phone rang. It was Ronica Barrows. She sounded very terse and businesslike today, preoccupied.

"Peggy, I'm sorry it's such late notice. But things have

been hectic here. Look, I have to cancel our appointment
this afternoon. Something's come up."

"Oh, is everything all right?"

"Yes, but I'm very, very busy."

"Ronica, you don't have to be there when I interview
the patients and Dr. Lincoln."

"Dr. Lincoln's tied up, too. We have this real important meeting."

"What about the patients?"

Ronica was getting testy. "It just isn't a good time,
Peggy."

Peggy, in turn, was getting annoyed at Ronica's attitude. "Ronnie, you told me you'd level with me all the
way if I wrote this article. How can I—it's been *weeks.*
I've already stuck to all your rules and regulations and
appointed times and all that, and I think—"

"I'll call you in a few days, Peggy. Good-bye." Ronica
hung up.

"Well!" Peggy said. What was *that* all about?

She was startled by Ronnie's uncharacteristic rudeness.
Very peculiar. Were complications developing in the patients' treatment? She could understand why Ronica
wouldn't want anyone to know, but nevertheless, surely
Ronica and the others would have expected some unfore-
seen side effects in some clients. That didn't necessarily
mean the makeup was unsafe or the treatment hazardous.
What was going on?

She was wondering how she would spend the afternoon
now, when the phone rang again. It was a man's voice,
youngish. He introduced himself as Harold Eberson and
said he was a close friend of Jennifer Lindsey's, the writer
doing a piece for *Medicalstyles.*

"I'm sorry to bother you, but the people at the clinic
gave me your name and number, and that of a George
Burke, whom I've already spoken to."

"What can I do for you?"

"Jennifer has disappeared," Eberson said bluntly. "I
was out of town for a while. I didn't hear from her when

I came back. She didn't answer her phone for a week, so I asked the super to let me into her apartment." Peggy was getting a bad feeling. "She wasn't there and there was no sign of trouble. I've called her parents, her other friends, even the police." His voice cracked. "Jennifer's simply *vanished.*"

Vanished! Peggy's heart went out to the man who was so obviously at wit's end. She didn't know what she could possibly say to console him, and she had no idea where Jennifer could be; they were not friends, after all.

"That's horrible, Mr. Eberson. I don't know what to say. I'm sorry, but I haven't seen Jennifer. When was the last time you spoke to her?"

He told her. Peggy felt a chill run all through her body. It was the day before she and Jennifer had coffee, the day before Jennifer implied she had some scheme up her sleeve to find out more about the mysterious makeup.

The woman had been missing for over two weeks.

She knew it was foolish and paranoid, but she couldn't help wondering if the Barrows clinic had anything to do with it.

CHAPTER TWENTY-FOUR_____

Ronica hung up the phone, bit her lip, and walked back to the conference table. She was in a neatly appointed room on the second floor of the Barrows clinic, with floor-to-ceiling windows, discreet beige drapes, lush blue carpeting, and in the very center a large round table around which sat her brother, Romeo, Dr. Betty Lincoln, and Victor Asmodian. Victor wore his usual slick and expensive suit. He was head of Barrows Industries' legal department, and he was in a foul mood.

Banging his fist on the table, he said, "For the ninetieth time, Dr. Lincoln, I have to know the full facts before I can decide upon a plan of action. This firm may be facing more lawsuits than you can imagine, and I'll need to know just how bad it's going to get before I can formulate any possible defense. Is that makeup safe? Are our patients going to get better? Did you anticipate any of this happening? . . . Well?"

Ronica took her seat beside her brother, and waited with the others for Dr. Lincoln to reply. She almost felt sorry for Betty.

"You're overreacting, Victor, as usual," the doctor said. "You have a petty lawyer's mind and you're obsessed with petty lawyer's tricks. I tell you that makeup is safe. Look at me—I applied the cosmetic months ago and I'm fine, aren't I? Yolanda Vasquez is getting better every day. And didn't we release Matthew Douglas several days ago, his treatment completed, his face as perfect as before? And may I remind you, Douglas and Vasquez were the two patients submitted to us by cosmetic surgeons, who've looked them over and seen for themselves how successful our techniques are."

That only brought on a fresh flood of Victor's fury. "And why didn't we release that fact to the papers, to the journalists who are writing about the process, hmmm? We both know why we didn't. Because even though Mr. Douglas *seems* to be all right, there's still a chance something terrible will happen to him as it has to some of the others."

Everything was happening so fast, Ronica mused. First Dennis, totally unexpected, comes back into her life. Then Cecily Crenshaw, her brother's girlfriend and one of their patients, has an ugly rash break out all over her face—pimples, pustules, lesions, everything. She had locked herself in her apartment and not come out since the night it happened. She would only admit Romeo or Dr. Lincoln, and them only on rare occasions. Romeo said the girl's face looked awful but at least it hadn't gotten any worse.

And then the others: Tarramonte and Stuart.

Everything was falling apart, and Ronica realized that she hadn't the slightest idea what to do. Betty had assured her the makeup was safe. Betty's own face still looked fine. Still . . . Why hadn't they waited until after these "tests" were completed and they were sure everything was okay to hold that press conference? How could they have been so stupid?

Absently Ronica scratched the top of her left breast through the white cotton blouse she was wearing.

"We mustn't panic," the doctor said. "That's the worst thing we can do. We've kept the press at bay while working out these temporary—I repeat, temporary—difficulties. There have been some extreme reactions to the makeup . . . No, I take that back. It's not the makeup that's at fault. It's the patients."

Victor threw up his hands and screeched in that oddly vibrant voice of his. "The patients' fault! Dr. Lincoln, *you* should have been a lawyer!"

"I'm right, I tell you! Ronica, Romeo, and I have all been using this makeup, with no adverse effects. Matthew Douglas came through his treatment perfectly. If we made any mistake in choosing our patients, it's that we didn't subject them to enough psychological tests beforehand."

"Psychological tests?"

"Yes. You see, the makeup is stimulated by psychic waves, the thought projections of the patients, their positive attitudes—"

"Spare us your science fiction, Doctor, and let's stick to facts."

Betty looked as if she could have throttled him. "These are the facts. And this is not science fiction. Yolanda Vasquez and Matthew Douglas had no doubts or insecurities or troubling nightmares. They did as they were told and constantly *visualized* themselves getting better. Which is why Douglas's scar is completely gone, and Yolanda's tissue is healing itself and healthy cells are growing rapidly."

"And what about Emily Stuart? And Mr. Tarramonte? And that poor girl, what's her name?"

Romeo's brow furrowed. "Cecily."

"Yes, Cecily. What about them?"

Dr. Lincoln rolled her eyes and made a face that suggested she was talking to either children or the mentally deficient. "Cecily Crenshaw is a model whose greatest fear has been a simple, common, everyday blemish. One pimple can ruin a photo session if it's large enough and in the wrong place. She has had nightmares for years about such blemishes. Her negative thoughts were more powerful than her positive projections. Her thoughts reacted with the makeup and caused these pustules and lesions to grow on her face. She's hysterical and this only worsens her condition, which in turn worsens her emotional state. Only when the girl calms down, allows us to convince her of *what she is doing to herself,* will her condition reverse itself."

"I'm confused," Ronica said. "If makeup was applied to her nose and chin, how come the rest of her face is also affected?"

Dr. Lincoln stammered for a moment, then replied: "Makeup was rubbed into every part of her face, as it is with all our patients, to ensure a clear, younger complexion, as well as even skin tones."

"I see." Ronica's nails moved slowly, silently, across her breast, worked their way down to just above the nipple.

"This all sounds crazy to me," Victor said, "but you people are the experts. Is anything being done to treat these people in the meantime? I don't mean with makeup. I mean, have you brought in dermatologists and skin-care professionals to treat the skin conditions they've developed? Barrows does employ quite a few of them at other labs."

Now it was Betty's turn to bang the table with her fist. "No. *No!* Because these lesions and rashes are all in their minds! There is *nothing* really wrong with their skin. Their apprehensions have simply become externalized. Cecily's rashes aren't *caused* by anything. The makeup on her skin is simply mimicking the very conditions she's afraid of."

"Are you certain of that? Couldn't it be a real rash, some kind of allergic reaction?"

"Impossible. We tested them for allergic reactions and the like before treatment."

"Why didn't you anticipate this, Doctor?" Asmodian grimaced. "Those people must be suffering terribly."

Ronica watched Victor shaking his head and swearing and thought that he looked like a gibbering troll or monkey. She was afraid his mop of hair might fall off onto the table even though she knew it was not a wig. She wondered if he had planned on undergoing "beautification" himself—who would blame him?—and if part of his anger was due to his bitter disappointment in the process.

"We didn't anticipate this," Ronica said, "because it never happened to any of us three. I mean, Dr. Lincoln, Romeo, and I all had the makeup applied. If it was safe for us, it should have been safe for everyone. I guess Romeo and I trusted Dr. Lincoln more than our patients do. We didn't have such anxieties." Even so, she thought, she was glad Peggy had decided against undergoing treatment. She had only wanted her friend to be happy, as beautiful on the outside as she was on the inside, but instead she might have endured terrible anguish.

"And as for their suffering," Lincoln added, "we're doing all we can for them, but they *must help themselves.* Cecily won't even let most of us in to see her. She refuses to come to the clinic. Ralph—Ralph Tarramonte—keeps himself doped up with painkillers at his townhouse. He's so groggy all the time he can't possibly visualize himself out of his predicament. The pain obliterates all other thoughts and it won't go away until he accepts my advice. We've got Emily Stuart sedated upstairs. Her condition comes and goes. She, at least, realizes that she's better off with us here at the clinic than by herself."

Asmodian sighed and ran his hand back through his massive knot of tangled hair. "You've all gotten yourselves into a big mess, haven't you? What if the three patients who have not responded so well to treatment decide to talk to the press—or even to other doctors?"

Dr. Lincoln spoke up quickly. "Ralph won't—he promised me he wouldn't."

"Cecily talk to the press in her condition?" Romeo said with a bitter chuckle. "No way. She won't go near a reporter or a camera until her face clears up. She doesn't even want to go out to see another doctor."

"Emily Stuart is under observation at all times," Betty added. "And she's too tranquilized to go far in any case."

"This is awful," Ronica said. "I feel so sorry for them. It's as if they were locked behind bars or something."

"It's for their own good," Dr. Lincoln told her. "Only we can help them. No other surgeons or dermatologists can deal with the human mind. Conversely, no psychologist knows the inner workings of our cosmetic."

And they wouldn't believe it if they did, Ronica thought. Even now she had trouble accepting the macabre truth about what the makeup actually was and where it came from, its remarkable properties. She was torn between thinking they should never have brought this mad scheme into practice and the feeling that none of this would have happened if they'd decided to go public about it in the first place, totally above the table. Maybe Betty was right: considering what this makeup could do, the public might not even care (at least not for long) about its unusual origins. Now it was too late.

"We can help them, we can cure them," Betty was saying. "They will be all right, you must have faith in that. When they're back to normal, better than normal, we can forget this nightmare and go on with our plans. In the future we'll do psychological profiles of all prospective patients. Those who are too anxious, too nervous, too imaginative—we'll simply refuse to give them treatment."

"It seems a shame," Ronica said.

"Consider the alternative." The doctor turned back to the lawyer. "So for now, Victor, do nothing. None of our patients will sue. Vasquez certainly has no money to sue anybody, and she's doing fine anyway. The others will be all right in a few days, I guarantee it, no more than a week or two. They just need to calm down, to learn to trust us, and accept our help. They will. They have no other option."

She started to get to her feet, but the lawyer's voice stopped her. "Tell me, Doctor, just how does a person's —brain waves, did you say?—how does a person's brain affect this makeup you've put on them? I can't understand how it works."

Dr. Lincoln tapped her head and smiled. "And you never will, Victor," she said, gathering her papers. "You never will. It would be like discussing quantum physics with a five-year-old."

Victor frowned as she walked out. He made some kind of irritated gurgling noise and opened his briefcase.

When the doctor had gone, Romeo went to the lawyer's side and said, "Now, what do we do about the CDA?"

Victor sat there for a moment with a rather incredulous expression on his face. "I think," he said, "that it's a little too premature to worry about the CDA, Romeo. Let's see if these poor people *survive* before we take on the Cosmetic and Drug Administration, all right? I'll handle it, okay?"

"All right, it's just—"

"I said, I'll handle it."

"All right."

Ronica wondered just how Victor would handle it, when the time came. How would the CDA ever approve a cosmetic that worked miracles on some people and wreaked havoc on others? She saw all their plans crumbling like so many clumps of caked face powder.

When Victor departed, Romeo kneaded his chin and said, "I'm worried."

"Me, too."

"You haven't told anyone about these developments, have you? You haven't told your friend Peggy?"

"I hung up on her," Ronnie confessed. She felt guilty just thinking about it. "She'll probably never speak to me again."

"Just as well. Until this whole business is cleared up, let's forget reporters and articles."

"Assuming it ever will be." There was a pause. "I'm seeing Dennis again," she said after a moment.

"Dennis! That one! Is he still married?"

"Not anymore."

"Never understood what you saw in that ugly bastard. *He* could use some of our makeup."

"Now, now, be charitable to the less fortunate, Rom. Besides, I sort of like his looks. It goes with the rest of him." She paused. "A girl can get tired of pretty boys."

"Like me?"

"I didn't mean you, silly. 'Sides, you're my brother." Yet Ronica wondered if perhaps it was a flight from prettiness and vapidity that had attracted her to that married man when she met him at a party. She loved Rom, but he could be so . . . limited. Dennis was warm and giving and possessed of a passion and sensuality that in the bedroom turned him into the handsomest man in the universe. When first he had initiated her into his ritualistic sadomasochistic playacting, she had been repelled and alarmed, but gradually she realized what harmless fun it was; she became his "master" and he her slave, though she never really hurt him. He said his wife was a bloodless soul who would never have the imagination or boldness to play these games with him, and Ronica wondered if her willingness to do so was all he saw in her. Finally it was his refusal to divorce his wife that led to her decision not to see him anymore.

He got the key to her new apartment by bribing the super with a one-thousand-dollar bill. They'd seen each other practically every night since then. He brought his whip for her to use on him. And she used it, wondering how Ronica Barrows, former debutante, cheerleader, and all around "Suzy Creamcheese" had ever come to *this?*

"Are you getting serious about him again?" Rom asked.

"As serious as you are with Cecily."

He only grunted. "I'm going to go see her now. Want to come? Maybe she'll talk to you. I'll tell her to put a bag over her head."

It wasn't really funny, but they had a good laugh at the macabre humor of the whole situation. They laughed so long, loud, and hard it was as if they were trying to keep everything from falling in on top of them with sheer vocal power; as if some kind of uncanny sonics would work when all else had failed.

When they finally quieted down, Romeo heard a peculiar, rasping noise.

"What are you doing?" he said, pointing at her chest.

She didn't understand. Then she looked down. Her fingers even now were scratching, clawing really, at the material of her blouse, nearly shredding it, scraping at the itch in her breasts that would simply not go away. She hadn't even been aware of it. She'd been doing it so much lately she'd become quite unconscious of it.

"Silly," she said, embarrassed. She pulled her hand away from her chest and winked at her brother.

As they left, Ronica kept her hand off her breasts . . .

But all the while she wanted to scratch and scratch and scratch until the odd sensation, the terrible itch that was not an itch, went away.

CHAPTER TWENTY-FIVE_____

Matthew Douglas was probably higher than he had ever been in his life.

The bar was crowded. A luscious lovely sat to his right, a more voluptuous brunette sat on his left, and the booze was flowing. They had snorted some coke before leaving his buddy's apartment. Matthew had lost track of Hank three bars ago and figured his friend was probably doing some heavy-duty sacktime with a pickup from Odeon's. Meanwhile, Matthew was wondering which woman he wanted to spend the night with: the blonde, the brunette, or maybe the cute, big-chested barmaid who even now was mixing him another rum and Coca-Cola. He could have any one of them, he knew.

All his life he had wanted to be irresistible to women, to everyone he met, because he knew that was the ultimate power, and a shy, skinny kid who had been ignored and disdained could only triumph over his adversaries if he had lots of power. When he grew up he had become handsome enough that most women found him desirable. Now that his scar was gone he looked as good as ever. But even his sexy looks didn't insure that *everyone* would go for him.

Until now. Now that he had the power to look like anyone's and everyone's dream prince.

He hadn't realized he had the power until a couple of

days after his release from the clinic. Those first few days he had been getting in touch with old acquaintances and contacts, calling his parents with the good news, hitting the bars to celebrate, making appointments with old agencies. He spent a lot of time looking in the mirror, feeling like a silly Narcissus, but not caring. Now that he had his looks back, he could do anything he set his mind to.

If only, he thought one night, *I had told them to make the tip of my nose a little longer, the upper lip a bit bigger.*

And it happened. Right then, as he looked in the mirror, *it happened.* His nose and lip looked exactly the way he had wanted them to. But how?

The makeup must have some *incredible* properties: at times he could swear he felt it tingling all over his face, as if it were alive and somehow separate from him. His hair felt funny, too—as if that were possible. At night he thought he could feel the skin on his face and scalp *move around.*

He thought about calling Dr. Lincoln and asking her about it, but something stayed his hand. Maybe he was afraid she'd tell him it was a bad sign, or that he shouldn't be playing around with his face. But why not be as perfect as possible?

Part of him still wondered if it all wasn't a by-product of the drinking and drug-taking since his release from the clinic: if he thought about his nose getting smaller, it got smaller. If he thought about it getting bigger, it got bigger. Back to normal?—back to normal. It was weird. He would probably have been scared to death had the drugs in his system not made it all seem dreamlike, if he had not been under the illusion that he was totally in control. The drugs made everything that was happening seem detached from him, and prevented him from taking any real action.

Some nights before, he was coming on heavily to a pert redhead in tight leather pants and vest at a downtown bar, and she started looking at him peculiarly. Excusing himself, he rushed into the men's room. Was the scar returning? Had the clinic gypped him? No, but *his features were changing,* all by themselves. They had been discussing comic books, and she had mentioned how as a girl she'd always thought Superman's pal Jimmy Olsen was awfully cute and she still had a thing for cute redheads with freckles. All of a sudden he had freckles all over his face. Even his hair had turned red, and he was starting to look just like Jimmy Olsen in the comic books. He had run out of the bar. By the time he was home his face had returned to normal.

Dr. Lincoln and her "visualizing"! Somehow the human mind activated or controlled the makeup, that must be it. And not only *his* mind, but that of anyone else who was physically close to him and concentrating on a particular image. The girl had thought *Jimmy Olsen,* and suddenly he was a boyish kid with freckles and red hair. Think *Charles Bronson* and he'd have a broad craggy face with heavy eyebrows. *Arnold Schwarzenegger* and he'd have blunt features and for all he knew a gap between his teeth. But it was crazy. It didn't make any sense. How could it be possible? How could his hair have changed color? He must have imagined the whole thing. It was nuts.

His friend Hank had come over a few days later, and they did some coke. He told Hank to concentrate on changing his, Matt's, face, to look like Hank's own. Hank laughed, but did it. After a few minutes he wasn't laughing. Matt rushed into the bathroom and looked in the mirror; it was Hank's face looking back at him! He screamed and splashed water in his face. In a little while he was back to normal.

They pretended it was the drugs, but they were both freaked.

"I can look like anybody."

Hank was ever practical. "You can *fuck* anybody," he

said. "You can look like every girl's dream man. You can change your face to fit their fantasy."

"How do I know what their fantasy is?"

"Ask 'em."

"Maybe I don't have to. In those pickup places their heads are full of the type of man they want to meet. I just have to get close to them, talk to them. It'll happen without my doing anything, like it did downtown the other night. I'll start to change—I'll look like their heart's desire, like the one man they've been looking for their whole life."

"Wild, man."

From that moment on Matt never came down to earth, constantly loaded with booze, stoned on grass, or high on cocaine. He was afraid that once he was sober he'd have to confront the scary ramifications of this odd ability of his, and that was one thing he didn't want to do. In the meantime, he was going to enjoy it.

He thought of all the things it might mean. It could have much more benefit than merely getting him into bed with different women. As a model, his "type" would never go out of style, because he could change his face as the styles changed. Impersonating important people, he could give himself big contracts or acting jobs. Hell, he could take over a country if it came to that, look like Dan Quayle and get into the White House (though he'd hate to look older and less attractive than he already was for too long a period). There was no limit to what he could do.

In the meantime he would make up for all the time he'd missed during his "Two-Face" period. He loaded up on condoms and always carried some in his wallet; the girls were skittish these days. He found that with a little willpower he could hurry the process along: the waitress at the diner across the street preferred dark, Italian types; the girl in the cardshop on the corner had a thing for Swedes. Right in front of their eyes he'd pick up their most secret thoughts and turn into the one man they had wanted all their lives. He was careful to do this when no one else was facing in his direction. With more willpower he could turn his face back to normal in only a few seconds. It was a trip, all right, a trip.

Except for the time he found his face turning into a woman's, and he looked like a female drag queen for more seconds than he'd care to remember.

More drugs, more booze, this is scary, this is wild, never want to come down, more drugs, more booze.

So tonight Hank and he set out to paint the town purple. It was a riot. At a disco he danced across the floor, his face changing just as frequently as the different-colored lights flashing across his features did. He danced with one girl as a Robert Redford lookalike, with another in the mold of Mel Gibson, a third as a variation on Telly Savalas. There was no accounting for taste. Some ladies wondered what had happened to the handsome guy they had been talking to a moment ago; others were just as glad that he had gone and been replaced by someone who was more their type.

At one bar he talked to a brown-eyed lady for a few minutes, while he suppressed the change until he could excuse himself and go to the men's room. In the john, he let the change fully overtake his face, and walked back to the bar with completely different, if equally sexy, features. Although he couldn't change his height or general body shape or the clothes he was wearing, the girl didn't notice it—they never did. Why should they when his face was so *different?*

Sometimes his face wouldn't change at all, and then he knew he had found a woman who really went for him.

Tonight his face had changed over a dozen times. Now, he couldn't make up his mind which woman he should bless with an appearance straight from her heart's desire. The blonde on the right, the brunette on the left, the . . . *Wait a minute!*

He saw the woman sitting alone at a table in the corner. It was hard to tell her age. She wore a yellow slicker and sunglasses and was smoking from a holder. She looked like something out of a commercial. Her pink, glossy lips left a stain at the end of the holder and looked quite luscious. Her skin seemed smooth and pale; her hair was long and black, down to her shoulders. An interesting animal. Matthew wanted to get to know her. He didn't want to change. He wanted her to want *him*.

But as he approached her he felt the change happening and knew he would probably resemble the man—or woman—who most obsessed her before he reached her table.

"Hello," he said. He bowed at the waist and was about to ask her if he could sit, when she screamed:

"No! NO! I killed you! *I killed you!*"

Matthew had been out of circulation for quite a while. He had never heard of the notorious Lady Emerson, who had shot her husband six times in the shower and claimed she thought he was an intruder bent on sullying her virtue. She had managed to beat the rap with a shrewd combination of high-powered legal strategies, dubious witnesses, and rather well employed acts of blackmail.

Now she saw the man she had killed, but still loved, bowing before her in a seedy Tribeca bar.

Foolishly, she still carried a gun with her for protection against muggers and other fools when she went out on her all-night drinking sprees. She pulled it out of her purse and shot Matthew Douglas dead.

By the time the sixth shot penetrated his brain, Matthew's face had converted to "normal," but was so damaged by the bullets that he would have to be identified by the driver's license in his wallet.

When Lady Emerson told police that her husband had returned from the grave, this time, at least, she'd be telling the truth.

CHAPTER TWENTY-SIX

Now things were really getting spooky.

Peggy sat at the kitchen table beside a bowl full of cereal and a hot cup of instant coffee. David had gone out late last night and still not come home. The TV set was on in the background. Peggy had been watching Popeye cartoons until she'd started leafing through the paper. Something on page eight of the *Post* had caught her eye.

Playboy *writer hospitalized after beating.*

Playboy writer? Could it be—? Yes it was! George Burke! Apparently he'd done enough free-lance work for Hefner's mag to become well associated with it.

According to the article, George Burke had been set upon by muggers—eyewitnesses reported seeing at least two men—while walking up Lexington Avenue late Monday night. They took his wallet and beat him so severely he had to be rushed to Bellevue Hospital. Police assumed that Burke, who was still unconscious, had tried to fight back against his attackers and suffered because of it. But the eyewitnesses claimed the men came up from behind Burke and started hitting him without taking time to make any threats or demands for money.

Perhaps taking the wallet was an afterthought, Peggy thought. Perhaps the object had simply been to beat the man up.

Perhaps he had been digging too deeply?

She thought back to a couple of days ago. Knowing that they were not writing for competing markets, Burke had called to tell her that he had uncovered some unsavory facts about Dr. Lincoln and others associated with the Barrows clinic, but he wouldn't go into what they were. "I'm beginning to think the whole operation is a setup," he said. "You wouldn't believe the trouble I've had getting info from the nurses and the staff, as if they're *scared* to talk to me—even when I offer money!"

Peggy knew the man was utterly livid at Ronica's refusal to let reporters back into the clinic to see how the patients were progressing. "We were told we'd know the whole story, good or bad," he said. "Those were my terms. Your friend Ronica has broken them."

"If you think I'm getting special treatment because I went to college with Ronica, you're mistaken," she told the excitable gentleman. "She's not returning my phone calls, either."

"Well, with what I have on them they better return mine."

She wanted to warn him to be careful. For one thing, they both were wondering what had ever become of Jennifer Lindsey, who was still among the missing. Her body had not turned up and her distressed boyfriend had heard no news from her.

"Believe me, if I could help you I would," Peggy said. "But I told Ronica not to expect special treatment from me because I was a friend, and I guess she decided that would work both ways. I really haven't heard from her. I don't know what's going on at that crazy clinic."

Burke sniffed. "Maybe all the patients are slowly turning into wet, crusty scabs or human artichokes."

Peggy repressed a giggle. "Or something worse."

"I think the Barrows clinic is cursed," Burke said, half-joking. "Jennifer Lindsey disappears. Matthew Douglas gets shot to death in a bar by an acquitted murderess . . ."

Peggy said, "I don't think they'll acquit her *this* time. I can't believe it happened. Just when things were going great for the poor guy. It's tragic."

"Well, that's life." Burke wasn't the type to waste time or sympathy on other people's misfortunes. "Hey, Peggy —give me a call if anything comes up. You help me, I'll help you. I wouldn't mind giving you some of the info I've got as long as you give me something in return."

She was certain he wasn't after her body. "Sure, George. If anything develops, I promise I'll be in touch."

That was four days ago—two days after Matthew Douglas's murder. Now George Burke was in the hospital, unconscious. Only days after telling Peggy he had uncovered damaging information about people who worked at the clinic.

Jennifer. Matthew Douglas. George Burke.

Who was next?

George had been right. Something about this whole business stank to high heaven.

Then she leaned back in her chair and chided herself for her raging paranoia. She couldn't be certain that Burke's assault had anything to do with the article he was working on. He could have been beaten by a jealous husband and an accomplice for all she knew. Maybe his assailants were only muggers who decided incapacitating the victim first was the best way to get off with the money without being recognized in the bargain.

But there were witnesses nearby. Of course, the witnesses had been in a doorway across the street. Probably the assailants hadn't known they were there.

Yes, in this dangerous town there were any number of reasons why someone could wind up in the hospital. George Burke's hospitalization may have had absolutely nothing to do with the Barrows clinic. She spooned the rest of the fiber-rich cereal into her mouth and chewed it diligently, in spite of its absence of taste.

The same went for Jennifer Lindsey's disappearance, she mused. Anything could have happened to her. What did she think—the woman broke into the clinic and ran into a maniac or something? She could have had very good reasons for disappearing. *Yeah, like what?* she thought. Perhaps the poor woman had been attacked, like Burke, in the street, raped, her body dumped in some abandoned cellar where police might not find it for months. God, she hoped not. *Poor Jennifer!* The fact remained her disappearance might also have nothing to do with the Barrows clinic.

She finished chewing the cereal, swallowed the whole gooey, unappetizing mess, and washed it down with some coffee.

Yeah, right. A woman doing an article on the clinic disappears, and weeks later a man doing an article on the clinic is beaten up in the street by unknown assailants. And the two aren't connected.

Sure they're not. Just coincidence, huh?

It wasn't coincidence.

She finished the coffee, put the cup down hard on the table, and leaned forward on her elbows to clearly think things through.

First of all, even if something rotten was going on at the clinic, it didn't mean her friends, Ronica and Romeo, were involved. Burke had said he had info about Dr. Lincoln and some others; he hadn't mentioned Ronica or her brother. She couldn't imagine Ronica doing anything evil or dishonest. She was upset, behaving funny, but that didn't mean she would ever be a party to criminal activities—kidnapping people, beating people up. Not Ronica. And not that charm-boy, Romeo. They were too nice, too classy, to do anything so totally filthy and vulgar.

But what about that hairy man she had seen at the press conference and outside Ronica's apartment? Such an ugly, appalling creature. Mr. Hyde, she'd call him, though she thought his name was Victor. Now, there was a suspect if ever there was one. And that Dr. Lincoln— she had more to lose than anyone. They might be doing all these terrible things right under the noses of Romeo and Ronica.

Yes, that was probably it.

Peggy went to the phone and called the clinic. As usual, Ronica was in conference. Ronica had not returned her calls or spoken to her since she'd hung up so abruptly that day.

She put down the phone. She was going to get dressed and go directly to the clinic in person. She would make Ronica talk to her if it was the last thing she ever did.

CHAPTER TWENTY-SEVEN _____

Ronica hated not talking to her friend, not taking the opportunity to apologize for hanging up on her last time, but Romeo had warned her not to speak to anyone. "I know you," he said. "You like and trust Peggy, and before you know it you'll be telling her too much. I don't care if she's a friend—she's a writer after a story, isn't she? Wait until we've got everything under control."

Ronica felt terrible about the way she was treating Peggy, and knew she was just as much to blame as Romeo. It had been her decision not to allow the reporters to watch the patients being treated (aside from that brief time with Matthew Douglas), because she'd been afraid they might ask too many questions about the makeup's origin. Stupidly, she'd only increased their curiosity. She didn't particularly care about the other writers, but she did want to make it up to Peggy. However, with these new developments she felt it was better to put everything on hold.

So she told her secretary to tell Peggy that she was in conference. It wasn't entirely a lie. For half an hour later she was in the second-floor conference room with Romeo waiting for Victor to show up. He had said he needed to speak to them, and under no circumstances were they to tell Dr. Lincoln about this meeting.

Romeo stood in front of Ronica like a taut, youthful replica of their late father.

"Keep up a brave front, Sis," he kept saying. "Don't tell anyone what's going on until we're ready. Until the patients' conditions have changed."

"When will that be?" she asked.

"We have to trust Dr. Lincoln."

"We've done nothing but trust Dr. Lincoln," she said. Unconsciously her fingers had lightly touched her breast; she quickly removed her hand. "We've trusted her with our lives, Rom. How do we know something awful isn't going to happen to us?" She wanted to scratch her breast, but for the past few days she had been determined that she wouldn't give in to the impulse. If she ignored the itchiness it would go away. Her breasts even seemed to be getting larger. She wore a looser blouse to hide it. In the past she had always been self-conscious about her small breasts, but now she thought she would have been only too happy to return to the way she had been if it would relieve her of the terror and near hysteria she was feeling.

What made it worse was that everything seemed to be happening at once. It was a madhouse. Reporters had been ringing up constantly since the murder of Matthew Douglas and they'd had to hire extra part-time security men to turn away the TV crews camping at the doorway. Ronica and the others entered and exited the building through the garage. Police had already gone through the building on the odd chance that the missing Jennifer Lindsey was somewhere secreted within. Dr. Lincoln had been prepared for that. A fake plywood "wall" had been hastily put in place across the corridor leading toward the lab with the tanks. Fortunately, no one really assumed Lindsey's disappearance had anything to do with the clinic, and the search had been perfunctory at best.

Romeo had instructed the receptionist only to read a carefully phrased statement to interested parties regarding the Douglas murder.

Barrows Industries regrets the untimely death of one of

our patients, but his death was in no way related to the Barrows clinic or to his treatment, which was completely successful. He came in with a large scar across his face, and weeks later left with his face completely normal. It is doubly tragic for this to have happened to him when he was about to embark on a new life and a reactivated career. We pass our deep regrets and sympathies to all his friends and loved ones.

Matthew Douglas had been shot in the face, among other places. If death had reversed the beneficial effects of the makeup it would not have been easy for anyone to tell, given his condition.

The conference room door opened and Victor Asmodian walked in. "Good, you're both here," he said. Victor was accompanied by an obese man with sharp features, thin lips, and a receding hairline who wore a suit and tie and carried a briefcase. Victor introduced him as Stephen Jeffries, a friend of his, and a noted dermatologist.

"I don't care what Dr. Lincoln says," Victor said with his customary terseness. "She's not a skin specialist, she's a biochemist. I want Stephen—a neutral third party who's unassociated with Barrows—to take a look at our patients and tell us what he thinks. He's promised to keep this in the strictest confidence. Shall we go, Stephen?"

Ronica felt as much relief as alarm at the doctor's presence. If anything was seriously wrong with the patients, perhaps this man could start doing something for them. *And for her?* They were about to exit the conference room when the phone rang. Romeo grabbed it.

He hung up a moment later, looking upset. "Cecily's gotten worse," he told his sister. "I'm bringing her to the clinic. Dr. Jeffries can examine her. I should be back in half an hour."

As he left, the others went out into the hall. Ronica was following Asmodian and Dr. Jeffries to the back staircase when she heard her name being called. Her secretary was at the top of the staircase at the end of the corridor, motioning to her furiously.

"You gentlemen go on without me," Ronica said. "I'll catch up."

She walked over to the woman and said, "What is it?"

"Peggy Antonicci is here. She brushed past me into your office and says she won't leave until she talks to you." She bristled with indignation. "She practically knocked me to the floor."

Ronica thought a moment. Romeo was gone. Victor had gone upstairs and Dr. Lincoln was either down in the basement lab or at Ralph Tarramonte's.

"I'll see her," she said.

"Scottie. I want to see Scottie. I want to see my nephew. Why won't you let me see Scottie!"

Dr. Stephen Jeffries had no trouble figuring out why the powers-that-be at the Barrows clinic would not allow Emily Stuart to have visitors. The sight of the woman thrashing and writhing in the bed would be enough to give anyone the willies. In all his years as a dermatologist, he had never seen such a variety of skin disorders afflicting one single human being.

He could not believe that his friend Victor and his associates had waited so long to call him in for consultation. Whatever treatment they had been giving this woman had gone horribly wrong, or else she had come into the clinic with a whole series of already existing skin ailments which had taken this opportunity to surface. Although the room she was in was filled with a slew of the latest medical devices, the woman really belonged in a bona fide hospital.

Luckily she was so drugged she was probably not aware of how extreme her condition had become. And to call it extreme was an understatement. A nurse stood in one corner looking as if she wanted to bolt the room and run screaming in horror, although she tried to affect a bored, professional expression.

Jeffries made quick diagnoses as he examined her. He saw various types of rashes and eruptions, but neurofibromatosis, the "Elephant Man's disease," seemed to be the major ailment. Or perhaps elephantiasis. "Has this woman been in the tropics recently?" he asked Victor.

"I don't know," Victor replied. "Would it make any difference?"

"Worms. There are worms inside me!" Emily suddenly screeched.

Worms. Jeffries knew that elephantiasis, which was common in the tropics, was caused by filariae, tiny worms carried by mosquitoes that became lodged in the lymph vessels after a person was bitten; a less common form of the disease was caused by bacteria. He felt Mrs. Stuart's head—she had a raging fever. He asked the nurse to move the blankets and open the woman's flannel bathrobe. It was one of the worst cases he had ever seen.

"How long has she been like this?" he asked the nurse.

"Days. I guess her skin started getting rough like that weeks ago, but the swelling didn't get this bad until last evening."

Emily Stuart's face had swelled to almost three times its normal size, particularly on the left side; her eyes were almost enveloped in folds of thick, grayish, wrinkled flesh with the look and feel of elephant hide.

"Now, tell me, Stephen," Victor demanded. "Could a person do *that* to themselves psychologically, as Dr. Lincoln suggests?"

"I don't know the properties of this 'makeup' she's developed," Jeffries said carefully. "But I suspect not. And it wouldn't explain why the rest of her body has been affected. The skin on her legs and stomach has also thickened; and the arms and one leg are starting to swell."

"I want to see Scottie. Where's my nephew? The worms, the *worms.*"

"Dr. Lincoln claims this is all her own doing, that it's

psychosomatic. But as you say, if it isn't just her face being affected, she has to be wrong."

"I expect she is."

"What's wrong with Mrs. Stuart?" the nurse whispered.

"I'll have to make some tests, take blood and skin samples, before I'm certain. This might be caused by anything from a hereditary disorder to bacteria or parasites. I seriously doubt it's 'in her head' or even an allergic reaction to a makeup, no matter how esoteric."

Jeffries felt very bad for this poor woman. Both neurofibromatosis and elephantiasis were incurable diseases, although the latter was treatable with drugs and surgery. He also knew the horrible skin swellings caused by elephantiasis would get bigger and bigger with each attack until they became permanent, if they weren't already. To have to walk around with a face as hideously disfigured as this . . . the woman would probably not want her life to be prolonged.

He looked down at her hands, which were also rough and grayish and were slowly turning into gnarled, scaly claws. Her feet had also been affected. She must be in terrible pain. If it were neurofibromatosis, the bones and nervous system—even the vital organs, as well as the hearing and vision—would be affected.

"This is a very sick woman. I think she should be removed from this clinic immediately and taken to a hospital where she can be properly cared for. There are a great many tests I have to take and—"

"I'm not in the position to authorize it, Stephen."

"You won't have to authorize it, Victor. As a doctor I *insist* she be transferred immediately. You can tell your associates that I'll take full responsibility. Are the other patients like this?"

"The only other patient on the premises is Yolanda Vasquez, the burn victim. She seems to be recovering quite nicely, actually."

Jeffries had heard about her. "I want to see her."

Before making the necessary phone calls regarding Mrs. Stuart's transfer, Victor took Jeffries down the hall and into Yolanda Vasquez's room. The doctor braced himself. What new horrors would await him in here?

But he was surprised. Yolanda was sitting up in bed, unbandaged, looking quite literally in the pink of health, with glowing, flourishing skin all over her body. Victor introduced the dermatologist, who asked Yolanda if he might examine her. She readily agreed.

"Isn't it a miracle, Doctor?" she said gaily as he poked and probed the skin which he knew had been savaged by fire only weeks ago. It seemed impossible. He didn't know what this Dr. Lincoln used but it was better and faster than artificial skin. She seemed practically back to normal.

"Dr. Lincoln said I could leave the clinic tonight for a few hours," Yolanda said. "The mayor heard about me—can you imagine, the mayor!—and he's taking me to a party tonight to honor the city's firemen. I would have died without them—and without Dr. Lincoln. The mayor said I'd be the perfect date. I'm so thrilled." She pointed to a cocktail dress hanging in the open wardrobe in the corner. "Ronica Barrows even bought me a dress to wear. I'm so excited." Her eyes started tearing. "I feel like I've come back to life, Dr. Jeffries."

Jeffries was glad for her; she seemed a sweet woman. She'd lost her whole family, gone through countless physical and emotional agonies. He hoped things worked out for her. She was entitled to some happiness after so much pain. But where had she gotten this fantasy about going out with the mayor? There had been virtually no publicity since that first press conference . . .

"Does your skin feel okay?" he asked her.

"Fine—except it itches a lot."

"That's probably normal," he said, smiling. "It's still healing."

She smiled back. "I try not to scratch."

"Good."

When they left Yolanda's room, Victor reminded him that Romeo Barrows was bringing a third patient to the clinic shortly, and that there was a fourth at his town house uptown. "We have to be careful there. Dr. Lincoln will probably be with him and I know she won't appreciate your visit."

"What's this Yolanda was saying about going out with the mayor?" Jeffries asked.

"It's true."

"But how? You told me you've put a tight lid on publicity, swore the nurses to secrecy practically upon threat of death . . ."

"The surgeon who brought Yolanda to us is a cousin of the mayor. Luckily he's one of those rare souls who's more interested in helping patients than in self-aggrandizement. He thinks Dr. Lincoln's work is miraculous. He suggested that if Yolanda felt up to it, his bachelor cousin, the mayor, should take her to an event honoring the city's firemen. They did, after all, save her life. Since her treatment has been so successful, we agreed."

"No wonder you don't want what's happened to the other patients leaking out."

Victor nodded. "Exactly."

Although Jeffries's opinion of this Dr. Lincoln had risen a bit since examining Yolanda Vasquez, he no longer felt guilty about examining her patients without permission. He could understand the clinic's reluctance to go public with all this, but what had happened to Emily Stuart convinced him that Dr. Lincoln had no business keeping such seriously ill patients out of hospitals, or suggesting their condition was due merely to a psychological disorder.

He couldn't help but wonder what condition Ralph Tarramonte and Cecily Crenshaw would be in when he finally got around to seeing them.

CHAPTER TWENTY-EIGHT

Peggy had been talking to Ronica in the latter's office for half an hour now. Ronica spoke like a mannequin that had been equipped with a tape recorder that played the same messages over and over again.

"Everything's okay," Ronica said. "There's nothing to worry about. The makeup's safe. Everything's going perfectly."

For her part, Ronica was going to do what her brother had told her. Oh, she'd be friendly, but she'd say *nothing*. Apologizing for hanging up on Peggy was her main reason for talking to her now, and she explained that she'd been in the middle of an important meeting.

Ronica was glad that Dr. Jeffries was on the premises. Perhaps he and Dr. Lincoln could get to the bottom of the patients' problems and iron out the difficulties with the makeup before things got entirely out of control.

"Ronica," Peggy said, "I don't think I'm getting through to you. I'm not accusing you or Romeo of any wrongdoing, believe me, but perhaps some of the people who are working for you are not as up front as you two are."

Ronica lit another cigarette and leaned back in her chair. "Peggy, I appreciate your concern," she said, "but I think you're overreacting. I don't know why Jennifer Lindsey disappeared, but there's no reason to believe it has anything to do with us. And that goes for the assault on George Burke. Lots of people disappear and get attacked in this city. A certain percentage of them are writers, I guess. Why make more of it than that?"

"Ronica, please don't—"

"Why would you think anyone here would want to hurt either of those people?" She put down her cigarette and folded her hands together as if she wanted Peggy to join her in prayer. "Peggy, our makeup could help so many people, why look for ulterior motives or problems? It's *safe.*" She mentally crossed her fingers. Her breasts were itching badly; the more emotional she became the worse it got.

She told Peggy how her breasts had actually been enlarged by repeated applications of the makeup which eventually changed into flesh, or something very much like it. Again, she resisted an urge to scratch. "Nothing bad has happened to me. We have nothing to hide."

Peggy found Ronica's news so astonishing she could hardly keep her mind on what she was saying. *Big breasts from makeup!* She forged ahead.

"George Burke said he had found out some . . . unpleasant facts . . . about Dr. Lincoln and others. Doesn't that indicate something's fishy about what happened to him?"

Ronica had a funny image of Betty Lincoln stalking her prey on city streets and she nearly laughed. "But he didn't tell you what those 'facts' were, right? Maybe he didn't find out anything. Because there's nothing to find out."

Ronica wouldn't tell Peggy this, but she was secretly dying to know if the man had actually uncovered anything, and if so, what. She knew Dr. Lincoln's career and reputation were not without blemish, but she didn't think the woman was a quack or a criminal. At least she hoped not. *God, what if she was?*

"And Matthew Douglas's death had nothing to do

with this clinic. He was shot by a crazy lady. He was cured when we released him."

"Which you never bothered to inform me of. Or George Burke, for that matter. We didn't know he'd left the clinic until we read about his murder in the papers. Why?"

Ronica had to think fast. Damn her brother for insisting on such secrecy.

"Matthew wanted it that way. He didn't want a big fuss. He wanted to get used to his new face first. We had to respect his wishes."

Actually Dr. Lincoln didn't want him talking to anyone. *But why?* she asked herself. Dr. Lincoln hadn't even wanted Yolanda to go out with the mayor tonight, but Ronica, Romeo, and Victor had vetoed her. There'd be TV cameras there, and important people: it was a perfect opportunity to show the whole city what Beautifique could do. The mayor would dance past the cameras with the lovely Yolanda in his arms, and everyone would see how the ravaged skin of the burn victim had rapidly turned into pink, healthy flesh. She was convinced—and wanted to convince others—that if the makeup could do that, it could do anything. She was sure the itching in her breasts was just nerves—no wonder!—and nothing more.

She had wanted to call Peggy and tell her about Yolanda, but Romeo had protested: "Who needs those penny-ante writers anymore? It's too risky having them around while Cecily and the others are sick. Let's let Yolanda have her fling tonight. It'll be good for all of us, and it will give us more free publicity than any ten writers could give us—without the risk."

Dr. Lincoln hadn't looked too happy when they told her of their decision.

Ronica now decided to tell Peggy about their triumph with Yolanda Vasquez. When she was through, her friend seemed genuinely pleased. Ronica thought it safe enough to add: "Between you and me, Peggy, there have been some . . . minor complications with other patients.

Nothing serious. They're just not responding to treatment as quickly as we'd hoped. Naturally, they don't want to speak to the press—just yet. We can't force them to."

At last Ronica was leveling with her, Peggy thought. "This just isn't working out the way I thought it would," she said. "With your triumph with Yolanda Vasquez, why worry about disclosure of some initial problems with other patients? That won't negate what you've done with Ms. Vasquez."

Oh, yes it will, Ronica thought. *You haven't seen Emily Stuart.*

"Why haven't you let me talk further to Yolanda? I would think you'd want me to."

Yes, you would think so. But Dr. Lincoln wasn't crazy about that idea, either. "We figured Yolanda would have to deal with the press enough tonight," Ronica said. "She's not quite one hundred percent yet and she needs her rest. She's been through quite an ordeal."

Damn it, Ronica, Peggy thought, *you have an answer for everything.* "Ronica, do you want me to write this article or don't you?"

Ronica sat there for a few moments, staring into space. She wanted desperately to confide in someone, talk to someone who was not involved with Barrows Industries or the Beautifique makeup. Wasn't that really why she'd decided to talk to Peggy? She was sure she could trust her old friend.

"Peggy, I—I can't talk now, okay? This isn't a good time. But how about tonight? I'll call you, and . . ." She lowered her voice. "I've got to talk to you, Peggy, about what's going on. I've got to tell someone or I swear I'll go crazy. I need your advice."

"Okay," Peggy said. "I'll be home all night. Call me anytime. We'll talk. It will all be off the record, too—just friend to friend—if that's what you want. Okay?"

"Okay. And thanks."

Just then Victor Asmodian walked abruptly through

the open door of the office. Romeo trailed behind him. Ronica hoped they hadn't overheard her talking to Peggy just now. She knew neither Victor nor her brother would appreciate her telling anyone exactly what was happening.

Peggy recoiled from the sight of Victor Asmodian, the man she'd suspected was behind all of Ronica's troubles, but she was glad to see Romeo. She nodded curtly as Ronica introduced her to Asmodian.

"Cecily's here," Romeo said, nodding perfunctorily to Peggy, then glaring at his sister as if in afterthought. "We've brought her upstairs."

Ronica figured she'd better hustle Peggy out of there fast. "I've got to go, Peggy." The men left and Ronica rose to her feet. She escorted Peggy out past the secretary's desk and into the outer lounge where another man was waiting on a couch, reading a newspaper. When he saw Ronica, he got to his feet.

"Peggy," Ronica said. "I want you to meet Dennis Reckler."

Dennis? *This* was Dennis? Peggy wondered, as she shook his hand. Dennis, whom Ronica had spoken so fondly of, who had once been her lover? Peggy didn't understand—Ronica could have had her pick of some of the most gorgeous guys in the universe and she chose this middle-aged, downright homely creature out of all of them? It simply didn't make any sense!

Ronica took Dennis by the hand and pulled him toward her office. She turned to Peggy. "I'll call you," she said, using her professional, noncommittal voice now that they were no longer alone.

"Okay," Peggy said, walking toward the entranceway and wondering why she was throwing a looker like David back into the ocean and why Ronica was throwing herself at a man like Dennis Reckler.

She looked at her watch. Three o'clock. She thought she'd treat herself to an ice cream sundae.

* * *

That evening David filled in for a sick bartender at Maxie's on Third Avenue. He left a note for Peggy, giving her his whereabouts, hoping she'd come down as she always wanted to and keep him company. He'd slip her a few free drinks, have her feeling all sentimental, and get her to tell him he could keep living with her. Her deadline was fast approaching and he still hadn't found a new place to stay. Even the advent of Christmas would not deter her. It was getting scary. He had little money and very few prospects of a job, at least one that he wanted to have permanently.

Maxie's was a swinging singles joint in the late evenings, but now it was empty except for a few of the tables in back. A guy in a raincoat was sitting at one of them, watching him. He'd come in around six. He made David nervous. David ignored the man, washed the bar off with a dishrag, and thought some more about Peggy.

He had formerly felt a kind of affection for Peggy, but after her recent behavior, all he felt for her was contempt. Sure, she was right, he wanted to use her. She should have been glad he was willing to be her boyfriend; few other men with his looks would have bothered. He figured he more than made up for the free rent and the money she gave him with his bedroom skills. If worse came to worst, he would tell her he was in love with her, propose marriage. It was drastic, but he thought it would work. Then when he could afford to move out, he'd dump her, laugh in her face, tell the pig what he really thought about her. Yeah, that was what he'd do. Nobody fucked up David Kravitz's life and got away with it.

The couple at the bar got up and left. David picked up their glasses and went down to the corner to put them in the sink. When he turned around, the guy from the table in back was sitting on one of the bar stools. "Can I talk to you?" the stranger asked.

David was wary. There was something about the guy.

He had never seen a face quite like his before. "What do you want?"

"How would you like to earn one hundred thousand dollars?" the man said.

David was all ears.

CHAPTER TWENTY-NINE⎯⎯⎯⎯

Dr. Lincoln wished that Frank Eddington was still alive. Ever since his death at the laboratory in New England several years before, she had missed his advice dearly. He could have told her what to do now. As the taxi took her to her beloved Ralph's town house, her mind flowed freely from thoughts of her late associate—*what a horrible way to die!*—to the hours she had spent with him and the others at the Barrows Research Labs in the country. *Those were the days, all right.*

They'd had such camaraderie, such fun arguing and debating with one another. It was all so stimulating. Not like today, which was as much full of fear and apprehension as it was anticipation. Nobel prizes—or ruin? Which would it be?

Early in her career she'd been accused of falsifying test results in an effort to speed up completion of one phase of a project and ensure necessary funds for its continuation. The faked results were no different than they would have been had she done it properly. Though she was guilty, the charge was hard to prove and she was publicly exonerated. Privately she was considered poison by virtually every lab and university in the country. If Judson Barrows hadn't taken a chance and hired her . . . of course, he knew he could get a desperate woman for a lot less money.

Barrows had been into everything in those days; still was. The beauty company was only one division. They'd had so many projects at the labs, in the hopes that one of them would develop into something useful and profitable. Who would have suspected that crazy genetic engineering experiment would be the one to pay off? Of course, it had taken the life of Frank, and of that pretty young scientist, Susan Raymond, in another tragic accident, before it was over. *And there'd been another, more recent victim, hadn't there?* But Betty didn't want to think about that.

She remembered it was after Frank's death that they finally realized what they had stumbled across. Even "trial and error" would not be the correct term to describe how the cosmetic was discovered. It was really only a series of bizarre accidents that led to the development of the makeup with which they now hoped to revolutionize the world. In part it was their own imaginations, and the perverse qualities of those *creatures,* that had led to the product as it was now.

And now, after so much time, so much work, it was all in danger.

She must not let it happen.

She couldn't understand why the makeup had worked so well for her, and the Barrowses—not to mention Yolanda Vasquez and the late Matthew Douglas—when it had been so disastrous for Emily Stuart, her Ralph, and the Crenshaw girl. She'd been reluctant to let anyone interview Douglas or Vasquez until she was absolutely *certain* nothing would happen. Ronica and Romeo were letting Yolanda go to that public function tonight despite her strenuous objections.

She found their contradictory natures tiresome. First Ronica didn't even want her to talk about the makeup or let anyone see it. Now she let one of their patients go out waltzing for the TV cameras! Those two spoiled brats didn't know if they were coming or going. If only Judson was still alive . . .

She was convinced she was right about it being the patients' own minds screwing up the process; it was the only explanation. It didn't matter that in some cases parts of the bodies that had not been touched by the makeup were being affected. She knew better than anyone how unusual, how downright weird, this "makeup" was. It could penetrate cells, replace cells, it could shift, change, and shape body structures, flesh and bone, it could *move* anywhere you—*or it?*—wanted it to go. Sometimes it was as if it had a mind of its own.

Good God! Was it invading, infecting, the patients' healthy tissue of its own volition? *Was it picking up their nightmares and subconscious fears, following those impulses, and changing them accordingly, or was it acting on its own? Was it a combination of both?* How could she find out? Ralph and the others were in such a mental state they seemed completely unable to follow her instructions. She'd spent practically the whole day in the lab going over their blood and tissue samples, but to no avail.

There was no more time to think about it. She'd arrived at Ralph's town house. She paid the cabbie and went up the walkway past well-kept flowerbeds to the imposing structure. She was taking out the key she'd gotten from Ralph to open the door, when she heard screaming.

God, it was Ralph, yelling so loudly she could hear him from his bedroom through the thickness of the front door!

She opened the door hurriedly and ran down the corridor, throwing her coat onto the floor.

She found Ralph in his bedroom.

It had gotten worse. At first, weeks ago, had she not known better, she would have assumed her lover had contracted a case of leprosy, combined with several fungal diseases. The signs were all there: patchy spots and thickening of the skin, large lumps all over his body. In addition there were ringwormlike circles on his chest and back, as well as rashes and growths of all kinds. He didn't look as bad as poor Cecily Crenshaw, but that wasn't the worst of it.

Instead of receding, his jaw was widening, lengthening; the bottom half of his face was horrendously swollen. He was in constant pain. She shot him up with tranquilizers and painkillers and monitored him almost constantly. She assigned Olga, a nurse from the clinic, a stout woman of Russian descent with strong arms and short legs that could move fast when they had to, to watch over him here.

"Ralph! Ralph!" Betty cried. He was lying on the bed, still screaming. *Where was Olga, the silly bitch? How could she leave an hysterical patient alone like this?*

She stepped back from the bed and found Olga.

Olga's head stared up at her from under the end of the bed.

Olga's body was halfway across the room.

She had put up quite a struggle. The nurse's uniform was splattered with blood, and the thick, stubby hands clawed upward grotesquely as if to ward off an attacker.

Betty Lincoln turned to one side and threw up.

Obviously Ralph was not always paralyzed.

He opened his eyes, stopped screaming, and saw her. "You bitch—you did this to me! *You bitch!*"

He got up off the bed. Betty could imagine how in his maddened rage he could literally tear a person's head off, but she saw the meat cleaver that he was pulling out from under his pillow. She suspected what had happened. He'd knocked down Olga, run off, gotten the cleaver from the kitchen, and tried to kill himself with it; she saw the slices he'd cut in his chest and on his arms. Olga had followed him to the kitchen and tried to stop him. Instead he'd chased her back to the bedroom and murdered her. Now he wanted to kill Betty.

"You miserable bitch!"

Betty was so terrified, she couldn't move. Even as he stood there screaming at her, she saw that something was happening to Ralph's face. His jawbone was beginning to *tear free* from the surrounding skin. She saw the muscles and blood vessels burst, spurt out liquid. She heard the tearing of flesh, the parting of individual strands of skin, heard the crunching, snapping of the emerging cartilage and bone. Teeth started falling out of Ralph's mouth, plopping onto the mattress like unpopped kernels of corn. The jawbone which squeezed out of his skin was twice the size of a normal one. Finally it popped out with such force that it literally flew out of the man's head and hit Betty in the face.

She prayed it was only an hysterical illusion, but the sharp edges of the jawbone bit deeply into her cheeks. She felt blood running down her neck. She tried to pry the jawbone off, but it was stuck, a perfect fit. She screamed as Ralph raised his meat cleaver. The bone fell off her face as she shivered uncontrollably with terror.

"You bitch!" Ralph said. The cleaver went up and down, up and down, until Ralph's whole head collapsed inward with a sickening outpour of blood and brain matter. The sunken lips in the boneless maw continued to mouth the words: *You bitch, you bitch, you bitch.*

The cleaver fell out of his hand. Ralph Tarramonte fell face forward, stone-cold dead, onto the floor.

CHAPTER THIRTY_____

By the time Peggy stepped out of the subway station at Fourteenth Street she had still not entirely absorbed all there was to know about Beautifique makeup and why it was having such odd effects on some of the clinic's patients. Her mind was still reeling. It was like something out of a weird science fiction novel or horror movie. Such things simply didn't happen in real life!

At around five she received a call from some woman asking where David was. It was a familiar voice—Michelle Green, maybe? Peggy had found David's note asking her to join him at Maxie's and saw no reason not to tell this woman where she could find him. She herself had no intention of going to the bar just to hear more of David's pleading.

Ronica called her a short time later, and told her to come to the clinic. By the time Peggy got there, Ronica's secretary had left, and there was only a weary night receptionist snuggled behind a dog-eared paperback at the front desk to greet her. Peggy went straight to Ronica's office, where Ronica started telling her all the details of what had gone wrong, now and then stopping to wipe tears from the corners of her eyes.

At first it had been all right—pretty horrifying, yes—but nothing Peggy couldn't handle. But then Ronica took her down to the basement labs and showed her just *where* the makeup came from . . . the tanks of writhing gray flesh in viscous fluid.

"You've got to be kidding me," Peggy told her.

Ronica just looked at her. "I wish I was."

Ronica swore Peggy to secrecy, a promise Peggy had no trouble making because she doubted anyone would believe her unless she had photographic proof. Ronica rushed her out before Dr. Lincoln or any of her staff, who sometimes worked late, could return from supper. When she left the clinic Peggy had more questions than when she'd arrived.

She was torn between feeling sorry for Ronica and thinking her a contemptible idiot. Who would allow such stuff to be put on people's faces? Or *breasts!* But Ronica insisted it really had worked wonders for Dr. Lincoln, herself, and others, and that in spite of everything she had faith in the makeup's abilities.

"Everything will be straightened out," Ronica told her. "I know it will. And then you'll be right on top of the story of the decade! You can write a book about it and make millions."

Peggy reflected that back when she was younger the ultimate agenda in this country was to change the world for the better; now it was just to make money. But she was more sure than ever that the disappearance of Jennifer Lindsey and assault on George Burke—maybe even Matthew Douglas's murder—were related to the Barrows clinic and what they kept hidden in the basement.

If I had that in my basement, Peggy mused, *I'd sure kill to keep it secret, too. Especially if there was a billion billion dollars riding on it.* She wasn't certain she was glad Ronnie had taken her into her confidence. She couldn't imagine Ronnie ever hurting her, but she had visions of that creepy Victor Asmodian hunting her down before she could "talk" to anyone. She was always wary during her walk from the subway to the apartment, but tonight she was doubly careful. She turned and looked behind her at the slightest noise, studying the shadows in alleyways before she walked past them. Although she had learned how to handle a gun when she wrote a piece on the right to bear arms, she didn't own one and wished that she did.

Her paranoia was multiplied a thousandfold when she got to her apartment and found the door wide open. *Robbed again? Oh no!* But when she stepped inside she realized that this was much more than a simple robbery.

Her first thought: *Ronica told someone that she spoke to me. The fool!*

The apartment had been trashed. Nothing appeared stolen, just wrecked, shredded, pulverized. The couch had been slashed with what must have been a butcher knife, and the stuffing pulled out of it. The kitchen table was overturned. The cabinets were open and all the food pulled out. The contents of cereal boxes and the like had been poured on the floor and the crumbled containers thrown in a heap to one side. Books had been pulled off shelves, torn apart, and thrown to the floor, and piles of magazines and papers had been hurled haphazardly across the room, making it look like one big wasteland.

They hadn't taken the TV set or VCR. No—they'd only kicked in the screen, torn out the wiring, and overturned the whole worthless unit, then accumulated bashed videotapes all over the toppled machines as if they were building a mechanical bonfire.

Peggy broke down and cried.

Soon she went to the bedroom. *What have they done in there?* she wondered. The door was closed. Scrawled on the door in red ink were the words: STAY OUT OF BARROWS'S BUSINESS.

Mingled with the terror of having her fears confirmed, she felt an odd kind of relief. For a moment she had suspected Davey of inflicting all this damage, or perhaps some of his drug-freak friends. She knew it wasn't burglars—they would have taken the TV and VCR instead of breaking them. She opened the bedroom door and saw that this room, at least, had been left untouched.

"What the hell happened here?"

Peggy nearly jumped out of her socks. She turned around. It was only David. Immediately she relaxed, sighed with relief, nearly crumbled with the release of tension. She had forgotten he had an early shift tonight.

"David, David—look what they've done!"

"Shit! Did they take anything?"

She stepped back and showed him the writing on the door. "No, no, it wasn't burglars. It was somebody at the clinic. David—" All thoughts of keeping her promise to Ronica were forgotten. "Wait till I tell you what's going on there. You won't believe it. David, I think they're going to kill me."

He pulled her to him and hugged her fiercely. "Relax, baby. Davey's here. I'm here, babe." He stroked her hair. "Tell me all about it, baby. Tell me."

David let her go for a moment and righted two kitchen chairs. When they were seated facing one another, David's hands holding hers, she told him everything: the makeup, the horrible disfigurements, *the things in the basement.*

"Ronica must have told someone she spoke to me. She *must* have. Or else somebody overheard us. I know too much, David. They're going to kill me. I'm going to disappear like that poor Jennifer Lindsey. Thank God I wasn't home. You would have come back and found my dead body. At the very least I would have been beaten to within an inch of my life like poor George Burke. Oh David, what am I going to do?"

"First of all," he said, "I think we both could use a drink."

She sniffled into a handkerchief. "The liquor's all gone."

"Got a fiver? I'll run down to the liquor store and be right back."

"Don't leave me alone!"

"They won't come back tonight. They figure you must

have called the cops already. Lock yourself in the bathroom and I'll be back in a jiffy."

She opened her purse and gave him the money. She
only had a twenty. "H—hurry." She did have to go to the
bathroom anyway, and the liquor store was right at the
corner. "I could use a drink," she said.

He kissed her above her right eye. "We'll figure out
something," he promised.

CHAPTER THIRTY-ONE

Things at the clinic had gone from bad to worse.

Ronica had gone out for a bite to eat after talking to Peggy—something she was still quite apprehensive about. When she returned, she learned from Victor Asmodian that Emily Stuart had "escaped" from the clinic before the ambulance could arrive to transfer her to Clinton East Hospital. In spite of the reduced number of personnel on the night shift (there were never that many people in the building even during daytime) the whole clinic seemed to be in an uproar. The nurse Mitzi had been hit on the head with a bedpan, and was crying hysterically in the nurses' lounge. Dr. Lincoln was missing and no one—not even Olga—answered the phone at the Tarramonte residence. Victor and Dr. Jeffries had gone to his town house much earlier, but for some unknown reason Tarramonte had refused to admit them and Olga didn't come to the door.

Cecily was still having hysterics in room thirty-two, and Romeo, Dr. Jeffries, and a nurse were trying without success to calm her. She had refused to see Dr. Jeffries, and dispatched Romeo to get some more clothes from her apartment. Finally she'd relented and allowed the dermatologist to look at her, but was refusing, when Ronica arrived, to go to the hospital where many more people might catch a glimpse of her.

At least Yolanda had been picked up by the mayor's limousine and gotten off to the banquet without mishap. That would be a great public relations coup—but Emily Stuart hideously disfigured and running wild through the city? That would cause a black eye that no amount of cosmetics could cover.

In Ronica's office, Victor reported, "She took one of the cars in the garage." The clinic had a private garage attached for official cars, visitors, and ambulances. "One of the security men noticed it was missing."

"Security men?" Ronica said. "Where were they when Mrs. Stuart was sneaking out of the building? The poor woman is not exactly hard to notice."

Victor shrugged. "Some of these guys your brother hired on the cheap couldn't find their feet if they fell over them."

Ronica knew he was right. "Where's Romeo now?"

"Still with Cecily."

She was about to leave when she had a second thought. "Victor, should we call the police about Mrs. Stuart? She needs medical help badly."

Victor looked as if he agreed with her but still felt obliged to say, "If it hits the papers, everything you've worked for will go down the tubes."

"Even with Yolanda and her remarkable recovery all over the television?"

Victor snorted. "One swallow doesn't make a summer. Let me make a few calls. I know people who can be discreet. Like you said, she won't be hard to find in a crowd. I'll also make some inquiries with her nephew. Discreet."

"I feel so sorry for her."

"Don't worry. We'll get her back. She couldn't have gone far in her condition. Let's just hope she doesn't crash the car. In the meantime, I suggest you and Romeo give a lot of good, hard thought to salvaging what you can of this mess. And to kicking our dear Dr. Lincoln out on her ass. That bitch has caused enough damage."

He swept through the door of the office and was gone. Ronica sat there a moment, wondering what to do. She felt so helpless. She was glad Victor had insisted on bringing in a skin specialist to look at their patients. She should have asked Dr. Jeffries to look at *her*.

She was just thinking that it had been quite a while since her breasts had itched, when a sharp, prickly pain flashed across her bosom. She was about to open her blouse to investigate, when she heard horrendous screeches coming from the third floor. Cecily. It had to be Cecily. What on earth was happening to her now?

She didn't really want to see, but she had a morbid need to know. Dr. Jeffries had told them that the once-pretty model seemed to be suffering everything from psoriasis to painful plantar warts. As well, cysts, tumors, and boils had broken out all over her skin. But by the way she was screaming now, something even worse must be happening to her. It was a good thing Cecily's mother was traveling in Europe and her father was dead, or her parents would undoubtedly have mustered a whole battery of lawyers already.

Ronica made record time dashing up the front stairs to the third floor. The squeals, wails, and keenings grew louder and louder in her ears. She darted down the hall and opened the door to Cecily's room. *What was happening?*

Only one low light was on in the room, and the drapes had been drawn. Cecily was standing at the end of her bed, between Dr. Jeffries and Romeo, who were trying to restrain her. Cecily was half out of the flimsy nightgown she wore, and the shapely figure that was revealed only made the absurd head crowning it seem more grotesque.

Ronica stopped in her tracks and raised her hand to her mouth. Cecily Crenshaw bore little resemblance to the attractive woman she had been only a few short weeks ago. She did not even look as she had a few *hours* ago; her face had become an exaggerated manifestation of her worst apprehensions.

Instead of decreasing the size of her nose and chin, the makeup had done the opposite. She looked like a hag, a wicked cartoon witch. Her nose was a lengthy sharp rod of flesh sticking out nearly a foot from between her eyes; and her chin had grown to an enormous tapering wedge jutting out from the bottom of her face. She was still covered with all manner of growths and rashes, the latest manifestation of which was a series of ugly translucent boils that had broken out all over her body. The thin membrane that covered them—some were as large as an inch or more across—stretched with a quite thick liquid or pus, as well as a thinner liquid that resembled water.

Cecily had apparently chanced to touch her face, felt the abnormally distended nose and chin, and determined then and there to commit suicide. Ronica could not blame the girl; her anguish must have been unbearable. Seeing Cecily standing there writhing and struggling, trying to reach the window—and put an end to her agony—Ronica couldn't help but think with sharp, sudden clarity that it was odd how suffering made even shallow, superficial people like Cecily seem noble. Whatever the woman's flaws, however, she had certainly done nothing to deserve this.

Jeffries and Romeo had managed to get Cecily back to her bed, when the nurse came in to administer an intravenous sedative. Jeffries was shaking his head. "I'm not even sure this will work," he whispered to the others, as Cecily squirmed on the bed. "I've never seen anything like this. She must be transferred to Clinton East immediately." He turned to Ronica. "Has Emily Stuart been located yet?"

Ronica shook her head.

"Honestly, I don't know what's with you people. This place is run like some sort of chamber of horrors. I'm afraid your Dr. Lincoln may have to be brought up on charges. Letting this poor girl's condition go this far—"

Cecily murmured from the bed. "Don't look at me.

Don't let anybody see my face. I'm too ashamed. *Don't let anybody look at me."*

The doctor sat beside her, patted her heaving shoulder compassionately, and tried to calm and console her. He had almost succeeded when a sudden popping sound blasted out across the room.

Romeo looked about in alarm. "What's that?"

Ronica felt terribly afraid.

"Ohhhhh." Cecily was moaning, shivering. She rolled over as if in a trance and began to squiggle out of her nightgown. "Hot, so hot." The doctor tried to stop her but she batted his hand away. Ronica saw with disgust that those boils had broken out all over her breasts, abdomen, trunk . . . what could be causing it? Before she could turn her eyes away there was another popping sound and one of the boils below her neck burst open.

Cecily screamed with pain and tore out of the bed and out of her clothing before anyone could stop her. Her whole body was one festering mass of boils. Ronica swore she could see something moving underneath the skin, as if there were an animal squirming throughout her subcutaneous tissue, causing each painful, wretched boil.

POP. Another boil burst. POP. Another. Ronica hung back while Romeo and the doctor went after the girl. The nurse was too thunderstruck to be of any use. Cecily seemed possessed of unnatural strength. She was pulling both men toward the window. Ronica feared for her brother's safety, so she finally acted. But as she moved toward the girl a boil on Cecily's back popped open and splashed Ronica's face with a loathsome mixture of pus, blood, and water. More pops and more of the hot liquid hit her in the face and splattered her clothing.

The liquid within the boils was under pressure. The force generated by the explosions made it seem as if they were miniature geysers or volcanic fissures under her skin. POP. POP. More and more of the boils erupted until Ronica, Jeffries, and Romeo were splattered with horrible fluid. The stuff burned where it hit and the two men were forced to break their hold on the girl and back away.

But there was no chance of Cecily taking a dive for the sidewalk. She stood there moaning, a study in warped ugliness and misery, gobs of saliva dribbling down her face. There was a widening crack in the middle of her nose, and all at once the heavy distended end of the proboscis simply dropped off. To the astonishment of all, her chin did the same. Ronica looked at the girl's feet in disbelief and saw the two fleshy sections lying there like discarded snakeskin or cocoons. Twin streams of blood poured from the resulting craters and spread out into rivulets lining her trunk and legs. In a matter of moments there was a crimson puddle of blood on the carpet.

Cecily's skin—what remained of it—was stark white, wet, and steaming, like a huge piece of boiled meat.

More boils formed. Romeo and Jeffries looked too exhausted and helpless to do anything. Cecily collapsed on the floor. This time the boils were each several inches across. They popped explosively, spraying shreds of skin into the air, thrusting Cecily's body a foot or two away in the opposite direction. POP. Her body heaved upward, seemed to snap, almost float, then collapsed onto the floor again.

There were more monstrous pops; flesh and organs flew up into the air. Blood saturated the drapes and wallpaper. The nurse fainted. Crazed, Romeo went to the window, broke the panes open with his fists, leaned out precariously above jagged glass, and threw up. Dr. Jeffries turned his head and covered his eyes with his hands.

Cecily Crenshaw was simply *blowing up*, splattering all over the room. Ronica could take no more. She thought she had gone mad—that they had all gone mad, been mad since the very start of this project, since the day they announced the creation of Beautifique.

She realized her breasts were aching. If that could happen to Cecily—could it happen to her?

She flew out of the room, hurtled down the corridor,

and into a rest room. Gathering her wits, she washed away the gore. Then she went downstairs and got her coat out of her office. She had to get out of here, run away from this place and her fears before she went utterly crazy.

Dennis. She would see Dennis. He would make things better.

With Dennis, she would finally be back in control.

CHAPTER THIRTY-TWO_____

David didn't come back.

Peggy had given him a twenty-dollar bill to buy liquor—and he hadn't come back.

After a half hour passed, she came out of the barricaded bathroom and started cleaning up the living room. First she put a chair up against the door; the invaders had broken the lock and it was useless. As she picked up the papers and used a broom to sweep rice and cereal up off the floor, she was torn between mourning David and cursing him. Could he have been waylaid on the street or on the stairs by someone from Barrows or an ordinary mugger? Was he lying somewhere hurt and helpless? Dead?

Or had he taken her twenty dollars and gotten drunk somewhere? Maybe with that woman who had called earlier asking where he was? Or his drug cronies? *What a wonderful Christmas season this was turning out to be!*

He had probably never intended to come back. In a weak moment she had allowed herself to think he cared about her welfare. Right now he was probably getting high in some bar, making time with a woman, laughing at the thought of Peggy shivering in terror behind the locked bathroom door. He would probably expect her to still be there when he got home.

Well, she told herself—not entirely believing it—she

was made of sterner stuff than that. She would clean up the apartment (should she call the police, or would that only make it worse?), then make herself a cup of tea. She'd get her thoughts in order and then decide what to do. (Should she call Ronica?) All she knew was that she was too disoriented and tired to make any decisions right now. Besides, what could the police do? Or Ronica for that matter? What could anybody do? She suspected this had only been meant as a warning; if she spoke to no one else about what she had seen at the Barrows clinic they would probably leave her alone.

Peggy Antonicci—how do you get into these messes?

She was in mid-sweep when she decided upon a course of action. Just in case anything happened to her, it might be smart to write down everything she had learned tonight. She'd mail it to her mother with a covering letter, telling her to keep it safe and open it only in case of death or accident. (She could imagine the look on her mother's face if she snuck a peek beforehand!) She knew she was being perhaps a touch melodramatic, but she didn't care.

She got the typewriter out of the closet, put it on the kitchen table, and started writing. Within half an hour she had put down most of what she wanted to say.

There was a knock on the door that nearly made her jump a foot out of her chair.

"Hey—let me in, babe."

David. She debated whether or not to open the door, then decided to go ahead. For one thing she was anxious to hear his excuses. They were almost always amusing.

He was drunk, or pretty near it. He leered at her as she let him in. "Sorry," he said, "lost track of the time." In his hand he held a tiny bottle of vodka, about the size they served on airplanes. "Brought you the booze you wanted."

She swiped the bottle from his hand. "I don't suppose there's any change."

He took off his jacket and flung it on the remains of the sofa. "I knew you'd be all right. Those creeps aren't coming back. Sorry, babe, but I hadda go somewhere and do something for a while. I knew nobody would bother you. Already been cleaning up, I see—that's great."

"Thanks, David. I was worried and frightened, and you've been such a comfort. Your concern for me is truly overwhelming."

His booze-dopey grin turned downward and became something quite the opposite.

"Look, lady. We're on the outs, aren't we? I have to get out of here, don't I? Who are you to expect my concern, huh? You're not concerned about me. You're throwing me out on the street. Why should I worry about you, huh?"

He was doing his Marlon Brando, tough-guy act—he was really so pathetic—but somehow Peggy didn't think this was completely artificial. He was angry, she could tell, full of a seething, quiet madness that could burst outward at any moment. He was full of self-righteous, alcoholic courage. There was no telling what he might do. He'd never actually become violent before, she reminded herself, but there was always a first time. She would have to watch herself.

He went over to the typewriter, menacing, swaggering. "Whatcha writing?"

He pulled out the sheet and started to read it. "Barrows—*wha?*"

He flipped quickly through the sheets she had already typed. "What is this? This is the whole damn story you were telling me!"

"It's true, every word of it. Now don't get it messy, give me—"

His hand flew out so fast she didn't see it coming. WHAM. The back of it hit her in the face. She stood there, trembling, shocked. A trickle of blood came out of her left nostril and stained her upper lip.

"God—Davey—you're drunk." She trembled with fear and fury.

She was gratified that he looked as shocked by his actions as she did.

"I didn't mean to do that. It's just that—" He crumbled the pages she had typed in his fist. *"You cannot write this shit!* Do you understand me? You cannot write this shit! I thought you were terrified what they'd do to you! Haven't you learned your lesson, for Christ's sake!"

She wiped away the blood on her lip. *Don't hit me. Don't hit me again, David. Please.* "It isn't shit. I told you it's the *truth.* And that's why a letter to my—"

"That's just it!" he screamed. "That's why you can't write it."

"What do you mean?"

"Shit, shit, shit, I shouldn't've told you." He banged the wall repeatedly with his fist. He was really very, very drunk. Peggy saw the knuckles bleeding but had no desire to restrain him from hurting himself as he had hurt her. Then he suddenly thrust out and slapped her again. "Don't make me do this." Another slap. In panic, she backed away from him, fell across the sofa.

"You gotta stop writing this crap. You gotta forget all about this story. All about the Barrows clinic. Shit." He looked around, gestured at the room, while hovering above her. "Wasn't this enough?" He pointed to the words written on the bedroom door. "Wasn't that enough? Stupid bitch—I thought you'd drop the story. I promised him I would make you keep your mouth shut. I have to make you keep your mouth shut."

"What are you talking about?"

"One hundred thousand dollars, you stupid bitch, that's what I'm talking about. Just if I make you keep your mouth shut."

She stared at him with a blank expression, but it was dawning on her. "You did this!"

He nodded repeatedly like a jack-in-the-box. "That's right."

"David. Why are you doing this? Who offered you one hundred thousand dollars?"

"Ha, ha. Wouldn't you like to know? He overheard Ronica saying she'd give you a call, and he was afraid she might tell you too much."

Victor Asmodian, she thought.

He hunkered down beside her and grabbed her head in his hands. Strong hands. "I'll split it with you, babe. One hundred thousand dollars. Fifty thousand for each. I need that money. I need a place to stay, somewhere to live." He started crying.

The bastard, thought Peggy.

"I don't want to wind up on the street. I'm getting old. *Going bald.* I can't stand it, I just—"

She pulled her head out of his grip before he could hurt her. "Don't expect me to feel sorry for you. Not after the way you've used me. Your life didn't have to turn out this way. You could have tried harder. You didn't have to give up so soon."

His teeth were clenched and he made twin fists. "Tell me you'll do as I say. Tell me you'll forget this story— and I'll give you half. *Half.*"

"No," she said emphatically. "I don't want you to get anything. I don't want their money. They're killing people. I'm going to the police—right away." She made fists of her own and started beating his chest, his face, tears running down her cheeks. "You destroy my apartment, everything I own, and expect me to want you to get fifty thousand dollars for it? You bastard, you *bastard.* I knew you were low, but I never knew how low."

She knew she had gone too far. She braced herself for the blows that would follow. She tried to get up off the couch, find something, anything, to defend herself with, but she wasn't fast enough. Deep down, she'd never thought it would be this bad.

But as she felt his fists and feet on her face, in her ribs, in her stomach, as she tried to get away, hit him back, save herself, as she screamed and bled, she thought, *It's going to be very, very bad.*

CHAPTER THIRTY-THREE _____

Emily Stuart's mind had retreated into a tiny place where the sane and insane intermingled, where one's body and brain could go through the worst contortions and distortions, and yet view it all as if it were happening to someone else in some other dimension. She drove herself forward as if in a dream, secretly aghast at what had become of her but not allowing the thought of it to surface on a conscious level where it might incapacitate her. The itching inside her skin that had earlier made her feel full of wriggling, burrowing worms had ceased and all that remained was a tingling numbness.

Emily had only one consuming purpose. To see Scottie again, even if it were only a dream-Scottie, to see Scottie and ensure him that she was well, that she would never desert him. She had to make sure her Scottie was safe and happy. Underneath his cruel words and sarcastic demeanor, she knew he loved her and, more importantly, counted on her. She was certain of that, if nothing else.

She had kept to the shadows in the halls of the clinic, and slowly made her way down to the garage. She'd had trouble for some reason sliding behind the wheel of the limousine, but as in all dreams, she eventually had her way. She drove the car out of the private garage—there was no attendant—and drove as fast as she could toward her Scarsdale estate. Even though it was a dream and she should have been able to just glide through traffic, simply roll over the other automobiles, or even take to the air, she somehow sensed it was important to drive as if this were real life. She got halfway without mishap, but then had to pull over to the side of the road. She felt unaccountably dizzy.

Ah, I'm waking up, she thought. *Soon, I'll see Scottie for real.* But instead of waking up she only fell asleep. The last thought she had was *Why am I wearing such an odd body?*

An incredible metamorphosis had taken place. Her arms and legs had become more like claws—the skin had become not only leathery but scaled, and eventually plated. She was hunched over, her head thrust forward by two horny outgrowths from her back. Her condition worsened as she slept.

When she awoke a few hours later it was pitch-black out, and her shredded clothes were hanging off her body. It was even more difficult to sit comfortably in the car, to drive, to steer, to see where she was going, but somehow she made it. Somehow she made it home to Scottie.

She fell asleep again after parking a short distance from the house. Further change occurred. What finally emerged from the car was a scuttling humpbacked hybrid that walked in a partial sideways motion on all fours like a giant crustacean. The skin had almost completely converted to hard plating or a shell-like crust. Among the only human remnants were the misshapen head with one tiny, darting eye, and the scaly upper arms and thighs. The feet were huge forklike objects; the hands had metamorphosed into pincers.

The Emily-creature had no trouble covering the distance from the car to the house. It traversed the grounds quite quickly, then stopped at the edge of the driveway to peer at the large, two-story structure. Scottie had not been attending to the grounds, Emily thought; she saw that the flowerbeds needed work, and there were tools lying about when she had expressly told him to clean up. She would have to talk to him.

Emily entered the house.

Scottie lay on a rug in front of the enormous living-room fireplace, his hands on the breasts of a seventeen-year-old girl he had met in Central Park on Sunday. He had lied and told her he was older but he didn't think she believed him. Not that it made a difference. He'd pumped his dick into her twice already this evening, and he had a hickey the size of Nova Scotia on his neck. He figured he had to thank his sweet Aunt Emily for teaching him the tricks of the trade. But it was such a relief to have fine soft flesh to work over for a change instead of some wrinkled old prune in a bathrobe and lipstick. The phone and doorbell had rung several times that night, but he hadn't stopped for anything.

There was a crashing sound. The naked girl jumped to her feet, breasts bouncing. "What was that?" Scottie would have thought one of his friends was playing a joke on him—if he'd had any friends. He looked at the girl—perhaps a boyfriend of hers?

He was about to get up and investigate when something smashed into the room from the hallway, trailing pieces of the kitchen door behind it. It was enormous.

When the thing screeched "Scotttiiie" and advanced on them, he knew it wasn't a man in a crazy costume; it was real. He recognized the voice but didn't think it could be possible. He'd tried to visit Aunt Emily at the clinic again, but each time they'd given him some story and refused him admittance. This could not have happened to his aunt! This did not happen to people outside of nightmares.

As the creature rushed toward them, he grabbed the fireplace poker. He took a swipe at the thing, but the poker just bounced off the hard shell of its back. Under the shell Scottie saw familiar breasts—the small, withered breasts of his aunt Emily, the brown mole that lay between them and which she had often insisted he suck on.

Knowing, accepting, what the creature really was only made him more determined to beat it out of existence. He crashed the poker down again and again, but it did no good. The swollen, mutated face slobbered and roared with anger. He repositioned the poker in his hands and tried to hit the underside of the creature, tried to hit its breasts. The monster backed up and away from them.

Scottie stepped back, dazed, as the creature jumped forward and attached itself to his ladyfriend. The girl let out a frightened squeal and tried to escape—to no avail. The pincers were working, working, splattering Scottie with blood. The girl was lifted off the floor by the scuttling horror and thrown toward the fireplace with such force that she crashed right through the firescreen and hit the burning logs.

"AHHHHHHH!" The girl wailed in agony as her hair caught fire and her flesh began to blister and sizzle. She tried to crawl out of the enclosure, but the creature thrust out its pincers and clawed and slashed at her. The upper part of the girl's body became a roiling mass of blood while her lower body caught fire.

Scottie had already run the length of the enormous living room when the creature turned from his dead girlfriend and came after him. It was much faster than the boy. A pincer caught his foot and flopped him hard onto the floor. He tried to squirm, squiggle, crawl away, but the pincer held tight. When the creature began to pull itself up and over him, relaxing its hold on the ankle, he saw his opportunity and quickly darted forward on hands and knees.

Too late—the pincer reached out again, thrust under his stomach from the right, and caught hold of his dangling penis.

Terrified, Scottie gingerly rolled over on his left side, afraid to perform any movement that might endanger his manhood. The creature moved with him, and he saw the terrible face hovering right above his own.

It was—at least, in part—the face of his aunt. One half of the head was unbelievably rough and distended, hideous. Her puckered slash of a mouth was dripping spittle and she smelled like a million sick rooms put together. With each movement the beast made, Scottie could hear its joints creaking, the hard shells and crusts covering the skin cracking and snapping.

"Please, please," he groaned piteously. "Please don't hurt me."

His aunt Emily had a terrible time forming the words, but eventually she managed. "You . . . little . . . bastard . . ."

One pincer went up his rectum as the other snapped shut on his penis. Enduring unimaginable pain, Scottie was lifted up several feet into the air.

Emily pulled the boy's body back, back . . .

Then hurled it with whiplash force against the wall, breaking his neck instantly.

Minutes away from her own expiration, the Emily-creature lifted her pincer . . . and the small flaccid piece of dismembered meat, as if in triumph.

CHAPTER THIRTY-FOUR

It seemed to go on for a lifetime, the hitting, the kicking, the slapping, the cursing. She had nearly gotten away from him, crawled between his legs, when suddenly he was on her once again. They wrestled together, rolled across the floor. He tried to choke her. He begged and pleaded for cooperation, but she knew he was too far gone to let her go. She threw everything at him that she could lay her hands on. Twice she nearly made it to the door when he threw himself at her and brought her down to her knees. She was bleeding, heaving, crying—black and blue in a dozen places.

"David, *please,* David!"

"You bitch—you lousy bitch!"

How could she have ever been fooled? How could she have been so wrong about someone? What made it worse was that she knew that on some level David was just as dismayed as she was, but that he had gone past the point of no return and that in his mind every blow necessitated the blow that followed.

He was through, it was finished. He'd be out on the street, in jail, locked up behind bars. And there'd be no one hundred thousand dollars, not even fifty thousand—and no place for him to stay once he got out of prison. Everything had gone too far, too far. She was afraid he was figuring he'd be better off with her dead. The severity of his assault indicated that her death might well be his objective.

She couldn't believe it was happening. Not even while it *was* happening.

Then she heard the banging on the door. She remembered hearing it earlier, but it had stopped that time. She screamed for help. David only hit her harder. "Get lost!" he screeched at the door. "Get the fuck outa here! This is none of your business."

But they made it their business. The chair Peggy had placed in front of the door toppled to one side and the door burst open to admit a heavyset black neighbor, his wife, and two cops they had apparently called in from the street corner. *God bless them,* thought Peggy.

"Get out of here, bastard!" David said when he saw the neighbor. Then the two cops brushed past the tenant into the room.

David bolted, but the cops followed him into the bedroom. The neighbor's wife helped Peggy to her feet, and Peggy turned to stare in the direction of Davey's flight.

She heard a shattering sound, glass breaking—a high-pitched scream.

Then silence.

Peggy nearly fainted at the thought of what must have happened, but her anger sustained her. The cops came out of the bedroom and confirmed her suspicion.

David had jumped through the window and landed in the alley several stories below.

She was numb, but she had to see this through to the conclusion. Waving aside everyone's objections, she followed the police down the stairs to the alley.

David lay beside some toppled garbage cans on a pile of refuse. He was barely alive. He was out of his head, covered in blood. Bones had shattered and the pain must have been indescribable. Peggy pushed her way past the cops, and repressing her hatred of him, knelt beside his body. One cop went to call an ambulance.

"I'm sorry," David strained to say. "I should never

have tried to hurt you. I'm sorry. But Romeo . . . Romeo Barrows offered me so much money. After a while I . . . recognized him from . . . from pictures you showed me . . . weeks ago . . ."

Romeo! God—it couldn't be! Was David still trying to lie to her, hurt her, even now? But she knew David was too sick to lie.

"You didn't want me anymore—I hadda do something." David turned his head carefully, in excruciating pain, and spoke directly to the police officer. "Romeo Barrows . . . of the Barrows clinic uptown . . . offered me one hundred thousand dollars if I'd make her shut up. Make him pay."

Peggy was confused. Was he talking about the money? Did he think he'd live to spend the money? That she'd allow it? But no, that's not what he meant.

"Make him pay for what he did to us," David said.

In spite of herself Peggy felt tears welling in her eyes. She had loved this man for a long time and letting go wasn't easy. She was torn between mourning his wasted life and hoping the miserable wretch would expire before he could do to other women what he had done to her. Romeo Barrows's part in this certainly did not absolve David of guilt.

A funny look came over him. He cocked his head and asked in a high sing-song whisper, "Who was the little boy in the pictures, Peggy?"

And then he collapsed.

A short while later Peggy could hear the sirens, but it was too late. David was dead.

The cop who had remained near the body asked her if she was all right. He wanted her to go with them to the hospital for a checkup, but she had other things on her mind. *That bastard Romeo Barrows—did he think his money gave him a right to do anything he wanted?*

"I'll be okay," she stammered. "I'll be all right. There's no time for this now. I know who's responsible. I know who did this to David and me."

The cop was unimpressed. "Seems to me your boyfriend beat you up, and that's all there is to it."

"Yes, but he was promised *money* to beat me up," she told them. "And I know who's responsible. Now either come with me to question that man, or I'll go there myself. I won't go to any hospital until he's arrested. People are being killed—there's a whole conspiracy. . . . I'm a writer working on a story and they're trying to keep me quiet!"

They thought she was being hysterical, and who could blame them? Her clothes ripped, blood all over her, her hair in tangles—what a pretty picture she made. How could she convince them? She would not sit around in an emergency room for hours, knowing her condition looked worse than it was, while the third act of this melodrama was played without her. She wanted to *face* Romeo, to see this through to the finale. And she wanted to see if she could somehow protect Ronnie; Peggy was sure she knew nothing of Romeo's actions.

"Please—you heard him say Romeo Barrows. That's the man who wanted me silenced. I know too much about his operation. I'm telling you—what harm would it do to come with me to the clinic?" She explained that most of the damage to her apartment had been done *before* David started beating her. "The clinic was responsible!"

The ambulance departed with David's body. After a few more minutes she finally persuaded the cops to do as she said. If this did turn out to be something big it might not hurt their chances for promotion if they followed through.

One cop used the radio to confer with an associate. Officers from the precinct in which the clinic was located arranged to meet them there.

"One more thing," Peggy said, as the car set off toward the clinic. "I think I should tell you about these . . . things . . . in the basement."

CHAPTER THIRTY-FIVE_____

When Dr. Lincoln finally woke up at ten P.M., her head was throbbing and she was covered with blood. Ralph Tarramonte—what was left of him—was lying on the floor nearby, next to Olga's severed head. Betty Lincoln was too dizzy and defeated to get sick again; she simply didn't have the energy. She had no idea how long she had been lying there. She wasn't certain if she had passed out from sheer horror, from the shock of one of Ralph's blows, simple blood loss, or a combination of all three. Luckily Ralph's hands had been too weak near the end to deliver killing strokes with the cleaver, although he'd done some minor damage.

She got to her feet, looked herself over, then looked at the splattered blood and mayhem in the bedroom. She let out a howl and sobbed hysterically for several minutes. Ralph was dead, one part of her life was over—and she knew what was responsible. She knew what had done this to her and it was time to pay them back.

She kept spare clothing in a closet down the hall, for those weekends when she and Ralph would stay snuggled together in the town house. Sniffling back tears of loss and rage, she stripped out of her soiled clothes, washed off the blood, and changed into a fresh outfit. She left the building, hailed a cab, and made her way back to the clinic.

Something had gone terribly, terribly wrong with the makeup. She suspected it was only force of will that kept her own face and body from breaking out, mutating, metamorphosing the way Ralph's had. She had honestly thought it was safe, or she would never have subjected anyone else to it. Ralph and others had paid for her mistake. She knew that her theory about the psychological state of the patient affecting the makeup still held water, but now she also knew that was only part of it. The makeup itself was responsible. The makeup—and the unhealthy influence of the creatures from which the "cosmetic" was derived.

When she arrived at the clinic, she rushed past the startled night receptionist with nary a comment. As the receptionist ran after her, yelling, she headed for the door at the end of the hallway. She slammed the door in the receptionist's face—the woman was not allowed down here—and made her way down the narrow staircase. The other members of the research team had long since left the building. She went to the left—the fake wall had been removed—entered the laboratory, and stood above the nearest tank trembling with outrage.

She stepped back out into the corridor, grabbed a fire axe from its holdings on the wall, and returned to the lab. In her mind she saw Elliot Lester using the fire axe on the animal that had killed Frank so many years ago.

These creatures—*Porodynean mariscrotii*, they were called—had had their day, and that day was now over. Barrows should never have let them live. They didn't belong in this world, and they were far more dangerous—cunning, conniving—than Betty had ever realized. They treated them like slugs when they were probably as intelligent as dolphins. Instead of being greedy they should have shared the news of the *mariscrotii* and the makeup years ago with other scientists, learned men and women who could have helped control the species and neutralize whatever danger they might have presented.

She went to the first tank where the "fleshopod" was

resting, and opened the lid. This particular creature had not been fed much since Dr. Lincoln came back from dinner one night and found it chomping on the remains of Jennifer Lindsey. She had found her purse lying on the floor nearby, amid a pool of blood and gore. Betty had quickly cleaned up and kept her mouth shut. The body of the woman would sustain the beast for quite some time, even though it was almost always hungry.

Betty assumed the writer's curiosity—or nosiness—had gotten the better of her, but still the woman's death shocked and appalled her. *What had possessed her to open the lid of the tank? Couldn't she get a clear enough view of the creature through the glass?* This made Betty wonder again about a subject she hated to consider: the possibility of the fleshopods having limited psychic control over humans.

There were six tanks in the laboratory. Six creatures born of one mother who herself had been born of genetic engineering, molded together from many, many different animals to form one unique hybrid. Holding the axe behind her back, Betty looked down at this, one of the children of that first beast, and wondered where would be the best place to strike.

The fleshopod was approximately ten feet long. Its shape was that of a giant snake or tentacle or an outsized elephant's trunk, with a thicker middle section and two tapering ends. There were several flapperlike appendages spaced evenly along the bottom of the creature to help it move. It measured two feet at its widest, and was a foot and a half high. The creature had two flat, black eyes level with its skin on either side of its "head," and two holes at the same end through which it breathed. Its hide was extremely thick, bumpy, and mottled, the color of drying blood. At the same end as the eyes and "nostrils" there was an opening at the very tip through which it fed. Inside this circular opening, which could expand to engulf an object many times its size, were many layers of tiny serrated teeth, as well as a series of muscles that could pull the fleshopod's prey down into its gullet. There was a series of tiny orifices on top of the beast which almost continually leaked a viscous fluid from which Lincoln, with some refinements, had derived her wondrous cosmetic. How the fleshopods smelled depended on who was smelling them. Some people thought they had the aroma of seawater; others, the countryside after a rainstorm. Betty found them as odorless as nasal mucus.

She could remember the day when Frank Eddington was killed by this creature's parent. The day they looked into the dish where he had collected some of the fluid it secreted and saw that the outline, the distinct impression, of Susan Raymond's face—she was the one who fed the creature—had formed like a mold or mask of clay. They realized then that this creature, this substance, had qualities they had never dared to dream of. Qualities that could be put to use for mankind. They'd experimented in dozens of ways.

First they tried the makeup on injured animals. The material would heal the wounds almost instinctually, even making minor changes that Betty had only thought about. Finally, after much work, they determined that the living cells of the makeup would respond to psychic stimuli from an outside source and change an animal's, or even a person's, very flesh and bone structure. A lower animal was not smart enough to affect the makeup by itself, but with humans it was a different story. Betty tried it—again, with great success—on herself. Before too long, with minor adjustments and additives, they had developed several "types" of makeup each of which worked best on different sections of the body and on different problems.

They had at one point intended to see if they could somehow develop a fast-acting cream that could heal scrapes and cuts, instantly seal up life-threatening injuries and surgical wounds, to assist doctors. The time it took the psychic factor of the makeup to work made it

ineffective for such use without modification, but they'd
all realized the *real* money was in cosmetic application.

Betty hadn't told the entire truth when she spoke
about the makeup. They were all largely in the dark as to
how it worked. She did know that the makeup—acting
upon conscious or subconscious thoughts transmitted by
the patient—could affect a person's DNA, which in turn
gave instructions for protein production to the RNA,
which in carrying out these instructions changed cells on
a small scale and hence human features on a much larger
one.

Therefore the makeup, like artificial skin, had the ability to eventually turn into, or at least promote the growth
of, actual human skin cells. But—and this was what
scared her—it also retained the ability, while on (and in)
the patient, to *move about independently* through the
skin. It looked like flesh, but in reality it remained just
what it was: part of an external organ of the fleshopod,
the animal's liquid outer skin coating. And apparently
through some strange bond this organ could still be influenced by the animal's "thoughts."

The fleshopods had no "motives" that Dr. Lincoln
could see, except to exist, to thrive, to "do their thing,"
so to speak. She could not really ascribe to them any evil
intent, such as "revenge" for their captivity. Chances
were they actually had no true idea of what they were
doing, or helping to do, to the patients. They simply did
it because they *could.* Perhaps they were as curious about
humans as Dr. Lincoln and her associates were about
them. Perhaps they were *experimenting* on Ralph, Mrs.
Stuart, and the other patients. Heaven only knew what
they might finally do before the experimentation was
over. She just didn't *know* enough about them, not even
after all this time.

Well, what did it matter? The fleshopods had to die, it
was as simple as that; for killing Ralph, they had to die.
Especially now that they were pregnant. Imagine! They

had actually planned to breed these monstrosities in clinics across the country and the world!

She lifted the axe and chopped maniacally at the beast in the tank, allowing its life fluids to spatter her face and clothing. She then moved away from the first tank, and went to the second. This time she did not bother lifting the glass case. She simply hurled down the axe with all her strength, heedless of the glass shards that flew into the air and into her skin. She hacked repeatedly at the writhing, terrible animal inside before the beast could lunge at her in self-defense. She moved on to the third case—and the fourth, the fifth.

The animal in the first case, not dead, slithered onto the floor and made its way silently toward Dr. Lincoln.

So did the second.

And the third.

Betty had smashed into the sixth case with the axe, was trying to butcher the fleshopod within, when the first three beasts, the fourth lagging behind, caught up with her. Her blows had simply not been strong enough.

Using muscles in the middle of their bodies, as well as their tiny "flippers," they lifted their heads off the floor and snapped eagerly at the offensive woman. One mouth bit into her shoulder. Another into her calf. She felt the sharp sting of the many teeth grinding into her cheek. Another mouth poked up in between her legs and bit into her groin. She flailed wildly with the axe, but she couldn't get the leverage, couldn't do enough damage from her position. The fleshopods reared their heads and she was raised up off the floor as they burrowed their way into her body.

A fifth fleshopod lunged out and engulfed her entire free hand in its mouth. Her other hand dropped the axe, and she screamed. The creature had already sucked her arm in up to the elbow. She could feel the little teeth stabbing, slicing, tearing away her skin. Blood did not drip out of the tubular maw but was sucked directly into the membrane of the mouth as if by osmosis.

One of the fleshopods burrowed its way into her vagina.

Instead of killing them, she'd only let them loose.

She had honestly wanted to help the world, to atone for past mistakes and do something that would forever benefit mankind. Instead . . .

As she was torn apart and devoured the thought finally came: *It's what I deserve, it's what I deserve, it's what I deserve . . .*

CHAPTER THIRTY-SIX

It would have been the happiest night in Yolanda Vasquez's life but for two things: the thoughts of her dead husband and children, who had not escaped the terrible fire as she had; and the constant, infernal itching that had broken out all over her body. It was simply unbearable, but she was determined not to scratch. She wasn't taking any chances of damaging her skin after all that fine doctor had done for her. Dr. Lincoln was a saint, she swore, a saint.

Otherwise, the whole night had been like a dream come true. Being driven in a limousine to Gracie Mansion, meeting Mayor Jason Clarke (who was not as handsome as his pictures, but even more charming than she'd expected), driving with him to the Waldorf Astoria and going up on the escalator to the ballroom, which was beautifully decorated and full of exciting, glamorous people. She got very nervous when the mayor told her she would have to make a speech, but she handled it better than she thought possible. She simply spoke with her heart.

"These fine men we are honoring tonight—I did not appreciate what they do until I was caught in a terrible fire which claimed the lives of my husband and children." She fought to hold back tears, though she was sure no one would have objected had she cried. She noticed a TV camera dollying forward just then to get a close-up. "I lived through that fire only through the bravery of these men, who risk their lives time and again. . . . I can now appreciate how courageous they are. I couldn't imagine going through that experience ever again, yet these men —and women—do it over and over and over, because it's their job. They risk their lives constantly." And then she did start crying. "God bless them. God bless them." The mayor came to her side and hugged her, and she was afraid she would get salty tears all over his shirt.

Then the dinner—she'd never had such a meal—and the dancing afterward! She tried as hard as she could to ignore the itching, the constant *itching,* but it was nearly driving her to distraction. Even up there behind the podium with the lights and cameras on her, her skin had been itching. The mayor and others tried to talk to her, but she had trouble maintaining her thoughts, and hence a conversation. Luckily everyone seemed to be understanding. Many knew she had just come from a clinic, that her late husband and children were still on her mind.

Oh, Roberto, if only you could see this, be here with me. And she knew she would have gladly traded this wonderful evening for the lives of her husband and children. This night was nice, but it was only a brief pause in the life of emptiness and loneliness that she was facing. Yet, while she was here, for this moment, she would enjoy it. What else could she do?

In the middle of a dance, the itching suddenly became so intense that she had to pull away from the mayor for a moment. She stood there, as he stared at her, waiting for it to subside, wanting desperately to scratch, to *claw,* at her skin and make it stop.

"Uhhhh."

The mayor's face was creased with concern. "Are you all right?" he asked.

"Yes, yes, but I think I should sit down. I don't want to get too tired."

"Of course, I'm sorry. I should have realized. Would you like me to take you home soon?"

"There's no hurry, Your Honor. I'm having a wonderful time."

Back on the dais, she sat and tried mentally to subdue the itching while the mayor and some of the other guests conversed. Absently, she began to stroke her face, then gently scratch it. Before she realized it, she was scratching at her skin so furiously she was drawing blood. She looked at the crimson stain on her nails in horror. She had to get to a restroom before anyone noticed.

Then a new wave of itching began and she had to—*just had to*—keep scratching—her cheek, her forehead, her neck, her arms. *Scratch, scratch.* Her fingers seemed to be ripping into some kind of moist material on her face, but she wouldn't stop to figure out what it was.

Ahhhh! This felt so good, wonderful. At last she could scratch and the itching would stop. At last there would be some relief.

"Oh my God!"

A waitress who'd bent over to refill her water glass began screaming. At what? At whom? *At her?*

Yes, Yolanda looked down and saw blood—*strips of her own skin*—clinging to her fingers. Flaps of skin that she had torn away were hanging down off her cheeks and chin and arms. There was a strip of skin lying across her plate, another lying on top of her wine glass. Everywhere she looked there was skin.

Others on the dais, alerted by the waitress, looked at Yolanda and also started screaming. The mayor turned to her and his eyes widened in horror. Still, she could not stop scratching. *The itching, the itching*—it would not go away. She had to make it go away. It was driving her quite mad . . .

The waitress's eyes were practically popping out of their sockets as she stared at her. The mayor and some others tried to restrain her, but *she would not stop.* Yolanda knew she was undoing everything the good doctor had done for her, but she didn't care. She had to stop the itching. *Oh God, why is this happening to me? What have I done? Haven't I suffered enough?*

Finally she dug her fingernails under her skin on both sides of her face and simply *ripped* the flesh down and off her cheeks. Then she tore off the remaining strip on her forehead, started clawing at her neck—throwing the flaps of skin onto the table as if they were confetti—and then her arms. Strip after strip came flying off, dripping reddish fluid, revealing a raw ruined layer of burnt flesh underneath.

Others on the dais fled from the gruesome display, while some regurgitated their two-hundred-dollar dinners. The waitress backed up with her fingers between her teeth, tripped on the stairs, and tumbled to the ballroom floor. Dots of blood and fluid were spattered all over the mayor's face and tuxedo. He, too, was beginning to get sick.

Yolanda felt hot, terribly hot. It was stifling in here. Everyone was running away, giving her room, more air. *Good, good.* She had to get out of these clothes. They were too hot, too confining.

Ripppp, *rippppp.* She tore the dress off, took the tatters in her hands, and flung them all over the platform. She tore off her stockings, her undergarments—and still she was stifling.

There was a terrible commotion in the ballroom. TV cameras were rolling toward her, and several uniformed men were rushing toward the dais. The itching had stopped, but now she felt terrible pain all over her body. There was blood everywhere. She kept tearing at her clothing, ripping it off shred by shred by shred.

And then, in mid-yank, she looked at the floor and saw that all her clothes were *already lying there* in a bloody pile.

Yet hadn't she been tearing at her clothes these past few minutes?

She became hysterical at the realization of what she

had actually been doing. Screaming, she rushed down the steps off the dais and ran around reaching out for help, leaving bloody hand prints on white dresses and tuxedos as people backed away from her in terror. A riot had broken out in the ballroom. People were screeching, shouting and fainting, running into each other in an effort to avoid Yolanda and her bloody outstretched hands. *"Help me! Help me! Help me!"* Yolanda screamed.

Yolanda's eyes rolled up in her head and she toppled to the ballroom floor, a miserable creature who had *skinned herself alive.*

CHAPTER THIRTY-SEVEN

Somehow Romeo had managed to keep himself together long enough to see to some details after
Cecily's unbelievable death. He felt terrible about the
death of his girlfriend, but there were still things he had
to take care of. Ronica had run screaming out of the
room—God only knew where she was—the night nurse
had fainted, and Dr. Jeffries, after vomiting copiously,
had made his way downstairs to phone for the police.

Luckily no one else was aware that Cecily had expired.
The receptionist had heard the screams and seen Ronica's hasty exit but otherwise knew nothing of what had
happened. There were no other patients in the clinic, and
the nurses, except for the one who fainted, had gone
home a little earlier. The security guards had been told to
stay on the first floor unless specifically called for, and
were on a break in the cafeteria. Victor had apparently
gone out to help look for Emily Stuart. So far so good.

Romeo caught up with Jeffries just as the man was
about to use the phone at the reception desk. He managed to persuade the doctor to go into Ronica's office
instead, where there was more privacy.

When the dermatologist's back was to him, Romeo
took a stapler and brought it down hard on the man's
head. Jeffries collapsed onto the floor.

Romeo went upstairs to get a syringe and a sedative.

He had watched the nurses do this often enough. He gave Jeffries a shot that would keep him under for hours. He would deal with him when the time came.

Victor would know what to do, he told himself. He called Victor's number, in the hopes that the man had given up his search for Emily Stuart and gone home, but there was no answer. He suspected Victor was sick of the whole lot of them and had ensconced himself behind closed doors, incommunicado, until he had figured a way out of this mess. Romeo left a carefully worded message on his machine.

Romeo went upstairs. Earlier they'd dragged the unconscious nurse out of Cecily's room and put her on a sofa in the nurses' lounge. She was waking now, but was still groggy. Romeo pinned her on the couch and quickly injected her with the sedative. *Good. She'll be out for a while, too.*

He debated gathering up Cecily's splattered remains and feeding her to the fleshopods in the cellar, getting rid of all the evidence. Then he might also let the beasts feast on Dr. Jeffries and the nurse. No, no, it was too monstrous. What was he thinking of? He must have been crazy to attack the doctor that way! But he *had* to have time to figure out what to do.

He hadn't been thinking straight for days now, weeks, so disoriented was he by all that was happening. Everything was going down the tubes—they'd sunk a fortune, almost their entire worth, into the development of this makeup. They were facing financial ruin, lawsuits by the cartload, terrible publicity from which neither they as individuals nor the company would ever recover. What this really meant, Romeo thought bitterly, was that he had failed again.

Victor had to come up with a plan; Victor had to tell him what to do. The police must not get into this. He had to get rid of Cecily's body. Where was Ronica? Where was Dr. Lincoln? *Where the hell was Victor?*

He told the receptionist to call him the moment there was any word from any of the others. *The stupid cow!* thought Romeo. She just sat there reading her novel and chewing gum. If she had had any idea of what was going on, she probably would have run for the hills. He went upstairs to one of the empty rooms to lie down.

Two hours passed. Romeo got up, went to the phone, and called downstairs.

"No, Mr. Barrows, sir, haven't heard from anyone, sir. But Dr. Lincoln rushed past my desk about twenty minutes ago like a bat out of hell."

"Dr. Lincoln! Why didn't you call me?"

"Sorry, sir. She went downstairs to the restricted area. I was waiting for her to come back upstairs."

"Of all the stupid—Where is she now?"

"Down in the labs, I think."

"Okay. I'll come down and talk to her."

Dr. Lincoln had gotten them into this mess, and she was going to know what had happened, what she had done, to Cecily. His own face, to which Dr. Lincoln had applied makeup in order to remove age lines, as well as an unsightly bloating from too many nights of partying, had been feeling funny for hours now, but he assumed that was only due to nerves because of what happened to Cecily. If anything like that happened to him, he swore he would kill Betty Lincoln!

As he made his way down to the first floor, he thought about all the things he had done since this project started, things no one—including himself—would have thought the well-raised Romeo Barrows would ever have done. The first mistake had been in letting Dr. Lincoln, with her dubious reputation and background, become the head of this project. The second had been in failing to bring in some other authority to double-check her work. (Perhaps he hadn't *wanted* the makeup to be proven dangerous or useless.) His third mistake had been in hiring security men and nurses, also of questionable background, be-

cause they were cheap and in no position to blow the
whistle on anyone. And perhaps worst of all . . .

Ronica could obviously not deny that she had finally
spoken to Peggy Antonicci, but she insisted that they had
just talked about their respective boyfriends. "She's
throwing her lover David out," Ronica said. "She needed
a shoulder to cry on." But when Romeo and Victor Asmodian went into her office to tell Ronica that Cecily had
arrived, Romeo overheard his sister telling Peggy in
hushed tones that she "had to talk" to her.

Romeo didn't trust Peggy Antonicci as far as he could
throw her. Later, he asked the receptionist to call Peggy's
number and ask for "David." It worked out as Romeo
intended. The receptionist got Peggy instead, who told
her which bar this David was working at.

During the dinner break, Romeo had gone to the bar
and offered Kravitz a small fortune if he'd keep his silly
girlfriend from writing any stories about the makeup.
The guy clearly had no love for Peggy Antonicci. However, after Romeo spoke to the guy, he thought he might
have made a mistake.

Of course he'd had no intention of actually paying the
loser one hundred thousand dollars—he'd only implied
as much. He just wanted Peggy neutralized until the
clinic cleared up all its problems, and figured an angry,
hungry boyfriend might still have some influence over
her, as well as the inclination to use it. Just a good "talking to" was all Romeo was after. It seemed a lot safer
than paying hoodlums to beat up people, as he had done
with that nosy George Burke. He had lots of unsavory
contacts from his days of trying and failing at one job
after another after another.

Well, if he'd gone that far to keep their operations secret, he might as well go a few steps further. When Victor
got here, he and Dr. Lincoln and Romeo would figure
out what to do about Jeffries, the nurse, and Cecily's
remains.

Romeo stopped when he reached the first floor. He

heard shouts and screams coming from the corridor leading to the labs. The door at the end of the hall had burst
open and there were large reddish things crawling on the
floor, whipping through the air, snapping and waving like
thick animated telephone wires with teeth.

The fleshopods were loose! Jesus! How would they ever
get them back into their tanks? Where on earth was Dr.
Lincoln?

It looked like all six of the fleshopods had broken free
and made their way upstairs. Two security guards—part-
timers who had rushed indoors a moment ago—began
firing their handguns at the monsters. One of the creatures darted forward and sank its mouth into the face of
the nearest security guard, who beat at it with his fists but
succumbed rapidly as the creature sucked blood and skin
into its maw. Romeo could see the "jaw" muscles working as chunks of the man's flesh were pulled off the bone
and down into the hollow cavity of the fleshopod.

For such bulky, heavy animals, they moved with amazing swiftness. Two of them converged on the second security guard—one swallowed his right hand, gun and all—
while the other concentrated on the man's leg. The guard
kept squeezing the trigger, but the bullets couldn't even
blast their way through the inner flesh of the monster.
Slowly but surely the creature ate its way up the screaming man's arm, as the second beast gnawed into his belly,
spattering blood and offal. Romeo feared that the fleshopods had probably already eaten the two full-time security guards. *God!*

Romeo stood there and wondered if there was time to
dash across the lobby and out the front door before the
fleshopods spotted him. He had just decided to take a
chance when he heard a scraping sound nearby on the
floor and noticed one of the creatures wriggling toward
his feet like an overgrown sentient cable. The receptionist
saw it, too.

As the fleshopod reared up off the floor and whipped

toward them, she tried to run past Romeo. Before the animal could sink its teeth into him, he grabbed the receptionist and threw her into the fleshopod's path, saving himself. As the fleshopod fed upon the woman, he made a mad dash for the second story.

On the landing he stopped to look back and see what was happening.

One of the woman's arms was sunk halfway into the tube-mouth of one creature. Another arm was lodged up to the elbow in a second fleshopod. A third creature had enveloped her leg up to the knee. The other three beasts were still occupied with the dead security men, whose bodies they were flapping through the air, supported by the very tentacle-like monstrosities that were devouring them. The fleshopods worked their way farther up the limbs of the thrashing woman; her body whipped this way and that through space, churning, struggling like a fly caught in a spider's web. It looked to Romeo like a bizarre form of intercourse, as if the woman were in the throes of a violent, thrashing orgasm. The jerking movements of the animals kept the suspended woman in constant motion, swaying from side to side, so that she would suddenly hurtle upward a foot or two, then snap downward to nearly touch the floor a second later. Meanwhile her limbs were being sucked farther into the animals' maws, her flesh neatly sawed off by the teeth and virtually vacuumed into the monsters' insatiable gullets. As repulsed as he was, Romeo could not tear his eyes away. The three victims seemed caught in a *danse macabre* in a theater of the damned, helpless puppets being consumed by their own strings.

That could have been me, he thought.

He heard a coughing sound and looked down to the right. Dr. Jeffries was stumbling out of Ronica's office, roused from his sedation. Romeo was about to warn the doctor about the fleshopods when he decided against it.

The good doctor would be no match for the fleshopods

once they caught sight of him. Neither would the part-time nurse, stumbling unsuspectingly down the stairs after she awoke.

Do nothing, Romeo thought desperately.

The secret of the Barrows clinic would be safe.

CHAPTER THIRTY-EIGHT_____

On the way uptown to the clinic, Peggy told the police officers all she knew about the Barrows clinic, the fleshopods, and the makeup which was the creatures' by-product. They didn't necessarily believe her, but they were all ears. She told a very convincing story. "I can show you these animals," she said. "They're kept in a lab in the basement. I know it sounds unbelievable, but it's true."

"Look," said the nicer of the two officers, a kindly middle-aged man named Robbins with a mustache and a big pot belly, "we're mainly going to this clinic to question Romeo Barrows about his hiring your boyfriend to terrorize you. This other stuff . . ." He shook his head. "Well, we'll have to see about that."

The other officer, a young rookie named Sloane who had slick blond hair and a neatly trimmed beard, said, "You say they get this makeup from these monsters?"

"Yes, yes, that's it. That's what Ronica told me. It's not as crazy as it sounds. Animal by-products are used for all sorts of things, only there have never been any animals like these before. The stuff they secrete is used to make the cosmetic, and it's composed of *living cells.* Apparently these cells can react to mental stimuli and—"

Robbins held up his hand. "Lady, let's worry about all

this later. Right now, let's just talk to this Romeo Barrows, okay?"

She leaned back in her seat and shut up. They wouldn't believe her until they saw for themselves.

When she'd looked into those tanks and seen those ugly creatures . . . just the thought of them gave her the creeps.

During the silence that followed she thought about David, about the last words he'd spoken. Funny what the human mind will think of at the oddest moments. But she would never have told him the truth about the "boy" in those early photographs: he was not a dead brother, but actually Peggy herself. . . .

It still hurt to think about it. Peggy had been born with a rare condition known as pseudohermaphroditism. Biologically, she was a female, with female sex organs, but she had the outer characteristics of the opposite sex. Even on the rare occasions when her mother made her wear a dress, she looked like a boy in drag. Everything about her was male, worse than any tomboy. Teachers and children who first met her refused to believe she was a girl until someone else she knew would confirm it. It was a constant humiliation; her voice, her way of speaking, her mannerisms, even her body shape, were those of a boy's. She developed a dread of wearing female clothes because she looked so funny in them.

Then, at puberty, a miracle happened. She sprouted breasts, which had grown bigger and bigger as she became a young woman. Even though she still had a big-boned boy's body in certain respects, there could certainly no longer be any doubt as to her sex.

The whole experience had left terrible emotional scars. She had lived her life in terror of reverting to the boyishness of her youth—losing her breasts, growing a mustache, waking up to find she was more man than woman. And she couldn't trust her own feelings. She had looked like—been made by her peers to *feel* like—a boy for so long that she was afraid the male side of her had not completely dissipated but simply retreated within her.

So she turned away from that hidden side of herself, refused to acknowledge it. She had taken up with men who were all wrong for her—anything to keep from facing the truth, from owning up to that side of her sexuality.

Yes, she was genuinely and truly attracted to men, but there was more to her than that. Wasn't it time now for her to admit to herself that her physical feelings toward Romeo were so intense—that she had "fallen in love" with him—because she'd been transferring, denying, her true feelings toward Ronica?

She knew—she just *knew*—that Ronica wasn't mixed up in any of this. Yes, Ronica knew about the fleshopods, she had participated in a cover-up—but she would never have done what Romeo had, offer David money to persuade Peggy to drop a story. Peggy would never believe it of her friend, never.

And then they were pulling up to the clinic and there was no more time to think about any of it.

Dennis Reckler had put the key in the lock of his apartment door and turned it to the right. He swung the door open and reached in to find the light switch.

"Don't turn the light on, darling," a voice said from inside.

Dennis was so startled he nearly dropped his briefcase. Then he smiled. He recognized the voice.

"Ronica. I see you used the keys I gave you." In the light from the hallway he could now see that there was a figure sitting on the couch.

"Yes, darling. Come in and close the door. But don't turn the light on."

"Okay."

He put his briefcase down on the table beside the door. He moved in the darkness toward the couch. It was pitch-black in the room. His knee hit the coffee table and he cried out.

"*Ouch.* Ronica, can't we turn on a light? At least light a candle?"

"No," she snapped, going into her act. "Just do as I say, you piece of shit. You ugly bastard. Are you *grateful* I've come to see you? Are you, you shit-faced piece of garbage?"

He chuckled, then restrained himself. Ronica performed better when he took it seriously, which in turn excited *him* that much more. "Yes, mistress, yes."

"Get on your knees, bastard."

He did. Something moved outward from the couch and hovered in front of his face. "Lick my foot, bastard."

He did, gratefully. He put the toes in his mouth and sucked on them.

"Take off your clothes, asshole. Do as I tell you, shitface. Hurry."

He wriggled out of his jacket, vest, and shirt. He took off his shoes and pulled down his pants.

"Hurry."

All the while he was doing this, he felt gentle taps on his face, shoulders, chest, even his back, but he couldn't figure out how she was doing it. He could tell from her voice that she was leaning back on the sofa, and could not have reached him with her hands. Her feet would have been much larger and could not have touched him with such softness, nor reached behind him. Was she holding something? A rod or belt of some kind?

"Kneel down," she said when he was naked. "With your back to me. Hurry, you ugly bastard."

Trembling with anticipation, he did as she instructed. A moment later he felt the whip slashing across his back. At least he thought it was the whip. There was something weird about the texture, the way it glided across his skin, almost as if it were alive.

"Ahh. Ah. Ah. *Ah.* Oh mistress, mistress—don't stop, *don't stop.*"

"Do you like that, my lover, my little troll? Do you like that, you diseased piece of *feces* . . . ?"

"Ah. Ah . . ." Yes, it was wonderful, though perhaps not as painful, as sharp, as he would have liked. Was she using the leather thing, the horsewhip? A belt, a piece of plastic? It felt so strange.

She stopped after a while, just to torment him. He loved it. Again he felt that odd probing on his back and neck. Strange little touches. Too big to be fingers, too small to be toes. What was she touching him with?

His curiosity got the better of him.

"What—what is that?"

"Same thing I've been whipping you with, my hideous lover boy."

"And what is that?"

"Turn around," she said. "Here, I'll turn on the light so you can see."

He turned—gasped. . . . *God, it's a joke, it has to be a joke* . . .

Something lashed out to wrap itself around his neck . . . *choking, squeezing* . . . He couldn't talk, he couldn't breathe . . . He was suffocating . . . His head was being yanked this way, then that way, was being wrenched from his neck. . . . Another warm noose lassoed his arm and held him fast upon the floor . . .

"How do you like my breasts?" Ronica asked.

CHAPTER THIRTY-NINE

Peggy and the two police officers rushed from their parked car to the entrance of the clinic as something large and brownish-red slithered out from the shattered glass door at the front of the building.

"What the hell is that?" Robbins hollered.

The animal was a snakelike creature, though much, much bigger than any python. Peggy recognized it immediately and shuddered. "Stay away from it!" she screamed. "It's dangerous. That's one of the things I tried to tell you about!"

Robbins pulled out his revolver and fired three shots at the fleshopod. The creature had been heading in their direction, but the bullets, the confusing sights and sounds of the city that confronted it, caused it to pause. It swerved abruptly and sank behind the row of bushes lining the front wall of the building.

"Did you hit it?" Sloane bellowed. "What was it?"

As they advanced toward the entrance, traversing the shattered glass, another large tentaclelike animal snaked out of the doorway and slid away into the bushes so quickly that Peggy wasn't even sure if it had been there. It was like a monstrous water hose being pulled out of sight by an unseen, cyclopean gardener.

The cops stood there openmouthed. "Another one? Did you see how fast that fucker moved?"

The officers who were supposed to have met them there hadn't yet arrived; they had either been held up or this case was not considered a high priority. "I'd better call for more backup," Robbins said. "Something's going on here."

He ran back to the police car.

Peggy and Sloane moved through the doorway.

How had everything gone so wrong? Why had it happened?

Everything had been so perfect, the future so bright. Now it was lost, all lost—everything was gone. Even his beauty.

Romeo stood before the mirror in a small private bathroom on the third floor, where he had retreated in case any of the fleshopods decided to come upstairs in search of him. Using flippers and muscles, they could traverse steps easily—hadn't they come up from the basement? He was still haunted by the screams of the receptionist and Dr. Jeffries, the nurse who'd finally gone downstairs, and the others who'd fallen victim to the animals. He was sure that he was now being punished for his cowardice, for all of the terrible things he had done. His father had left him and his sister the company he had founded, and his money, and they had squandered the money, let the company fall into ruin. Neither of them would ever recover from this.

But as he looked at the hideous visage of his once-handsome face, touched the unbelievably withered skin, he knew that none of that mattered anymore. Nothing mattered. He didn't want to live if it would be like this. He thought that Dr. Lincoln could save him—but not if it meant using that terrible makeup on him again. Besides, he had a feeling that the doctor was dead, along with the others; that her body had fed the fleshopods; her skin and blood and bones had given sustenance to the creatures she had helped to bring into the world and nurture.

He stared at his face, trying to deny what he saw, trying to figure out what had happened. He stood there trembling, trying to *picture, visualize,* his face as it had been only a short while ago. Striking, handsome, *beautiful.* He clenched his fists and closed his eyes and pictured himself normal again as hard as he could.

Images of horror, people being consumed, filled his mind instead. He saw David Kravitz's eager, greedy face, saw Peggy Antonicci, saw George Burke as he must have looked as the men Romeo hired beat him into a coma, saw all the things he'd done. He tried to fill his head with the Dr. Jekyll he had once been, but saw only the Mr. Hyde he had become. Ugly. Disfigured. Gloriously terrible.

Tears dripped down his face. Try harder, *try harder,* he pleaded with himself. Erase these images of death and betrayal. *Picture* yourself whole and handsome again. *Visualize* yourself perfect. Do as Dr. Lincoln said.

Dr. Lincoln was *wrong.* Dr. Lincoln was dead.

Try harder. *Try harder.* What is the point of living if you'll have to live like *this?*

"Romeo."

He was startled by someone behind him. The door was open. His first instinct was to cover his face, turn away, let no one look upon his visage. But he recognized the voice as Ronica's. He turned toward her, crying, to let her see what had become of him. Ronica would help him. Ronica would know, must know, what to do.

"Romeo—my God, what happened . . . ?"

Romeo saw that Ronica had changed, too. Not her features, not her face. But there was something in the eyes—a madness—a terrible hunger and loss of reason. He wanted her to take him in her arms—but something restrained him from asking her to do so. Her torso seemed larger. She could hardly close the cashmere coat she wore over her bosom. Beneath the coat, something was bulging at her chest and back.

Romeo didn't want to know what it was; he didn't

want to see. He needed Ronica to be whole and un-harmed so she could share her strength with him. He didn't want her to be as marred as he was.

"Oh, God, Romeo," Ronica sobbed. "What's happening to us?"

They stood there in the small bathroom, staring at each other, crying, reaching out with their hands but not touching, afraid to touch.

What had happened to the golden Barrows kids, the children who had been born blessed—blessed with beauty —and who should have grown up to have wonderful long lives? What had happened to them? This was not the future they'd envisioned. This was not the sort of thing that was supposed to happen to a Barrows—only to other people.

Then Romeo remembered: "The flesh . . . the creatures got loose. Didn't you see them? Down on the first floor . . . the fleshopods. . . ."

Finally he made Ronica understand what had happened, but she was beyond caring. She had stopped crying and now wore a strange, dazed expression. "I didn't see them," she said, giggling. She wrapped a strand of hair around her finger and twirled it. "I walked over from Dennis's. I came in through the garage—up the back staircase. Didn't see any of the monsters."

They probably have escaped into the night, Romeo thought. The part of him that retained sensitivity and empathy could only pity the innocents the fleshopods might come across. He thought he should call the police. . . . *Where is Victor? Why hasn't he returned my phone calls?* Victor had told him never to take a step without checking with him first. What would Victor say when he found out the awful things that Romeo had done? And now his sister was crazy!

There was a commotion outside. Gunshots? A few moments later, a distant voice. Police? *"Is anybody here? This is the police."* He should warn them about the fleshopods. He didn't want anyone to see him like this—but at the same time he didn't care. What did anything matter anymore?

Ronica froze when she heard the gunshots. When she heard the voices coming from the lobby, she shrieked, threw her hands across her chest, and hurriedly backed out of the bathroom. Romeo stepped out and saw his sister running into the nearest guestroom—she slammed the door behind her.

He was torn between going after his sister and going downstairs. Finally, the sounds of footsteps, shouting, helped make up his confused mind. *It was like something had taken over his brain.* He walked down the hall and descended the large front staircase. He had nearly reached the second-floor landing, when he saw two cops and Peggy Antonicci walking up toward him from the lobby.

Was that—could that be—*Romeo Barrows?*

Peggy saw an apparition walking down the stairs toward them, an apparition that wore an expensive business suit and had a carefully coiffed, masculine hairdo. The body was right, the proportions correct, there were no extra arms or legs or heads, no weird growths or outcroppings. But the face . . . *the face* . . .

The apparition spoke. It *was* Romeo Barrows. Peggy could hear the cops on either side of her sucking in their breath in dismay and disbelief.

"Be careful," Romeo said. "The fleshopods are loose." Sloane was a few steps higher than the others. Romeo took another step downward, which nearly brought him level with the policeman. Sloane backed up quickly before the apparition could get too close to him.

Romeo turned to Peggy. "I'm sorry, Peggy. Everything's gone wrong. I know you've always had a thing for me. But"—he lifted his hand to take in his horrible countenance—"as you can see, I'm not worthy anymore. Not worthy of anyone, not even you." His head sank down toward his chest. "I'm . . . ugly. *Ugly!*"

He's crazy, Peggy thought. *He's gone mad.*

Romeo's face had become wrinkled and gray like an old man's. Worse still, his forehead had broken out into bumps and growths in a variety of sizes. There were sore, reddish welts across his chin and neck. But the most terrible thing of all was that his cheeks had become transparent, gelatinous. You could see his teeth and gums right through the jellylike material.

Romeo saw Peggy looking at him, saw the look on her face, and his eyes widened until they seemed as big as twin moons, as wide as the madness in his mind.

Without warning, he took both his hands and placed them on either side of his face. He began to press inward, inward, on his cheeks, until the sticky transparent substance squished between his fingers.

Peggy screamed. The glutinous tissue started plopping in clumps onto the staircase. "Romeo! Stop it! We can get a doctor!" But Peggy knew it was too late.

He kept shoving his hands in, all the way in, disfiguring his face further. They sank up to the wrists in his cheeks. Romeo lifted his head and started screaming, roaring, at the top of his lungs, his fingers wriggling about in what was left of his face. He pulled one hand out with a *plopp* and a whole cheek tore away. He did the same with his other hand. Peggy had never seen anything so disgusting. The two cops just looked at each other. They didn't know what to do, or what could possibly be done, for the fellow.

"Ronica's upstairs," Romeo said. His voice had become a slurred, lisping choke. "The last bedroom on the third floor. She's . . . sick. You'll help her, Peggy, won't you? I know she's your friend. Help her, please. It's too late for me, but it may not be too late for Ronnie."

Peggy had spent so many years loving Romeo, or thinking she loved him, that it was hard for her to witness his ultimate downfall and despair. Even though she knew that his handsome countenance hid a heart that was cold and expedient, she still had pity for him. The cops had overcome their revulsion long enough to approach him, and were about to take him downstairs, when Romeo suddenly whipped out a scalpel from his pocket.

"Stop him. Romeo—no!"

Too late! He drew the blade across his own throat, releasing a spume of rich, red blood. He gagged on it, sank to his knees, keeled over on the steps.

She covered her eyes and cried.

For the second time that night Peggy had witnessed the destruction of a man she'd once loved.

Ronica knew they were coming; she could hear their footsteps. She had to hide, had to get away. She had killed Dennis, murdered Dennis, even if she hadn't meant to. It was her breasts that did it—they had a life of their own, they did things she didn't want them to do, she had no control. . . .

I'm crazy, aren't I? she thought correctly, *driven crazy, driven right out of my skull.*

Her clothes were too confining. It felt as if she were wearing a straitjacket or an old-fashioned corset. She tore off the overcoat, then ripped off her blouse, which could barely cover what was beneath it. Her whole upper body had been compressed by the objects that had wrapped themselves around it. Now they started unraveling, unwinding, ready to greet anyone who would dare try to hurt her.

It was Dr. Lincoln who was responsible, not her. She had done nothing wrong. She wouldn't let anyone hurt her. She wouldn't let anyone touch them, mutilate her. . . .

Her breasts were her own and she loved them.

CHAPTER FORTY _____

Although the police officers preferred to stay downstairs and wait for the tardy backup to arrive, Peggy wanted to make certain Ronnie was all right and persuaded them to accompany her. She hoped nothing had happened to her friend; it would be hard enough telling Ronnie what had happened to her brother.

Now she wished she had done as the cops suggested. When Sloane opened the door to the guest room at the end of the third-floor hall, the room was very dark. At first Peggy thought one of those awful fleshopods was waiting for them inside, for from the darkest spot, in the corner, something like a tentacle—no—two tentacles were lashing out in the direction of the door. She screeched and backed up but the cops stood their ground.

From her safer vantage point, Peggy saw Ronica kneeling on the floor, just behind the tentacles, quivering.

"Don't shoot!" Peggy screamed. "You might hit Ronnie!"

The tentacles whipped back and forth in the air. They were too small to be fleshopods. Due to their smaller size they were even more like elephants' trunks, although the skin was smooth and white—also these tentacles ended not in open maws or snouts but in dainty, tapering tips that resembled nipples. They were several inches wide at the thickest sections and appeared to be several feet long, as well as extremely versatile and maneuverable.

"What are they?" Sloane asked Peggy. "More of those things we saw outside?"

"I don't know."

The trio entered the room, carefully watching the swaying tentacles, trying to formulate the best way to reach the cowering Ronica.

And then Ronica stood up.

Peggy gasped.

The tentacles were not just swaying in front of Ronica —they were swaying *from* Ronica! They were *growing out of* the woman's chest, growing out from where her breasts should have been. Ronica Barrows was naked, snarling, and her eyes were full of a seething, terrifying anger. The breast-tentacles rose high in the air, then dropped to the floor, like miniature fleshopods, mesmerizing Peggy and the police officers. Peggy could not believe this was happening.

Before anyone could move or think of what to do, the tentacles shot out and wrapped themselves around the necks of Sloane and Robbins.

It happened so quickly they had no chance to defend themselves. Robbins dropped his gun. Sloane managed to get off one desperate shot which thudded harmlessly into a dresser, before his gun, too, fell to the floor.

Peggy clawed at the tentacle which was around Sloane's neck. His eyes were bulging, his mouth slobbering. She tried to get a good finger hold so she could pull it off him. No good—the tentacle was too tightly wrapped around the neck. It was too hard and rubbery to get a good grip on. God, the man was dying right in front of her eyes!

"Ronica, stop it!" Peggy screamed. "Please stop it! Please!" *This can't be real! This can't be real!*

Robbins was lifted into the air until his body scraped the ceiling. The incredibly strong tentacle bashed him repeatedly against the unyielding wood until blood dripped down from his cranium. Finally the tentacle let go and hurled the helpless man out into the hallway, where he lay sprawled across the doorway of the opposite room. Peggy was sure his neck was broken.

As for Sloane's neck, it was now spewing blood from both above and below the tentacle; the unnatural append- age was crushing his windpipe, slowly rupturing the jug- ular vein. Peggy was afraid in another moment his whole head might wrench free. She lifted a chair and batted the tentacle, trying to make it release its grip. Slam. *Crunch.* The chair cracked, a piece broke off, but the tentacle wasn't affected. She hurled what was left of the chair at Ronica.

Ronica ducked and the chair hurtled past her to break against the wall.

"Ronica, why are you doing this?!"

She heard a gurgling sound. Sloane dropped to the floor, bloodied and dead, as the tentacle unwrapped itself from him and slid, covered in his fluids, back to where Ronica was standing.

Ronica and Peggy—now about eight feet apart—stood there tensely, watching each other, waiting. Peggy did not want this to be happening; she did not want to fight or hurt her friend. She knew Ronica had been driven crazy by what had happened to her body. Now that she had acknowledged her true feelings for Ronica she wanted to tell her, even if those feelings could not be returned, tell her how much she had always meant to her. She was afraid she might never get the chance.

The tentacles swayed and swayed in front of her and above her. Peggy mentally calculated the time it would take her to race out the door before the appendages could whip out and ensnare her. She had never been more terri- fied in her life. Only the very unreality of what was hap- pening kept her from fainting or becoming hysterical, leaving herself wide open to an assault from which she would undoubtedly never recover. How could she get out of this alive? How could she get out of here without hurting Ronica? She didn't even have a weapon. And the injuries she'd received from David were crying out in protest.

"Ronnie—please let me go. I'll go and get help for you. They can help you, Ronnie, I know they can. They can . . . get rid of those things."

"Not my breasts. I won't let anyone touch my breasts."

Then Ronica lowered her head and started weeping in despair, overcome with the horror of what had happened to her. For a second the old Ronnie was back and Peggy thought she had broken through to her, past the madness. She knew her friend must be *terrified*.

But then the moment was over, and all that was left of Ronica was an enraged monstrosity who would rather kill than be touched or taken.

Peggy tried to move before the tentacles reached her, but it was no good. One started wrapping itself around her right arm; the other snared her left ankle. Before they could tighten their grip on her, however, Peggy lifted her other foot and brought it down hard on the second tentacle, causing it to let go. She wrenched as hard as she could with her right arm and managed to free that limb also. Her arm and ankle felt sore and contaminated. She'd been lucky that time—if her neck had been encircled, she wouldn't have gotten a second chance.

The tentacles slapped down at her as she darted about the room, trying to avoid them, trying to reach the door. But it was like a bizarre obstacle course in a crazy cartoon where the obstacles were alive and could move even as you did. One tentacle smacked against the wall with such force that it left a jagged crack. Peggy just managed to jump out of the way. Visions of what had happened to those poor policemen filled her head. She must not let either of those tentacles grab her. The other breast-appendage lashed out and might nearly have beheaded her had she not ducked beneath it. It smashed into the mirror above the dresser and broke it into a hundred pieces.

"Ronica—stop it, please!"

She dived onto the floor when both whipping appendages converged on the spot where she'd been standing. She rolled over and over as they followed her, continually pounding the floor where she had been just a moment ago. The hard slaps of the descending tentacles seemed only a fraction of an inch behind her. Suddenly Peggy bounced painfully off the wall—she could go no farther.

She looked up to see the two tentacles hovering above her, knowing that any second they would either crash down to crush the life out of her body, or wrap around her arms and legs to tear her limb from limb.

"My God! Ronica!" A voice at the door.

Victor Asmodian! He had startled Ronica long enough to delay the tentacles from killing Peggy.

Peggy rolled to one side at an angle. Her fingers hit something cold and solid—a gun! A gun Sloane or Robbins had dropped.

She fired at the tentacles, but they kept descending. One was pressing in against her neck. The other was slapping repeatedly at a defenseless Victor Asmodian. She fired and fired but it wouldn't stop them.

God forgive me.

She fired at Ronica.

The blast knocked her friend backward and through the window behind her. The tentacles flew away from Peggy's body and followed Ronica out the window and down three stories to the pavement below.

"Are you all right?" Victor Asmodian said, his face full of a surprising concern and benevolence. "God help you. You poor thing. Are you all right?"

Peggy just lay there, shivering, crying, wishing the world gave you easier options than having to murder the people you cared for.

EPILOGUE_____

T he backup that Robbins had called for arrived during Peggy's confrontation with Ronica. They burst into the room only seconds after Ronica's death plunge. A cop helped Victor get her up off the floor. They didn't realize that most of the bruises she had all over her had been sustained during her struggle with David, and not from her fight with Ronica. She had trouble convincing them who had killed officers Sloane and Robbins until they found the body on the sidewalk.

Victor Asmodian explained that he had been out and had not received Romeo's panicky message until half an hour ago. He could answer all the police officers' questions. Peggy sensed that he, too, was just another victim caught up in a madness he wanted no part of. Funny about Victor Asmodian. She had suspected him of all the evil doings in the clinic, when it had really been Romeo. And why? Because of his looks. Because he was ugly. She felt ashamed for not having known better.

Escorted by an attentive policewoman down the front steps to a patrol car, Peggy was still trembling, still crying. As the policewoman led her by the elbow toward the sidewalk, Peggy managed to lift her eyes from the ground to meet the world head-on. She would get over this as she had everything else—David's death, Romeo's betrayal, her murder in self-defense of a dear friend, Ronnie. *But*

*damn it! Why did Ronnie have to die? Why did life have
to hurt so much sometimes?*

The last time she had felt nearly this awful was when
she'd been a young girl, when the entire schoolroom
laughed at her, at the "boy" named Peggy. But she had
managed to live through that, to triumph over it, and
make her own way in the world. Perhaps no one—no
man, no woman—would ever love Peggy Antonicci the
way she loved them.

But she was forever through with hating herself, she
swore it.

The policewoman smiled and opened the door for her.

The scientists who'd created the *Porodynean mariscrotii* had been given a great deal of leeway. All they had to
do was create a great number of hybrid and multihybrid
animals—chimeras—in hopes that one or more of them
might serve a useful industrial, chemical, or biological
purpose.

The people on the project had gone a little crazy, adding more and more elements to their chimeras, creating
wildly outrageous life-forms as if to merely prove that
they could do it. They were full of a perverse, gleeful
curiosity. The creatures that resulted from their bizarre
combinations never failed to astound them. Most were
useless and were either killed outright or allowed to expire. Some, such as the fleshopods, seemed to show promise. There'd been rumors that certain creatures had
already escaped into rural areas in frightening earlier out-
breaks. These had been quickly contained by the corpora-
tion and kept from the media, but nothing could ever be
proven.

This outbreak, however, would be a different story.

Deep in the sewer system of New York, where they had
fled, the fleshopods consumed the filth, the debris, the
scum and feces of living beings flushed down the drains,
and grew larger, along with their appetites.

In this new environment, with new food sources, the

fleshopods underwent further changes. The babies they carried were mutating; the substance they secreted began to take on a strange, new life of its own. New creatures, new life-forms, were being created beneath Manhattan, unbeknownst to the rich supply of food that lived and worked overhead.

Soon the first of these new creatures would rise into the city streets in search of prey.

ABOUT THE AUTHOR _____

William Schoell is the author of over five hundred stories and articles for national magazines, and the author of numerous books in and around the horror field. He makes his home in New York City.